Ren

MW01674358

Bill Brooks

Table of Content

Dedication

To Al, for her patience

Thanks to Roy Damant for welcoming me into archaeology and tutoring me thereafter. A true gentleman.

Acknowledgements

Timeline of Conflict - Wikipedia (Anglo-Saxon Chronicle)

The team at Amazon Publishing Pros for their amazing support.

About the Author

This is the first offering from Bill, the idea which came to him while working as an archaeologist. Over the next couple of years, the idea grew until it could be contained no longer, and as the effects of COVID-19 took hold and the UK was plunged into an enforced lockdown, the seedling was re-potted and has since blossomed into the fully developed specimen you see before you. A second chapter to this story is already in the offing.

Chapter 1: Valhalla

Renweard stirred gradually from his sleep. His bed was warm and comfortable, more so than he had ever realised, and as the familiar sounds and smells of the Mead Hall came to him through the dim light of dawn, he pulled his heavy, woollen cloak up over his head and allowed himself to drift back into a hazy half-sleep. Inhaling slowly, he filled his lungs completely before releasing his breath in one long, contented sigh.

The aroma of woodsmoke, damp clothing and stale mead hung in the air, and across the hall, someone snored heavily. Wulfgar? he thought; Definitely Wulfgar.

Wulfgar was an old friend and ally; they had fought many campaigns together, shed blood together, and celebrated many victories in the great halls of the Bretwalda: the leader of the provinces. In stature, not the mightiest of warriors, but fierce as a boar and strong as a bull; it had taken five of the enemy to kill him at the battle of ……a thought hit Renweard…. Deorham…. Wulfgar was killed at Deorham. How, then, is he now snoring like a bull seal in this place?

A glorious encounter, Deorham was the battle in which the Britons had been driven from their hill camp at Hinton and their three leaders: Commagil, Condidan and

Farinmagil, were slain. Each time they had fallen on the Briton's lines, and each time they had broken through as the enemy collapsed under the onslaught of Ceawlin's finest, finally withdrawing far into the west where now they cowered behind their so-called 'Wansdyke'. It had long since been decided to let them rot behind that hastily constructed earthen bank; Ceawlin wanted nothing more from these wretches now than their absence.

The celebration that followed had become almost as legendary as the victory itself: Five days of feasting, drinking, poetry and song, all provided by the Lord of the Feast. Yes, Ceawlin is indeed a great king! He mused.

His thoughts drifted lazily through his mind like clouds borne on a gentle breeze, shifting and changing until once more they returned to the presence of his old comrade. Renweard shifted uneasily under his blanket and furs.

It must be someone who snores like Wulfgar…. no one snores like Wulfgar! he thought, arguing with himself.

Almost immediately, though, his eyes became heavy, his mind drifting into grey as he lingered briefly between worlds, and as the comfort of his bed lured him back into the world of dreams, he concluded: I'll not think on it now. Sleep on; It can wait.

~

The sound of people moving nearby brought Renweard abruptly from his sleep. With a gasp, he reached instinctively for the sword at his hip, ready to defend himself against his attackers. It was not there. He reached instead for his short-bladed Seax; it too was missing. Preparing to fight hand-to-hand, he leapt swiftly and deftly onto his feet and searched the gloom for his foe, fists raised, clenched into balls of iron; he was ready.

To his left, a group of warriors sat drinking and laughing. They barely gave Renweard a second glance as they listened intently to the wiry blonde man, clearly an accomplished storyteller, as he continued to regale his audience with the tale of a warrior whose horse, having taken flight at the sight of a large serpent, had left its rider face down in the mire through which they had been passing.

A pile of previously unnoticed, mud-caked clothing moved slowly and awkwardly in the gloom. As it did so, two eyes opened brightly in its midst. Clearly, this was the unfortunate soul to which the story related. At the sight of him, the group roared with laughter, one of them reaching over to console the poor man, patting him on the shoulder and causing flakes of thick, dried mud to fall into a loose pile on the floor as he said

"Be sure to remove all traces of the swamp Dreogan, lest you be mistaken for the creature Grendel!"

Laughter rose noisily once more, but this time a horn of ale was offered, which the man took readily.

Renweard was confused and frowned as he sank slowly back down among the wool and the fur, still warm from having swathed his body through the night, relaxing both fists and his posture as he did so. Realising quickly that there was no danger here, wherever 'here' was, he finally lay back, allowing himself to sink deep into the comfort of his bed, and closed his eyes once more as he tried desperately to recall recent events.

He had been dreaming of an old, long-dead friend; a message to him from the afterlife, perhaps? A warning? Why, then, he thought, had he chosen to communicate in the language of hogs? In grunts and snorts?

"RENWEARD!" the call resounded across the hall.

"Renweard, you're here! You made it!"

"It cannot be!" he said aloud.

Opening his eyes wide at the sound of the familiar voice, Renweard looked straight up at the ceiling. Normally a haze of smoke-filled thatch and soot-covered timbers, here instead, the glint of gold danced with the flames from the fire far below, and as his eyes adjusted to the light, he could clearly see that discs of gold lined the rafters, each shining magically in the half-day-half fire light. They were shields! Shields of gold!

"I knew it was you! I knew!"

"Wulfgar?"

"Yes, it's me!" his face was a mix of both exasperation and relief.

"Oh, my old friend. I feared they had carried you to Folkvangr to serve under Freya, but Woden saw fit to recruit you to his army, and his Valkyries brought you here instead."

"Folkvangr? Freya? Speak plainly. What do you mean?"

If Renweard had been confused before, he was more so now as cold fear rose and clung to him like a wet cloak.

"You're here, Renweard, in Valhalla, as we always said we would be - together. The Valkyries carried you here last night. You must remember?"

Renweard did not remember, and try as he might, his memories came to him as nothing more than a dream. And like a dream, they hid and played and tormented the dreamer so that every time he got near to an answer, it would wipe his mind of all knowledge of it.

He frowned, focusing inward in an attempt to recall that of which Wulfgar spoke; There was the vague recollection of an army on the move, another of a shield wall and another of searing pain through the back of his head. He winced at the memory of it. Then, just as he tasted the iron-rich tang of blood in his mouth, his concentration was broken as Wulfgar spoke again.

"...and look, your weapons, helmet, even your gaming pieces are here; though if you think I'm going to risk playing you for Roman pieces again, you're very wrong!"

As he spoke, Wulfgar gestured across to Renweard's side.

"They must think you're important too: to have given you a space so close to the fire, I mean!"

As Wulfgar spoke, Renweard turned his head to look. Sure enough, there lay his sword: Way Maker, sheathed in its wool-lined, leather scabbard, the simple yet elegant pommel and bone handle seeming to shimmer gently, as though viewed through the heat of a summer's day, as they too picked up the light from the fire. His spears lay alongside that and hanging from one of the hall's mighty upright oaken posts, eternally vigilant, as though bidden always to oversee and protect its keeper, his shield.

Fashioned from linden wood selected and harvested from woodland near to his village, its leather covering and central iron boss bore the evidence of the many campaigns in which he and Wulfgar had served. Its bronze icons: a boar and a bird, stared at one another across its breadth as if to do so formed an impenetrable barrier. Bejewelled too; It had been a gift from Ceawlin himself for loyal service to his lord.

His tefl board, folded safely away, its pieces secure in their leather pouch; they, too, awaiting the call to do battle.

And finally, his helm: the dome core, hammered from a single sheet of iron and lined with a leather skull cap, was then adorned with shining tinned panels, each fixed to the dome with minute rivets. Polished bronze eyepieces and a crested ridge gave the whole object a supernatural, wraithlike appearance as though it were alive, as though it were inhabited by the gods themselves.

There it sat, apparently suspended in mid-air, staring intently at them from its wooden stand, brooding, daring them to stare back.

"I can hardly believe it. I don't believe it! Show me the stag! Show me the tree, Glasir!"

"Shall I show you Heidrun too?" asked Wulfgar. "Will you believe me then, brother? If I show you the great goat?"

"I will, but this is a dream… I'm certain of it."

"Come then, dreamer; Come see for yourself!"

Wulfgar tugged at Renweard's elbow in an attempt to bring him to his feet.

"I won't. Wulfgar, this is absurd!"

Renweard hesitated as if to believe in it now would end the enchantment. To imagine that he may now dwell in that greatest of places, home of the two mighty beasts: Heidrun the goat and Eikthyrnir the hart who, born of a cloven sky, now serve Valhalla with both water and mead, was beyond him.

"Are you saying you won't believe in Valhalla? After years of waiting? Of inviting death to be here?"

Renweard searched his mind for an answer, his eyes darting desperately back and forth, settling nowhere and seeing nothing.

"I… I don't…. I can't take it in. SLOW DOWN, I COMMAND YOU!"

Wulfgar seemed hurt, offended, and Renweard sensed this.

"Wulfgar, I'm sorry. I … I don't know what…." He sighed heavily as he sunk back into his nest of furs.

Wulfgar placed a hand on his old friend's shoulder.

"I'm sorry, too, brother. I'm just so pleased to see you again after… how long is it?" he frowned as he tried to recall.

"Fifteen years," Renweard said matter-of-factly.

"Fifteen?" he said, taken aback. "It feels like…"

The shadow of a distant thought drifted across Wulfgar's face.

"…. I don't actually know what it feels like. I feel as though I've been here forever, but at the same time, it's as though I arrived only yesterday. Fifteen years you say?"

"Yes, Deorham was the last time we stood together."

They sat quietly for a while, staring into the fire as Wulfgar allowed time for Renweard to absorb this, his new reality, and he, his. The glowing logs crackled gently, occasionally spitting a hot ember into the surrounding hearth. It had a calming effect on them both as they drifted like the woodsmoke with their thoughts.

Quite suddenly, Renweard rose to his feet.

Looking around, he could see through the gloom that other warriors were rousing from their slumber, not least due to the laughter of the mud story warriors and Wulfgar's calls of excitement, and they were beginning to ready themselves for the day's labours.

Weary eyes and yawning, bearded mouths seemed to appear from all corners of the hall; it was as though the floor itself was coming to life.

Despite the unfamiliarity of his surroundings, Renweard felt strangely at home, as though he somehow knew this place. But just as he thought he was coming to terms with his new surroundings, he spotted something, someone, which unsettled him again.

"Is that....?"

Renweard pointed to an adjacent sleeping space from which a bearded, contented, ale-flushed face smiled out from the world of dreams.

"Isn't he......?

"Beadurof? ... dead, well .... Yes, I told you.... Come, this way, quickly," he said, half whispering now, recognising the need for tact.

If I must, Renweard thought. Yes, I must! He decided. If this truly is Valhalla, I must know it. Only then can I rejoice. A dream cannot be celebrated, however real it may seem.

They moved through a sea of blankets and fur, which cursed and moaned as they trod on a hand here and a face there, the garments making waves a Sea Wolf could sail on, until finally, leaving a wake of disgruntled, sleep-weary warriors behind them, they reached the enormous double doors whose job it was to protect the hall and its occupants after dusk as they drank, ate and slept.

As they did so, a shadow moved between them. A warrior whose stature seemed twice the height of them both, had they been standing one atop the other, moved quickly yet effortlessly into the space between Wulfgar, Renweard and the doors.

Looking up to where there should have been a face, they saw only a silhouette, all detail completely lost in its shade, and the shadow he cast enveloped them so completely that they, too, now seemed to disappear into its murky depths.

Yet despite this, neither felt fear nor malice, and neither felt the need to prepare for conflict. Instead, they were immersed in the warm, mellow tones of his voice as the giant of a man spoke.

"I do hope you're not running out on us!"

"Grimme! No! No, this is Renweard. He arrived last night from.... where did you come from?"

"Wödnesbeorġ," Renweard said, a strange, glazed look in his eye as though retrieving a memory from far off in the distance.

"Wödnesbeorġ? Ceol's land in the west?" Grimme asked, bemused.

"The same," recalled Renweard.

“Then all is not well in Ceawlin’s kingdom…” a look of contemplation spread across his face.

Grimme absorbed the news as though it might have an impact on all of them in this, of all places.

“It would seem so,” Renweard said, now fully present again.

“His nephew Ceol made war on him and drove us back eastwards.”

“That would explain the sudden influx of warriors overnight…”

It was Grimme’s turn to glaze over now. “It is good!” he said suddenly. “The ranks of the Einherjar will have swollen tonight. We may yet have warriors enough to face Ragnorök.”

With that, he punched Renweard hard in the upper arm in celebration. Renweard felt it but showed no outward sign of having done so. Show strength, he thought.

“So, where are you going? Asked Grimme, bringing them back to why they were all standing before the ornately carved doors of the Great Hall.

They stood some half a chain high and were at least the thickness of a strong man’s arm. Solid oak, hewn from Asgard’s own forest, and carving so fine; so detailed:

serpents writhed; Warriors fought, and beasts snarled, that only the Gods themselves could have commanded them to be made.

"Outside…?" said Wulfgar warily.

"A cryptic response; perhaps then you are running out on us?" Grimme asked playfully. Wulfgar was quick to respond.

"My Lord, no! He doesn't believe all this is real…" he pointed to Renweard before continuing, "…although one look at you…"

Grimme's eyes flashed briefly red, then seeing the mischief play in Wulfgar's eyes, he cocked his head to one side inviting candour.

Acknowledging this, Wulfgar finally answered as such.

"He really doesn't believe this is real. Thinks it's a dream or some such. I thought if he could actually see the golden tree..."

"Glasir?"

"Glasir," he confirmed, "he might finally believe me."

Grimme thought for a moment.

"Very well…" he said at last, "…but we break the fast before daylight returns completely, and Woden himself will join us before that. If you are not back before then, you may as well have been taken to Folkvangr; He may have but one eye, but Woden knows his warriors. That is why you were chosen. DO NOT betray that trust. Do you understand?"

Both men nodded as though scolded children. Grimme concealed a mischievous smile and stepped to one side, allowing them passage.

As he did so, both men saw properly for the first time, not just the size of the man but his grandeur. His golden armour, backlit by the enormous central fire, seemed to have a life of its own, as though it lived on Grimme rather than he wore it.

Chain mail, plate and leather covered a dark-skinned colossus who looked as though he were himself, a god.

The effect on them, however, was not to instil fear but respect, and outwardly displaying this via a look and a nod, they passed into the cool morning air.

"I'm glad he's on our side," said Wulfgar finally.

"He is undoubtedly a man of honour," Renweard replied.

"I'm glad he's on our side…" Wulfgar said again

"Yes."

They had walked no more than a few feet from the hall when immediately in front of them, a tree of unearthly beauty rose up out of the ground.

No taller than the height of a ship's oar stood on its end, yet it dominated the ground in which it grew. Leaves, gold and red, like the treasures created in the east for the Wuffings, moved silently in a cool, fragrant breeze.

Both men closed their eyes instinctively and breathed in the scene. Renweard had never seen such a thing; never felt such emotion swell in him such as it did now.

"What is this magic? What is this place?"

Wulfgar regarded his old friend warmly. Renweard's piercing blue eyes had moistened at the scene, and as he breathed heavily, it was as though he was trying to exert a degree of control over his situation.

Wulfgar recognised himself some fifteen years earlier, standing on the same spot. He, too, had been sceptical - unable to make sense of the one thing he had longed for all that long while in his Cyning's service. Finally, though, overwhelmed by the unquestionable truth, he had accepted his new life and now, he rejoiced in it.

The two men stood and watched as the sun rose slowly into the morning sky; a vast canvas of deep, deep orange accented by an occasional purple/grey wisp of cloud gave everyone and everything a soft, muted glow, enveloping and warming everything upon which its light settled.

“This is the most beautiful scene…” Renweard swallowed hard “…my eyes have ever been blessed to witness. If I were to look upon one last thing before my end, let it be this…” he whispered to himself.

For a moment, all was still; it was as though the earth held its breath, until suddenly and without warning, something bellowed loudly from above and behind them, long and low; A deep, rich tone that carried with it an air of both dignity and nobility.

Startled, both men turned, lifting their eyes to the hill behind them.

There on the slope, lit by the first amber rays of the day's light, stood an enormous stag, its vast antlers strewn with bracken, grass and even whole branches. Its short, rough coat accented the lean muscle beneath as it steamed, warming and drying in the first of the morning’s heat.

They were clearly downwind of the animal as his pungent musk came to them in the air, strong and irresistible.

Renweard, overwhelmed by its magnificence and unable to move, stared at the celestial scene through still-misted eyes.

The beast eyed them warily, snorting loudly several times through moist, flared nostrils before dipping his head as though bowing. As he did so, his antler's woodland adornments swung precariously forward, but none were dislodged, and then quite suddenly, he threw back his head and bellowed again. Once more, the mist of his hot breath drifting gently on the morning breeze seemed to carry the majestic voice away with it.

Then Renweard knew, and Wulfgar sensed it as he said softly.

"Welcome to Valhalla, old friend; Breakfast?"

Chapter 2: The Fallen

The morning's heat had given way to a dark, foreboding sky which seemed to match the mood of those present for the funeral of the fallen. Even the thunder god, Thunor, seemed restless, as though desperate to meet his new brothers-in-arms; as though he had bloody work for them in the afterlife, and as he moved back and forth across the sky, he hurled the occasional lightning bolt earthward to hasten their ascent.

Ceawlin had taken an army of some four hundred warriors, drawn from all of his provinces, with him to the ancient barrow of Wödnesbeórg in an attempt to force back the challenge from his nephew, Ceol. The whelp, not happy with his Wessex stronghold, had joined forces with his brother Ceolwulf and started to push east into the lands belonging to his uncle.

The battle was long; It had been brutal, and there had been great slaughter. Few of that four hundred had returned. Ceawlin himself was rumoured to have been exiled along with his son, Cuthwine. No one now seemed to know the whereabouts of their Bretwalda. No one knew what lay in wait for the fate of his kingdom, nor that of its people.

Only three score had returned, and eight of the best were now being carried to their final resting place on this earth. Some of those had died on the battlefield and had been carried home by their kin; others had made their own way home but with horrific injuries and had succumbed since.

Of those among the dead: Abrecan, Eadig and Waelwulf, none was more revered than Renweard - guardian of his lord's house and husband to Wilena.

The grief-stricken widow now walked quietly, yet proudly, behind her husband as they made their way to the burial ground, her eyes red but her back as straight as the sword that now lay in her husband's cold, pale hands.

All were to be buried in the ways of the old gods. There had been some pandering to the Roman religion which had begun to influence the people of this land, but Renweard and his kinfolk owed their allegiance to the old gods: to Woden, Thunor and Freya, and they were not about to change; not now.

Wilena had been key in organising Renweard's procession and burial. She had been the one to decide what should accompany her husband into the ground and on to the afterlife, and none would doubt her role as wife, counsel and decision maker.

The procession made its way quietly along the track from the river. They had arrived at the river bank in two of the Bretwalda's great ships, which had set out under oar from their settlement a few miles inland. The terrain between there and here was not suitable for such a journey as this and would otherwise have taken many hours and invited much risk of attack. They secured the great vessels, which were left under guard, and assembled the cortege.

Six bearers bore one warrior on a raft of Ash for protection and Yew; evergreen, marking the new path that now lay ahead of them. These led the family, who in turn led the rest of the mourners who were also charged with carrying the weapons and personal items that would accompany their master on this, his final journey. This was a great honour, and many had come forward to volunteer their service.

The climb was steepest at the bottom, but none complained. They moved silently and respectfully, each with their own thoughts and memories. Some wept gently, but none dishonoured their charge. These were great warriors who would now take their place in one of the great halls: Valhalla or Folkvangr, and all were honoured to be present at their release from this life.

As they climbed higher, they made their way through ancient woodland. This was the point at which the path began to level out and marked the boundary of the sacred burial site.

They were now around sixty feet above the river and once on the burial site itself, a further twenty. The warriors would be as close to the gods as they could be carried; the Valkyries would complete their journey.

As they passed through the trees, the crowns of the Ash, Oak, and Hornbeam seemed to bow in reverence to the precious cargo being borne way below.

All was quiet except for the wind blowing high above through their boughs - the growing storm was moving closer now - and the leaves seemed to whisper the names of the fallen as they jostled for position in their lofty seat; It was as though a message was being sent to the gods, enabling them to prepare for their arrival.

Finally, and after much toil, the procession moved out of the trees, leaving the fresh, earthen smell of woodland behind them. Despite the grey-green darkness brought on by the impending storm, it was noticeably lighter out in the clearing, which caused everyone to strain their eyes to adjust as they emerged, blinking from the tree line.

The rest of the village had assembled some hours before and had awaited the arrival of their warriors alongside graves that had been dug that morning. Deep openings had been lined with narrow planks of timber set vertically against the wall of each small chamber and horizontally to form a floor. Finally, a bed of woollen blankets and fur had been placed within.

As the cortege came into view, a lone warrior blew a long, mournful note from a war horn which seemed to circle the site before being gathered up and carried away on the breeze. This was the signal for the villagers to form a large circle around the graves.

It was also intended as a signal to the gods, asking them to despatch the Valkyries.

As many as sixty souls now gathered around the open graves. The village: Thegn, Freeman, and serf alike stood shoulder-to-shoulder to pay their respects. Some had come from the village itself, but many had come in from the land, such as the workload at the time of harvest. All were united today.

The slain were carried in through a gap in the circle which immediately closed behind them before being laid simultaneously in their respective graves.

There was no ceremony to this act, but a great gentleness and respect nevertheless, and as backs strained and brows dripped their labour into the grave, each man was settled and positioned among the fur as if sending them off to sleep.

As the bearers stepped away, the mourners, who had lovingly carried the possessions of the men, stepped forward and began placing them with their owners.

Most owned a helm which was placed in the grave above their head. That which belonged to Renweard held special meaning within his family; It had belonged to his grandfather, Borden, himself the son of a great house. A simple design compared to others on the field, it nevertheless consisted of a dome of highly polished iron to which the tinned, decorative plates had been rivetted. The whole piece was then embellished with bronze eyepieces and a crest decorated with intertwining beasts and animal heads.

As this was placed in the grave with Renweard, it sat awkwardly and needed to be supported by placing a pad of linen and wool beneath the damaged rear quarter, for where it had been struck and cleaved through by the blow that had ended his life, the iron had parted leaving a wide gash, the edges of which turned in toward the wearer as they followed the blade on its savage course, and despite attempts to clean it, blood, hair and bone fragments remained stubbornly intact; a testament to the manner in which he had met his end.

The warrior's spears were laid to their right, the sword gently removed from their hands to be placed at the left hip, once more back in its scabbard.

All were placed so that each could be called on to aid their master should the need arise.

Then came the personal items.

Some owned more than others, and Renweard more than most, and like Abrecan, Eadig and Waelwulf, he too was dressed in his finest clothes: chainmail; linen trousers and tunic; a woollen coat edged with finely woven, multi-coloured braid; leather shoes and a wolfskin cape. Most had some jewellery: a belt buckle and finger rings, but none were as noble as Renweard, whose lidded, leather purse contained coins, unworked garnets and small ingots of gold and silver from many distant kingdoms.

Food, drinking vessels, even a lyre, which belonged to Eadig - his verse and songs would be greatly missed, especially tonight - all were laid at the feet of their owner, ready for use in the next life.

The very last possession to be reunited with its owner was his shield. Each warrior had his own, and, like its owner, each was very different. Some were simple hide-covered timber finished with a plain central boss. Others, such as Renweard's, were more elaborate, adorned with magical beasts and decorated with gold and valuable gems - a gift from the Bretwalda.

But each told the same story: of standing firm, shoulder-to-shoulder with his warrior brothers; unyielding; an immovable wall pitted against many foes, and each bore the scars of combat, having withstood the onslaught of blade and spear alike.

The shields were placed over each warrior so that his entire upper body was covered; the boss was positioned centrally on his chest; one final act of protection in this world.

Then finally, when everything was placed in the grave, and the mourners and bearers had taken their place in the vast circle, all were covered with a shroud of the finest woven linen, weighed down at each corner with large stones. A number of white, glistening quartz stones had also been gathered. These were placed at the head and feet of each man, intended to shine out in the dark places the men may need to tread.

Halig, the village elder and speaker of ceremony, stepped forward into the space between the warriors. His tunic fluttered furiously against his thin body as the wind now tore through the site, and his cloak lifted into the horizontal, seemingly alive and wishing to break free.

He raised his hands into the air and opened his mouth to speak, but as he did, so there was a blinding flash of light from the sky directly above them and a simultaneous crack of thunder. *Thunor is becoming impatient!* he thought.

"WE HEAR YOU, MIGHTY THUNOR. YOUR PEOPLE ARE GATHERED, AND YOUR NEWEST RECRUITS AWAIT THE VALKYRIES!" he called over the wind.

Another bolt and another crash as the air around them shattered and tore. Then another and another....

"WE OFFER UP THE SOULS OF OUR FINEST! WE OFFER UP THE SACRIFICE OF OUR MIGHTIEST WARRIORS! WE OFFER UP THEIR SERVICE TO WODEN FOR THE GREATEST BATTLE WHICH IS YET TO COME!"

Each time Halig called into the wind, it seemed intent on forcing the breath back into his body, As though it could not bear to hear the words that spoke of such loss and sorrow.

The sky was now full of light and sound. People huddled closely together, nervously, as the great spectacle unfolded above their heads.

Yet no rain came.

The sky flashed blue and crimson above the dark, dark clouds, which seemed to boil as though heated by Thunor's exertions, and great dark, sinister faces seemed to be peering down at them from the sky above.

Yet no rain came.

"RECEIVE OUR BROTHERS GREAT WODEN, WISEST OF THE GODS. USE THEM TO DO YOUR BIDDING; RECEIVE THEM SAFELY INTO YOUR GREAT HALL AND GRANT THEM THE HONOUR OF MAKING

YOUR SERVICE! FOR AS HEL HAS CALLED THEM TO HER, SO DO THEY ANSWER!"

Halig signalled to the lone hornsman, who raised the instrument to his lips once more and blew a series of short, mellow notes. They were barely audible above the sound of the tempest, but on hearing the signal, the villagers moved, passing around each of the eight graves in turn, throwing, as they did so, a handful of soil and a personal tribute of either honeysuckle, kingcup or cornflower onto the shroud at the feet of the men.

The wind, having seized some of the tributes, carried both dust and petal back toward the river as though trying to hold some small part of the fallen in this world, unwilling to let them move on, and still the sky continued its violent display.

This is a great day! Thought Halig. *The gods have seen fit to witness our tribute to them and to our brothers.*

Then, as one, and without prompt, the entire village began moving reluctantly away to the temporary camp which had been set up a few hundred yards away some days earlier.

As the burial site cleared, the graves were closed by small teams of men and children who shovelled earth and stone carefully over the warriors, taking great care around the head and face.

All were honoured to have been chosen for this, but all were thankful that Wada, the water god, had seen fit not to send rain. They would toil until the graves were full and the surface lined with the sharp black tool stone that was so abundant in these fields. When their work was complete, they, too, would head for the camp and join in the feast to honour the dead.

This was to be a feast like no other. It would last for many days and nights. There would be singing, storytelling and drinking…. always drinking. Swine and sheep had been sacrificed and were already turning on the spit over the fire as the mourners streamed in and began settling into the camp.

And finally, as the darkness fell, it began, and as they celebrated the lives and ascension of the fallen, the storm began, finally, to abate.

Halig stood at the edge of the camp, staring back toward the burials. It was too dark to see them now. The indigo sky occasionally flashed far off in the distance, somewhere out to sea by his reckoning, but the storm had long since left them.

The night sighed, moving Halig's hair and beard gently as though it too found the day's events too much to bear.

Just then, Wilena, Renweard's widow, joined him.

"What is it, Halig?"

Her gentle tone brought him softly back to the present.

"Wilena. Forgive me. I was deep in thought."

"You look to the graves?"

At first, Halig did not reply and standing silently alongside the holy man, Wilena's gaze followed his off into the darkness where the man she had loved for the past twenty years now lay cold and quiet.

She remembered the words and the love they had shared, the homestead they had built together, and regretted now that she had never been able to bear him a son.

"If it is Woden's will..." He had told her the night before he left for his last great battle, "*...we shall raise a family, but it is you, my lady, you who command my heart, and I will not have you think of it."*

Out of nowhere, Halig suddenly replied, "I do."

Wilena frowned.

The spell was broken; her memories, her beautiful, precious memories, evaporated up into the night, at first leaving her a little confused and disorientated, but remembering that Halig was simply providing the answer to her original question, she composed herself and spoke

"To what end?"

"Mm…? Oh, none, child. Just an old man contemplating his own mortality. Do you see?"

"I do…" she replied wistfully "…I see all too well."

Understanding Wilena's pain Halig took her hand.

"You are the wife - the widow - of a great man and a well-respected leader of men: a warrior, and though he may not carry you with him to the next life… as yet…" he paused to allow the implication of what he had just said to find its mark "…there will come a time when you are reunited; The Web of Wyrd passes through all space and time and determines all things."

He attempted a smile which was met in kind.

"You are a strong woman, Wilena. Those who, like you, are without their men will look to you on this night and in the days and months ahead. You will draw strength from one another as it has ever been, and one day you will smile again…" he grunted stoically "…who knows: you may even learn to laugh again!"

Looking into the face of Renweard's widow, he smiled kindly.

"Come. Let's return to the celebration."

They turned together, arm in arm, and walked towards the light and the sounds of mirth and merriment.

***

Neither saw the eight small, pale-blue lights floating above the ground by the graves. Neither heard the thunder of hooves as the storm moved off into the night.

Yet both sensed a passing; nothing more than a tingle; a sensation that ran as though cold water trickled down their spine; a knowledge that passed between them.

And without needing to mention it, both continued on and joined the throng.

Chapter 3: The Unearthing

"OH, YOU'RE KIDDING ME!"

"What?"

"I could never be that lucky!"

"What? What have you got?"

Rab had been working as an archaeologist for eight years, but he had never found anything like this.

"I'm pretty sure this is Anglo-Saxon," he said as he gently removed the loose, sandy soil from around what appeared to be a shield boss.

"Wha....?"

Angela jumped to her feet and hurried to where Rab was working.

"Are you serious?"

"I'm pretty sure. I mean, it's only the very top, but it looks like a Carinated boss."

He removed more soil from around his find, his hands now shaking with excitement.

"The finial's gone, but look, you can see where it would have been?"

“Yeah, you’re right. And look, the sides drop straight down from that raised dome? I reckon you’ll find they stop suddenly, and there’ll be a flange with rivets. Nice find, Rab. Looks like Geophys’ were right then?”

“Doesn’t it just! I’d better get Colin over before I head any deeper.”

“I think you better have.”

The team of six archaeologists had been working on this particular field site for about two weeks. The first few days had been spent setting up the site hut, tool store, and fencing, the former of which had arrived late on the first day carried on the back of a low-loader lorry. Fortunately, though, the weather was dry and mild, so no one minded too much having lunch using an upended wheelbarrow as a seat. Actually, they were pretty comfortable when you knew how.

The site, on a raised promontory of land maybe eighty feet above a river, was bordered on two sides by steep wooded slopes - the slopes had been part of the reason that the site hut had arrived late: access. That, and the driver had got lost following the sat-nav!

The entire area had been evaluated about a year earlier whereby a series of thirty-foot trenches were excavated by a mechanical digger under the watchful eye of an experienced archaeologist, and at right angles to one another; the end of one trench lined up with the halfway point of the next, and so on. This tried-and-tested pattern of cutting trenches was the most likely way of uncovering evidence of archaeology while at the same time reducing the risk of missing anything important.

For the most part, on this occasion, they had yielded very little: the ever-present field-boundary ditch and the occasional ("possible") pit, but everything, no matter how seemingly insignificant, was excavated by an archaeologist and recorded in detail using GPS data mapping, drawings, and hand-written records. These would be added to the bigger site and geographical picture, and a decision would be made based on the likelihood of there being archaeology that needed to be further investigated and recorded.

This evaluation had indeed highlighted one area in particular. About one hundred and fifty yards from the tree line, just as the ground began levelling out, was an area that might just contain something of note. Seven or eight large, lozenge-shaped features appeared in the geophysics survey, and the signals from the magnetometry indicated the presence of metal, probably iron. The team on that dig had elected to record their presence but not open them up; time was against them, and they needed to be excavated properly, carefully.

Inevitably there had been something of a buzz back at the office as the data had revealed what appeared to be a cluster of eight graves, and everyone was hoping not only that this unit would land the contract to excavate - there was no doubt in anyone's mind that there would be an excavation - but that they would be on the team. This promised to be a productive and informative dig.

And so, one year on, the team was back.

Six archaeologists, including Rab and Angela, led by Colin Rhyll.

Himself an archaeologist with twenty-plus years' experience, Colin had a mind like an encyclopedia.

He also had the dress sense of someone who clearly worked out of view of the public. Mind you, if the public had ever seen him, he would probably still be wearing his signature "all-weather" shorts and red braces, lumberjack shirt and olive-green gilet - he found the many pockets "useful"- and the legendary "Benny" hat: A turret of 1970s military camouflage material, lined with wool and sporting an ear flap on each side; this was something that had seen many, some would say too many, days in the field.

"What ya got, Rab?" Colin walked eagerly toward the part-excavated grave, having been called on the hand-held radio.

"Ah yeah, cheers, Col'. I think it's an Anglo-Saxon grave. Well, I'm pretty certain, actually."

Colin dropped to his knees and sat back on his haunches, scratching his head in disbelief.

"Damned if I don't think you're right, fella! Carinated?" he gestured toward Rab's shield boss.

"That's what we thought," Angela said as she joined them.

"And if, as the Geophys suggests, these are all graves, we're gonna be bloody busy for the next three weeks," Rab added.

"You're tellin' me, boy, but it's still only gonna be the six of us!"

Rab flashed Angela a knowing glance.

"Mm… thought as much. What's the plan then, Col?"

"Well, Ange', what are you workin' on over there?"

Angela had been working about sixty feet away on a fairly indistinct 'splodge' in the soil.

"looks like tree roots or possibly an animal run? I was about to ask you if I could shut it down, actually."

"Oh, were ya?" Colin drawled with a glint of mischief in his eyes. "Fancy summat a bit more interestin' then, eh?"

Angela blushed.

"Can't say I blame ya, gal'. OK, look, grab your gear. I'll decide which one o' these I want done next, though I don't suppose it matters cos they'll all need doin'… Anyway, I'll let you know when you get back, alright?"

"Yeah, brilliant. Cheers Colin! Do you want me to record anything over where I am at the moment? The tree root thingy?"

"No, leave it, Ange. I'll finish up there for ya. Might jus' backfill it if it's rubbish. You crack on back here, yeah?"

"Yep. No problem. Back in a bit."

With that, she turned and headed back across the field, half running, half walking, barely containing her excitement. Colin turned back to address Rab.

"Right then, buddy. Better see who's under here, eh?" he said, pointing at the shield boss. "I'll see where the others are up to across the way, and once they've done, I'll draught them in over 'ere, yeah?"

"Yeah, do well. The soil is really light actually, Col, so it should hopefully be reasonably easygoing; better than that bloody clay site last month anyway."

They both frowned in mock horror at the memory of four weeks in a field and in the rain, which with every step, added a layer of thick, heavy clay that needed to be scraped off your boots; the tools slippery and virtually unusable and paperwork…. The less said, the better!

"On with the action then, fella. Looks like you've got most of that boss uncovered al…" He didn't finish the sentence.

"Good grief; is that what I think it is?"

"What? Where?"

"Jus' across to the other side from where you're working. Looks like a spear tip. No, a bit further up. Got it?"

Rab was navigating the grave with the tip of his trowel.

"What this?"

"Yep, you got it," Colin said as Rab reached the spot in the ground.

"Nah, it's just a bit of…. Oh blimey Col', you're right! God, you've got a good eye!"

"Got two, actually, bud. Tend to use 'em together!"

"Good spot. Looks like I've got my next target, then."

"Well, so long as you carry on taking it down in spits; Don't go burrowing after treasure!"

"No, I won't."

Rab knew that Colin wanted him to "empty" the grave from one end to the other by an inch or two at a time: a spit. This way, it would ensure that the feature was cleared evenly, level by level, and anything found within that level was recorded.

He also knew that this method of recording stratigraphy could often indicate what order objects had been placed in the ground or even whether one feature was older than another.

It could get pretty complicated if there were lots of features. Not today though, he thought.

With that, he carried on with the job of uncovering the shield boss, removing the soil carefully, sometimes with his fingertips, so as to not damage the fragile material.

"You were right about that flange, Ange'. Hey, I'm a poet!"

Everyone around him groaned.

"There's about five... looks like copper; it's green anyway.... five rivets and...oh look! The finial.... must've broken off. It's lying just off to the side."

Angela had just returned pushing a wheelbarrow into which she had haphazardly thrown her shovel, hoe and mattock, and a black and yellow toolbox, and as she prepared to excavate the grave Colin had marked out for her, he could be seen in the background, hurriedly shovelling soil back into her now abandoned feature which had indeed proved to be nothing more than the remains of a long-abandoned rabbit burrow.

She had hardly begun to dig when she came across something that was clearly metal but looked as though it might have been knitted.

"Errr…. I'm not sure…" she called, her voice shaking and not really listening to Rab, "… but I think this might be mail: chain mail."

No one had ever seen Colin move at such speed. He was by Angela's side in a flash and now stood looking over the scrapings in the sandy soil, his mouth partly open as though about to speak but having no words for this moment.

"I'm amazed that these are so shallow. I mean, there's what? 30? 40 centimetres covering them?

Colin nodded.

"What you've got to remember, Rab, is that these fields have never been worked; definitely never ploughed. Bit of a God-send, really!"

He had worked on many, many sites, but none had shown the promise that this one now did. The problem they now faced, however, was security. If word got out that something of this magnitude was starting to appear in the ground, those who sought to make a profit from it would appear overnight and rip the history straight out of the earth with nothing more than financial gain in mind. Quite apart from the trespass, the loss of so much knowledge, especially from a period as enigmatic and ephemeral as this: what appeared to be early Anglo-Saxon, would be a tragedy.

Fortunately, based on the geophysics results and the previous evaluation, the unit had already applied for and been issued a Home Office licence that gave them permission to excavate human remains should any materialise. Had they not done so, they would now be in the position where work on the graves would have to stop and an application for a licence made before continuing.

So, as the day wore on, work continued swiftly yet carefully, gradually returning the remains of what transpired to be eight souls to the world. But, as is ever the case, time was against them, and the working day was almost done.

"LISTEN UP, EVERYONE!" Colin said finally.

The team reluctantly stopped working and looked toward Colin, who, due to his attire, appeared to blend into his background.

The light levels were dropping now, it was late afternoon after all, but even so, there was an eerie look about the sky; a grey/green hue.

“It’s absolutely vital that we keep what we’ve found here under wraps. Do you understand?”

They absolutely did, which was reinforced by the fact that no one had ever seen Colin look as serious as this about anything.

“If word gets out about this site, we’ll have bloody night hawkers in here before you can say Danebury Metal Detecting Club!”

There was a ripple of laughter.

“I’ll see if the local constabulary can do a fly-by of the site overnight; I doubt they’ll have the resources, but I’ll ask. In any case, it means we’re gonna have to work bloody quick for the next few days, alright?”

Everyone nodded their agreement.

“Any questions or anything I might have missed?”

No one appeared to have any burning issues, so Colin closed the site for the night.

“OK, start packing up. Looks like the weather’s starting to turn against us anyway. And make sure you’ve taken out your loose spoil. Any finds you’ve got already, bring over to the site hut, and I’ll take ‘em back to the office tonight, yeah?”

The team went about putting Colin's instructions into action as he continued.

"Obviously, make sure you cover the graves properly before you leave them an' all. There's a few tarps in the tool store; weigh them down with your 'barrows, mattocks, whatever, yeah? OK then, let's get gone before this bloody storm arrives."

As he spoke, there was a blinding flash of light from the sky directly above them and a simultaneous crack of thunder.

It didn't take anyone long to secure the graves and pack away their gear; most had been surreptitiously doing so for the past 20 minutes anyway.

"Blimey, this looks really nasty!" Rab was packed up and ready to head for the van.

"Got everything, bud?"

"Yeah, all good, ta."

"Right, time to leg it, I think! Everyone else is in or on their way to the van already."

"OK."

They hurried to the waiting van together, placing their tools, bags, and boxes into the rear compartment before closing the doors, climbing into the front, and strapping themselves into their seat.

***

The sky began to flash blue and crimson above the dark, dark clouds which seemed to swarm and boil, and great dark, sinister faces seemed to be peering down at them from the sky above.

Yet no rain came.

And as the van slowly pulled away, no one saw the eight small, pale-blue lights floating above the ground by the graves. Yet everyone felt a tingle, like cold water trickling down their spine, but without wishing to mention it, they continued on and headed for the office.

Chapter 4: The Diminishing

Breakfast had been an almost festive event. There had been fish, eggs, bread, cheese, and mead, the latter drunk from enormous drinking horns, most adorned at each end with gold or bronze fittings, but one or two of the older warriors had blue glass horns which were ornately decorated, layered with spirals of molten glass that created intricate, plant-like swirls of Ivy and Honeysuckle, and which made the piece look alive; organic.

As Renweard drank from the horn that had been brought with him, he noticed that it never seemed to empty, and no matter how much he drank, the horn remained stubbornly full. He closed his eyes, lifted the tip skywards and took another long, slow drink from the heavy vessel. As he did so his nostrils filled with the sweet, heady scent of honey, followed soon after by the curious sensation of floating above the ground as the alcohol hit its mark.

"Have you ever eaten so well brother?" Wulfgar beamed at his side.

He had not. The food tasted…. divine, and there was so much of it.

It was carried into the Great Hall by a seemingly endless line of Valkyries, their silver platters full to the point of overflowing, yet from where, no one seemed to know. In truth, no one seemed to care; There was food, and there was mead, and this was a joyous time.

Renweard took a moment to savour the latest morsel, then spoke.

"Wulfgar, what do we do here?"

Wulfgar stared curiously back at Renweard, a half-smile playing across his lips, as he tried to decide whether this was another of Renweard's practical jokes.

"Here? .... Now? …. At breakfast …?"

"Valhalla!"

Renweard no longer doubted that he was in Valhalla. He had long since accepted that he had died a glorious death and had been chosen to serve in Woden's army: the Einherjar. He knew, too, that its purpose was to prepare for a great battle, but so far, this felt nothing like an army in training. At least, not one he'd ever served in.

"We train old friend; we train, we eat, we sleep, and tomorrow? We do it all again!"

"Woden spoke of a great battle…. This morning before the feast began; He spoke of a great battle."

Woden had indeed addressed the hall before breakfast.

He entered through a private doorway at the far end of the hall, his arrival heralded by the sounding of the great horn, which caused the air to pulse and the hall to shake violently under the weight of its tone.

He was flanked by a number of his personal followers: those who were sworn to protect him with their lives and accompanied to his throne chair by the golden colossus, Grimme.

Renweard's eyes briefly met Grimme's as they exchanged a nod of recognition, but the connection was broken abruptly as two enormous black birds: ravens circled the chair before settling gracefully, one on each side, upon a finial that had been provided for just that purpose. And there they sat, calling and preening.

Woden turned to face the hall, who stood proudly in front of their lord, and without blade or helm, he stared proudly back, his one, seeing eye glinting like a deep, dark pool in the firelight.

Raising both hands, he called, "Einherjar, be seated. There is much I would tell you!"

A murmur of activity spread like waves across the hall as men took their place around the vast, rectangular hearth, and Valkyries moved silently into the shadows. And then, as stomachs rumbled and men glanced longingly at the breakfast meal of fish, eggs, and mead already in place before them, he addressed them. There was, indeed, much to be told, and an hour later, as the hall ate and drank, Wulfgar recapped Woden's address.

"The greatest battle Renweard: Ragnorök. Has your memory left you? It is foretold that it will end with the loss of many gods and heroes and that a great flood will follow. But then? …."

Wulfgar leaped to his feet and appeared to be calling out to the thatch above them.

"…. then the world will be reborn, fresh and fertile, and those who are left will return to begin anew; a better world…."

Renweard had never seen Wulfgar so passionate, so animated. He tugged at Wulfgar's shirt pulling him back down into his seat on the floor where he landed with an undignified thump.

Wulfgar returned quietly to the present.

"…. but let's not get ahead of ourselves. There is still much work to be done here before that glorious day!"

Renweard looked deep into the fire in front of him hypnotised by the amber flames as they danced their sinuous dance.

“I think maybe my journey here has indeed left me shorn of some of my memory Wulfgar; I have no recollection of Ragnorök as yet, but the flood and the rebirth do seem familiar to me….”

“Good, good, but for now, eat… eat!”

Wulfgar gestured to the platter in front of them, which they shared with a small group of warriors; some seemed as bewildered as Renweard, others as enthusiastic as Wulfgar.

And so they sat, and they ate, and they drank. They talked long of battles and they talked openly of love, for as they all agreed: each came with a measure of both pain and pleasure.

And then, as was often the case here, Renweard thought to himself, it began. There was no signal, no blast from a battle horn or bellowed command, but almost as one, the gathering set down their plates and their drinking horns and rose to their feet to begin gathering their arms.

Men began pulling on chain mail aided by a second; some eased themselves into their helms, becoming at once other-worldly, peering out through eye holes that had become the mystical beast they had once only alluded to; others gathered spears and shields.

But all, to a man, buckled themselves into their leather sword belts, once again reunited with an old and trusted friend that now lay silently sheathed at their master's side, ready to do his bidding.

Renweard, too, now fully dressed, turned to gather his shield and spears. This was to be his first action in Asgard, and he was keen to show his new lord the prowess and fearlessness for which he was renowned.

He turned, expecting to find them still in the position they had been placed the night before, where the Valkyries had laid them after their long, stormy journey from Haligsfeld, but instead his eyes settled upon a sight which could only have presented itself in this place; for, other-worldly and ominous, it bore great ill.

His mind swam momentarily. Is this the mead? He thought to himself.

He blinked several times to ensure that this was not a trick of the light and with great anguish asked:

"What…. What is this?"

Wulfgar turned too.

"Renweard?"

"My shield! And one of my spears, look!"

They both peered into Renweard's sleeping space where the weapons had lain and hung since his arrival in the night.

Wulfgar was genuinely confused. He too blinked, doubting his sobriety.

"I've never seen this before, Renweard. This is not known to me!"

He sounded uneasy; alarmed.

He had good cause to be, for as they both stood fixed to the spot, Renweard's shield, his protector and overseer, appeared to them incomplete, as though great sections of it had been simply swabbed out of existence. Those parts that remained shimmered like water, almost ghostly in their form. The main structure was still present - mostly - but the central boss was transparent so that the post it on which it hung, and which it had once obscured, could now clearly be seen through it; The two guardians: the boar and bird, and all the Cyning's jewels seemed to be fading also, their sparkle fading like the creeping hand of dawn on starlight.

Wulfgar stepped forward suddenly.

"Wulfgar! NO!"

Despite Renweard's warning, Wulfgar placed his hand behind the shield. What had once been a solid structure of wood and leather now only seemed to exist as some form of light.

"What is this trickery?" Renweard hissed in disbelief as he too moved toward the unearthly scene. He looked on helplessly as his old ally, having saved him from flashing steel on many occasions, continued to fade out of this world.

"I...I don't know Renweard; I truly do not know. This is unknown to me. I swear it!"

Both men considered their next move, strong hands firmly gripping the hilt of their sword against the chance that they too were taken from them; ready to draw, ready to defend against who knew what, when a voice behind them issued another warning.

"Your spearheads appear to be fading too!"

Eadig had joined them now. One of the eight who had arrived in the night alongside Renweard, he had spent the morning in song with his beloved lyre. Much loved was his prose and his song, but devilish were the riddles that tangled your mind like the thorn.

"Eadig. Is your armoury intact?"

"It is my lord Renweard. So far, anyway."

He answered slowly, cautiously, as if to do otherwise might draw the phenomenon to him.

"Then what is this? Am I alone in my torment?"

"You are not!" Another, deeper voice joined them, its power echoed in its tone. It was Grimme.

Renweard, relieved at the great man's presence, looked to him for his counsel.

"Grimme! What is this trickery? What is this.... sorcery?"

"We are not sure, Renweard...." he said as he stared wistfully at the scene in front of him ".... We have seen it maybe a handful of times over the centuries, but in the past few decades, it has become more prevalent. We know it only as The Diminishing. What its true name and purpose are is a mystery!"

His statement ended on a note of concern, as though an idea was forming - had been formed. Nevertheless, it was an idea that he was unwilling to voice openly. He continued.

"My lord Thunor has witnessed events back on the old world that may explain these occurrences, but alas, Woden will not permit him to take earthly form and investigate in person."

Renweard, both affronted by and afraid of this unknown menace reacted in a manner consistent with his status.

"If there is mischief afoot, I would surely know who is at the heart of it! I would know who dares to tamper with MY WEAPONRY!"

Grimme offered a calming hand, gently patting down the air with his palm.

"Huginn and Muninn have already been despatched. You will have your answer soon Renweard...."

The birds, who took their names from thought and memory, were Woden's eyes and ears. Great fear for their wellbeing was felt, not least by Woden himself, yet still they travelled out across the world bringing news of happenings and events back to his hall.

Renweard moved to speak again, but Grimme intercepted his protest.

"…. The problem is known to us. The ravens will discover who is behind this mischief, and Woden will provide the solution." He spoke calmly but firmly.

The tension among the group seemed to ease a little, and as the concerned faces of warriors nearby looked on, Grimme continued.

"You have your sword; another spear and helm?"

"I do; for now!" He replied warily.

"Then continue to train with these; There is still much that can be achieved with them. As soon as word arrives from Woden I will call you and together we will resolve this mystery."

Grimme looked kindly into Renweard's troubled face.

"Renweard?" he said, looking for confirmation.

“Yes Grimme…. of course. Thank you….”

He returned the look of trust to his new friend and nodded, repeating, “…. Thank you!”

“Maybe Woden will have an answer for me too!”

As one they turned to face the direction from which Abrecan’s anxious voice had come and saw him standing proud, ready to do battle, except that his chain mail now bore the same ghostly appearance of Renweard’s shield, holed as though by some great iron-devouring moth.

Grimme spoke again, apparently more concerned now.

“You arrived in Valhalla together; last night?”

“We did, and from the same village, having fought our last great battle together.” replied Renweard.

Renweard and Abrecan made eye contact and stared proudly at one another - brothers in arms.

“Aye, that we did.” Abrecan spoke softly and with affection.

“Then there may indeed be a connection…” he stroked his beard thoughtfully as he stared into the firelight “…however, we will not know for sure until Woden’s ravens return. Until then, be the stout hearts I know you to be; continue with your training. I will call when they do.”

Both Renweard and Abrecan made to speak, impatient for a resolution.

"I will call…. when they do!" Grimme nodded, a friendly gesture which said: understand? This was confirmed in kind by the two men.

With that Grimme made his way out of the mead hall, his great bulk softened by the swirl and eddy of his cloak.

There was an urgent need now to relay this new information to Woden and his sons in order that as soon as the birds arrived home a plan could be formulated.

Never before had Woden's army been threatened in this manner, not to such an extent at least.

They had lost armour and jewellery; occasionally, a whole warrior had been taken in this way as if reabsorbed back into the old world. But if there was indeed evil preying on the men, and in greater numbers, it must be confronted, and soon, Ragnorök was closer at hand than any of those on the ground knew.

***

And so, as Grimme had instructed, Renweard, Wulfgar, Eadig, and Abrecan, their minds still trying to fathom the mysterious, disturbing events, began moving forward to join the rest of the army to begin training.

Gathering those arms that were, as yet, unaffected by the curse, they marched in column, fearless, courageous, but above all proud: proud to be men of Wandle's Ham. Proud to have been called.

Suddenly though, and without warning, Renweard stopped dead in his tracks. The entire column did likewise, albeit confused for having done so, and some cursed as they collided with the man in front. Was some other evil now among them? Had it taken Renweard?

They looked toward their leader who stood large in front of them, a look of determination on his face, a steely look in his piercing blue eyes, and they waited.

Ever the leader, Renweard had decided to rally the men against this new darkness. He had thought long and hard on their misfortune, and with each step, the rhythm of the march seemed to work on his mind. The steady footfall, the clank of steel and the creak of leather seemed to merge into one, overpowering voice, until finally, he knew what he must do.

The line waited silently as a soft wind blew playfully among them. Pennant and flag responded as they fluttered from spear top and pole proclaiming its bearer's house, and all eyes turned to Renweard who, mustering his consciousness, drew himself up to full height and spoke:

"Brothers! My brothers. Before we join the battle, we must focus. Wulfgar tells me that this…."

He gestured with an outstretched arm toward the training ground, where warriors were already forming lines as others prepared to fight one-on-one.

"…. is as brutal as any field in which we have stood together. No one will be giving us quarter, and you will still feel the bite of steel should your mind wander from its task."

He looked briefly at the ground, gathering his thoughts before continuing.

"There is nothing that can be done as yet to solve the ill that has befallen us; nothing that as yet that will stay our minds, and until we know what we are dealing with, that is in the hands, for now at least, of our lords Woden, Thunor, Grimme and the rest. We must therefore, push this from our minds and focus!"

The small band of warriors stirred, ready to do their duty, spurred on by Renweard's words.

"By night's fall, our worth shall be known to those in the Great Hall, not as the newly fallen; not as those yet to prove themselves; but as WARRIORS! As men of honour; and as proud, brave spirits!"

The men stirred again, rattling sword and spear as one.

"Forward then! Shall we show them what havoc the warriors of Wandle's Ham are capable of?"

"YES!"

"Shall we show them why WE were chosen for this fight?"

"YES!"

The roar of exhilaration filled the air, momentarily distracting those already on the field, and with the blood ringing in their ears, the warriors set off toward the training fields.

As they advanced Wulfgar leaned toward Renweard, a look on his face that Loki himself would be proud of, and whispered quietly.

"Good words, well spoken, my brother! A true leader of men!"

"Thank you old friend, but no; you may not have my space by the fire tonight!"

Both men smiled as they joined the chaos that is battle.

Chapter 5: The Corvid Return.

Mærsere, the messenger, moved swiftly through the heaving, clashing field of fighting men. Breathing heavily, he made sure his approach was from behind the shield wall, which was once more standing firm against the onslaught of yet another wave of sword-brandishing warriors.

"Come, Renweard. Make yourself known to me!" He spoke more to himself than to the man he sought.

He had been assigned to this quest but, in truth, had little time in which to complete it, such was the urgency of the mission, Woden's companions having been despatched on their errand three days since. Three days of uncertainty and misery, three days during which even more of the men's belongings had succumbed to the dark magic, and after what seemed like an age, long and torturous, there was no time, no time for this long-winded pursuit.

Huginn and Muninn, Woden's ravens, had returned from their quest in the old world and had been seen flying high above Asgard, and in little more time than it took for them to circle the city, land, and relay their findings to Woden and the others, he had been summoned by Grimme and tasked with finding Renweard and Abrecan.

Feeling the frustration rise in him, he was on the verge of asking a smiling, blood-streaked warrior - why so happy?

He mused - whether he knew of their whereabouts when he spotted them.

They were no more than a chain's distance from him, fighting as part of a skirmishing party who were in the process of rushing forward to reinforce the right flank and repel the onslaught of the opposing army.

"At last!" he cried aloud.

"What?" the happy warrior looked at him, puzzled.

"Sorry, friend. I was merely expressing my relief at having found my charge." He smiled.

The warrior looked none the wiser for Mærsere's explanation and carried on, still smiling, heading for the aid station to tend to his wounds, and without stopping or waiting for a response nor offering the man further clarification, Mærsere hurried toward Renweard, calling as he did so.

"Renweard! RENWEARD!" he called through the clamour of battle, but to no avail.

"RENWEARD!" he called again, but it was Wulfgar who heard him and, momentarily distracted, came close to receiving a shield boss to the face, which he side-stepped and countered with his own, bringing the hulk of a man crashing heavily to the ground, blood issuing from his now broken nose, his eyes glazed, barely a flicker of consciousness behind them.

He gestured Mærsere to wait at the brow of a small hummock just across from and behind them and made to rejoin the skirmishing party, skilfully avoiding the thrust of a well-aimed sword as he did so.

Side-stepping a small party of adrenaline-fuelled Geoguth: young warriors hell-bent on making a name for themselves this day, Mærsere climbed to the top of the grass-covered hill and waited, observing the fighting below.

The light was beginning to fade now as the day moved noisily towards its bloody conclusion, and as the last rays of sunlight swept lazily across the field, he looked down on the heaving, shimmering mass and pondered Asgard's fate.

Ragnorök will indeed be a mighty endeavour, but with an army such as this, we cannot fail. He thought.

Finally, as the assault on the right flank faded and the enemy troops re-joined the main force, Wulfgar was able to attract the attention of Renweard. He pointed toward the hillock and the figure that stood patiently, silhouetted against a reddening sunset, and Renweard knew at once.

"Grimme's messenger?" he called.

"He is. You are summoned to Woden; You and Abrecan."

Renweard called to Abrecan, who turned toward his lord's voice, the exhilaration of battle still bright in his eyes. Renweard was pointing across to a small hill where a single warrior stood. From his spear flew the banner of the house of Woden: a pair of stylised golden ravens against a ground of crimson, curling beaks entwined as they faced each other across the heavy woollen fabric. The emblem of the bearer's neutrality and safe passage across the field. Abrecan understood at once.

"At last!" he uttered as he drove the pommel of his sword hard down onto the back of an unhelmed head, and as the man fell heavily to the ground, he turned and left the field to join his lord.

Renweard, however, had one more duty to perform before they set off and gestured Abrecan to wait.

"Before we leave… WULFGAR!" he called to his old comrade, who hurried to his side.

"We are likely to leave the field for the night at any moment. Have the men make ready to depart, but DO NOT turn your back on the line. They may as yet send a further wave, and until the horn signals days' end, be prepared to fight on!"

"Of course, my lord. I will speak to the men now. They seem to think the day is already won!"

He nodded toward the skirmish party who were in the process of leaving the field, boisterously reliving the day's events.

"Over to you then, my old friend!" Renweard smiled knowingly.

With that, they parted; Renweard and Abrecan heading for the messenger, Wulfgar back to the line, issuing a series of Old English expletives towards the men as he went.

They reached the top of the hill just as the horn blew, signalling the end of training for that day. Instinctively Renweard turned to look back on his men, who were almost completely lost now in darkness, but saw them as they regrouped to begin the short march back to the hall.

All over the field, torches were being fired to light their way home, and splashes of flickering orange flame burst into life like angry, impatient demons.

"My lord Renweard; Abrecan…" each nodded a greeting as they met on the hill. "… Grimme sends word that the ravens have returned. He must speak with you both as a matter of urgency."

"What have they discovered?" Abrecan asked impatiently, whistling through a gap in his teeth as he spoke. Frowning, Renweard noticed for the first time that one of Abrecan's front teeth was missing.

“I am merely the messenger, Woden will address you all, Grimme too, as soon as you arrive. You are instructed to make haste for the High Hall. There is no need to reorder your attire or yourselves for this meeting, such is the alacrity required. We must leave at once!”

Seeing Abrecan’s confusion, Renweard clarified. “He means that we need to hurry, so don’t worry about cleaning ourselves up…”

“Oh… why could he not just say…?” Abrecan did not finish the sentence as a heavy-browed glare from the messenger cut him short.

With that, Mærsere hurried them away, following closely behind; He may not be privy to the conversation that was about to take place, but he would make sure that they arrived promptly so that they could be.

The march to the Great Hall took only a short while, and they approached its imposing entrance in good time. Through ranks of battle-weary warriors; lines of Valkyrie on their way back to the hall for tonight’s feast; past the goat: Heidrún; and Glasir, the golden tree, so that finally they stood before its majestic, towering doors, each fashioned from oak and adorned with gold, the stories of great battles and heroic deeds both embossed, and carved on their surface. Almost immediately, as though they had been anticipating the men's arrival, both doors swung open, moved by force neither seen nor heard.

They entered, but neither one was overawed as they might otherwise have been; such was their eagerness to learn of the fate of their belongings. More had since begun to fade, of others and of their own.

As they walked forward, Grimme greeted them with a smile of welcome. They returned it, glad of his presence, but their attention was drawn to the man seated high above them on the great fur-covered throne. There was no doubting who this was; the pair of ravens to either side would have been evidence enough, but as Renweard and Abrecan approached the plinth on which the throne rested, its occupant leaned forward, moving his face fully into the light, and considered them with his one, good eye, the other scarred heavily having long been sacrificed to the well of wisdom.

"Renweard. Abrecan. Welcome. Come, sit. We have much to discuss." Woden said.

***

It had been five days since Rab had first discovered the shield boss in the grave he'd been excavating. Since then, the entire team has made find after find. Artefacts associated with warriors, some of high status, had been found in eight graves which were arranged in a loose circle, their occupants having been buried with their feet to the east and head to the west. All had swords, although time and soil acidity had taken their toll.

Even so, they were easily identifiable as such despite the heavy corrosion.

There were spearheads too, their shafts of Ashwood long since having faded into decay; combs made from animal bone had somehow survived, and the prize: coins, unworked garnets, and small ingots of gold and silver which appeared to have been contained in a small purse, although it too had rotted away to almost nothing in the ground.

Nothing of this importance had been found since Sutton Hoo or the Prittlewell Prince, and what made those, and indeed, this site, important was that the burials had been found where they were originally laid, and the artefacts within had not moved or been moved.

There was so much that could be learned from a find like this which had indeed been confirmed as Anglo-Saxon, and the quantity and quality of the finds were what made it a rare one.

"Getting there, bud!"

Colin kneeled beside Rab as he worked to clear the rest of his features of finds.

His years of working in the cold and wet showed as he eased himself uncomfortably to the ground, sitting back on his haunches, which was his favoured position.

Sadly, there had been no sign of a skeleton in any of the graves, just the remains of a single tooth that the experts were fairly certain was a front incisor. In any case, it showed that the grave was just that and not a memorial as some had put forward as a theory.

The soil here was sandy and highly acidic so that any trace of bone, or anything organic such as wood, cloth, or leather, had long since dissolved away.

As such, the soil from each of the graves had been sampled in an attempt to, hopefully, find evidence of a former occupant. The samples would be processed in specialised laboratories that should be able to detect high levels of phosphate: one of bone's main calcium components.

"Oh, Hi Col. Yeah, another hour or so and I'll be done. Has the GPS arrived yet? Only, it still needs mapping."

"Yeah, Josette is just setting up over by the hut. I reckon that'll work nicely time-wise 'cos she's got some levels to record across the site first, then she'll be able to sort these out."

He gestured an arm across the series of graves. Most were at roughly the same stage of excavation now, as the team had worked hard to make sure they were cleared in a timely fashion, not least because of the threat of the cursed "Night Hawkers".

Those who were able had started earlier and finished later in the day to achieve this, such was the site's importance.

"OK, I'll crack on then to make sure. Have you seen the camera, by the way? Only, I think I'll make the photo record next; That way, Josette can get straight in here without having to worry about tip-toeing. Well, within a little!"

And I won't have to clean around my feature again afterward, he thought to himself. Footprints in an archaeological photograph being heavily frowned upon.

"Good idea. I'll bring it all over for you; Back in a tick."

Rab hesitated briefly, uncertain of whether to ask the question that had been troubling his mind for the past couple of days.

No, it's daft! He thought, but such was his dilemma. He took a deep breath before saying:

"Before you go, can I just quickly ask you something?

Colin looked at Rab expectantly. He seemed uncomfortable, embarrassed even.

"Yeah, sure, wassup?" he frowned, intrigued by the mysterious overtones of Rab's request.

"Well… oh, it's probably nothing…. no, forget I said anything…!"

"No, go on, Rab. It sounds like it's important. You look like you need to get summat off your chest anyway."

Rab continued.

"Well… have you seen those two blackbirds that have been around the site for the past couple of days?"

"Err… there's been loads of Blackbirds Rab…."

"No, not Blackbirds, blackbirds! Two of them. They definitely weren't Crows or Rooks - I know my Corvids - but I looked them up anyway, and just as I thought, they're Ravens!"

"What, like the Tower of London? And all that?"

"And all that! Thing is, we don't really get them over in these parts, not like this anyway, and the weirdest thing of all… oh, you'll think I've lost it…"

"No, go on, mate." Colin encouraged.

"… they talk to each other! There you are, I've said it!"

Colin's face froze in surprise, his mouth slightly agape.

"Oh, I knew you'd think I was loopy!"

"No! no… it's not that…" Colin saw the look of embarrassment on Rab's face. "… S'jus not what I expected, S'all. What do you mean 'talking', though? Like words and that?"

"No, I mean, I haven't actually heard words; it's more the way they interact like they're inspecting the site or something?"

Rab could see that Colin was more than a little confused, so he continued.

"OK, look; at first, I thought, oh, that's a rare sighting for round here. Nice! You know? Rare bird sighted and all that. But then I noticed that they always landed together and sat next to one another, chattering. Not just the usual chatter, though. One would 'talk' while the other sat quietly listening. Then the other would 'reply.' I'm telling you, Col', they're communicating!"

Colin sat silently for a moment allowing the information to sink in. This is a first! He thought, but the look on Rab's face told him that he really was spooked by this, and Rab was such a straight-up kind of guy; It wasn't in his nature to imagine things.

"OK, I believe ya mate. I can tell you're serious anyway."

A look of relief spread over Rab's face.

"Is that all of it?"

"Kind of, except that they only seem interested in what we're doing around the graves."

"I'll grant ya, it does sound a bit weird, but aren't Corvids and the like attracted to shiny objects?"

"Better keep your hat on then, Col!"

"Mm…? oh, the hair… yeah! Cheers, mate!"

They both laughed. It was a long-standing joke that Colin's hairstyle had been named "The Moses," given that it had long since parted like the Red Sea. Colin's riposte was that he was still waiting for the passage to close.

Emerging from his thoughts, Colin spoke.

"Thing is Rab, even if they're having a good ol' natter about the site unless they're Night Hawk spies, I don't know what you wanna do about it."

"Well, nothing really, I suppose. It's just been freaking me out a bit. Can't think why, to be honest… Just a feeling… I dunno."

"Well, look, we're almost done here now. You guys have sped things along nicely, so we're well ahead of schedule…"

It was Rab's turn to look confused now. Seeing this, Colin attempted to make things clearer.

"What I mean is, if you wanted to wrap it up here and head off to the new site…"

Another site, some ten miles away and in the middle of a small village, was in the process of being set up, and excavations were due to start in the next day or so. Rab was due to start there when he'd finished on this site.

"God, no!" Rab interrupted. "No, I love this site. It's got a really… peaceful feel to it. No, I'd like to see it through to the end… please!"

"All right, fella, don't worry. I'm not gonna banish ya!"

They both laughed again, Rab feeling slightly foolish now.

"It's one of the things I've always respected about you, Rab: you always seem to be connected to a site. It's not just about digging holes, it's about people and history."

"Don't see the point otherwise, Col'. Otherwise, it's just treasure hunting!"

"Exactly, boy. Exactly!"

With that, Colin headed off to the 4x4, which was parked nearby, to collect the photographic equipment he had promised Rab.

They continued to work; clearing, cleaning, recording, and sampling up to lunchtime and on into the afternoon. Neither Rab nor Colin discussed the Ravens further, although Rab occasionally checked to see if they were still there. They were. Neither felt that there was anything to add to the conversation and although Rab felt slightly less ill at ease than he had before he'd spoken to Colin, he definitely felt that there was something unusual about their presence.

Finally, at around three in the afternoon, as Rab completed the last of the paperwork which concluded his grave's excavation, and as the light began to fade, he again became aware of the birds. They sat together, as they always had, on the lowest overhanging branch of an old oak, its canopy having provided both shelter and sustenance during their visits. There they had remained all afternoon, chattering and feeding but, above all, watching. Suddenly, as one, they became silent and looked skywards as though they were being hailed. They were clearly listening, their heads cocked to one side when suddenly one of the birds chattered loudly as though answering, then together they took to the air, calling noisily as they flew off across the river before fading into the distance.

“That’s a new one!” Rab said aloud.

“Eh?” Angela was passing when he spoke.

“What? Oh, Hi Ange’. No, nothing. I was just thinking out loud. Are we off then?”

He had noticed that Angela had gathered her tools and was heading back to the site hut.

“In about half an hour, I think. The light’s fading already, and there’s not much point opening up that last feature till tomorrow.”

“Makes sense. I’m pretty much done here, so I’ll start packing up, too, I think.”

“OK. I’ll see you across there then. Do you need a hand with anything?”

“Ooh, actually, there is the camera gear. Would you mind?”

“No, sling it on.”

With that, the camera case, ranging poles, and other paraphernalia were balanced precariously among Angela’s tools and spare clothing: waterproofs and the like, and as the afternoon drew to a close, they and the rest of the team began loading their kit into one of the 4x4s.

They were ready to leave for the office when one of the team asked, "Where's Colin?"

They glanced back toward the site.

"He's there look; under that big old oak." Angela had seen him.

"What's he doing?"

"Dunno, just staring up into it." She replied again.

Rab felt a chill wash over him.

"Look…" he said wistfully, "…you take this truck, I need to talk to Col about that new site anyway, and we'll meet you back there? We'll take the other 4x4; Is that all right?"

"OK, yeah, no problem. See you shortly then." Angela agreed, sensing none of the foreboding that Rab now did.

Ian, the archaeologist who had asked after Colin's whereabouts, was more than happy to drive the truck and jumped enthusiastically into the driver's seat as the others took their place in the vehicle and as Rab set off across the field to meet Colin, he heard the enormous diesel engine cough and rattled into life, and the truck pulls away, its fat tyres slipping momentarily on the wet ground despite being four-wheeled drive.

The light was slipping away even more quickly now, and there was a slight chill on the air. Colin, seeing Rab approach, turned his back to the old tree and started to walk across the site to meet him. Rab's right: there's definitely something… different about this part of the site, he thought as he trudged back across the sandy soil; I'll grant him that!

As Rab reached the halfway point between the tree and the 4x4, he lifted a hand to acknowledge him, and as he did so, he noticed somebody standing by the graves.

I thought they'd all left for the office, he thought to himself. Is it Ange? No; he'd seen her climb into the back of the truck. Definitely female, though. Josette left ages ago; that only left Bernie, but she's been off sick today.

"Who's that Col?" he called as they drew nearer.

"Where?" Colin strained his eyes through the fading light but could see only Rab.

"The woman - I think it's a woman; standing by the grave pits!"

Colin strained his eyes again; still, he could see only Rab.

"Blowed if I can see anyone, 'part from you obviously, and even you're starting to fade into the gloom."

"There Col; plain as… well, not day but… you really can't see her? She's right next to my grave cut!"

Rab felt frustrated at Colin for not being able to see what he clearly could. Why can't he see her? He wondered

I hope this isn't another one of his "blackbird" moments! Colin thought.

"Hadn't we better go see what she's up to!"

"Rab, there's no one there! Come on, mate, this is getting daft; you're starting to give me the hecby-jeebys!"

Rab ignored Colin and turned and walked toward the unknown visitor, who appeared now to be strangely backlit by a bright orange light, which he assumed emanated from an unseen hand lantern, though in truth, none could be seen. He was within a few feet of her when he stopped suddenly, causing Colin to have to sidestep him.

"Wassup?... Rab?"

Rab did not reply; He had been about to ask the woman what she was doing when the hair on the back of his neck began tingling furiously, and a strange sensation, like that of cold water, trickled down his spine.

"What the….?"

Through the murk of late afternoon, he clearly saw an old woman who, as he looked on, stared intently back at him, her eyes black, all detail lost in the gloom. She wore a loose-fitting, ankle-length dress and was protected from the chill by a large, flowing woollen cloak; a head scarf covered most of her long, grey hair, and at her waist, something he recognised from his work as an archaeologist: a chatelaine.

Worn by women throughout the medieval period, a chatelaine was a decorative belt from which a series of chains were suspended, each terminating with day-to-day items such as keys, scissors, or sewing items: the lady of the house's tool belt, as it were. Such was this, but it also carried bunches of leaves and other unidentifiable but clearly organic items, each secured with a short length of twine. Her feet were bare and filthy from the soil underfoot, and everything appeared to be, strangely, sepia tone.

"What the….?" Rab tried again.

He stood, rooted to the spot, his mind racing. Colin, too, tried again.

"Rab; what is it? What the hell are you staring at? C'mon mate, this ain't funny now!"

Still, there was no reply as Rab continued to stare, wide-eyed, straight ahead into the darkness which now engulfed them both, and as Colin looked at his friend, he appeared paralysed: unable to move.

Gripped by fear but held by fascination, Rab watched as the woman continued to look straight into his soul. Slowly she raised both arms skyward as eight small blue lights appeared simultaneously; one above each grave. They hovered about two feet above the ground, shimmering slightly, and each seemed to emit a soft whisper.

"Col?"

"Rab? You alright?" He was really worried now.

One thing they had both noticed was that the wind seemed to be increasing now, along with the chill. Colin looked on helplessly, willing his friend to snap out of whatever this was, and whatever this was, he was convinced now that he was no longer faking it.

Without warning, Rab's expression turned suddenly to one of fear; his eyes widened, and his mouth began to open and close as though he were about to speak but was unable. Colin, sensing an imminent threat, called out, though he, too, now shook with fear for his friend's safety.

"RAB! SNAP OUT OF IT!"

There was no change, and Rab did not reply.

Unexpectedly, the old woman's arms dropped sharply to her side, her chin fell to her chest and her eyes closed, but the eight lights remained. Their whispers seemed louder now, and each carried an overtone of despair and frustration. She inhaled deeply, noisily, and as she lifted her head, her deep, black, empty eyes bore into Rab again. This time though, he felt her rage. Slowly, she raised her right arm and pointed at him, her fingers gnarled with age, and in a powerful voice that belied its owner's stature, she called:

"YOU MUST RETURN ALL OF IT!"

Chapter 6: Woden's Decree

Renweard and Abrecan moved forward to take the seat that had been provided for each of them. More accustomed to sitting on the ground by a fire, the seats were more comfortable than they looked. A simple cross made from two interlocking planks of wood, the seat was padded with a feather-stuffed seat cushion. I could get used to this, Abrecan thought as he reclined against the backrest, allowing it to support his weight. Had his status not afforded him similar luxuries in the old world, the experience might have been similar for Renweard. In any case, he relaxed into his seat, allowing the effects of today's exertions to drift slowly away.

Then Woden spoke.

"As you can see, Huginn and Muninn have returned."

He paused as he stood up from his throne and walked around to the two birds who had settled, one on each of its finials, where he hand-fed them the remains of what had once been a small mammal before continuing.

"They have kept a watch over your resting places in the old world where…."

"What did they find?" Abrecan asked, ever eager to know the fate of his belongings.

Grimme flashed him an angry look and was on the verge of scolding him when Woden spoke again, gesturing to Grimme with a calming hand that the interruption was both pertinent and acceptable.

"…. where they witnessed the removal of every personal item from within the eight deathbeds. Weapons, jewellery; nothing was left in the earth."

Renweard and Abrecan sat forward in their seat, comfort now quickly sliding down the list of importance.

"Every item?" asked Renweard.

"It would seem so, although, and I find this intriguing, the individuals responsible do not seem to be merely plundering for profit as has been the case in the past. It seems that they wish to learn of our culture by studying what remains of it on the earth."

"Do we know this is their aim? How can we be sure?" Renweard asked.

"Nothing is ever certain, Renweard, but my ravens have listened to the conversations of those involved…." All eyes turned to the birds, which were in the process of preening their feathers, having already consumed Woden's tidbits. "…and they observed the care that has been afforded to each item; The enthusiasm of the seekers is, according to Huginn and Muninn, quite palpable. They seem to have an equal interest in steel and gold alike."

"Are things so different there now, my lord?"

Abrecan proffered his question, remembering this time to observe protocol, and nodded to Grimme, seeking his approval. Seeing this, Grimme returned the nod with a smile as he acknowledged the gesture. Abrecan continued.

"Are the poems and stories no longer told? That they should have so little knowledge of us…" The sound of his voice faded softly into the rafters of the great hall.

All looked to Woden, their faces frozen in anticipation, awaiting his response.

"It would seem that there are those, such as these…. Seekers of truth, who aim to keep our name alive, but for the most part...? Woden sighed heavily "…we have become veiled to them; lost beyond all knowledge."

"I don't understand; What could have happened to have caused such a…" Abrecan searched for the word.

"An emptiness?" volunteered Renweard.

"Yes! Why do the poets and storytellers no longer keep our deeds alive?"

Woden looked down at his troubled warriors. He could see the pain and the hurt on their faces. Where are the bards? Why do they no longer speak of us?

"It would appear to be much more complicated than we might imagine, for the time being at least. Perhaps it is we who have turned our backs on the old world for too long; perhaps because of this, they now return the gesture? Whatever the cause, we must look to make it right, beginning with the return of your possessions."

The hall fell quiet as the men contemplated both the situation and the means by which to correct it.

It was beyond the comprehension of all but a few of them. Grimme and Woden had some knowledge, of course, but their work was here in Asgard. Of them all, Thunor: God of thunder, had seen things firsthand and, perhaps more importantly, had done so recently: It was Thunor who had first witnessed the desecration of the graves, and it was he who had tried to communicate Valhalla's displeasure through his bolts of lightning. When this failed, he brought word to Woden, whose ravens had been despatched and whose information they now debated.

Finally, Renweard broke the silence.

"Is there a way, my lord? Is there a way to have them returned to us?"

"I believe so, but I do not think it will be an easy task; the minds of men are not easily turned. Nevertheless, I have spoken with Kendra, the prophetess."

Grimme's eyes flashed astonishment toward Woden, who regarded them peripherally but offered no acknowledgement.

"Has she been asked to do what I think you have in mind, my lord?" asked Grimme.

"If what you think, Grimme, is that I would have her communicate directly with the seekers, to relay to them our woes, then yes; that is exactly what I have in mind. You doubt this is possible?"

Grimme's face had wrinkled into a frown, as had those of everyone else.

"My lord, I would never question your knowledge of such things. You are, after all, Wod…."

The doors to the Great Hall swung open. This time though, they did so with a deafening crash and recoiled on their hinges, bouncing heavily as the steel pins strained to keep them in place. A group of bedraggled, sweat-soaked warriors stood in the doorway, proud and exuberant. They moved noisily into the warmth and familiarity of the hall expecting food, ale, and a hero's welcome, but their enthusiasm quickly waned as their eyes met those of Woden and the men, and where, on their faces, there had been an expression of joy and reverence, there now lingered a look of horror at having disturbed such a distinguished gathering.

Woden broke the deadlock.

"We shall conclude this conversation later tonight, after the feast. It seems we have guests." He laughed aloud.

"Come, come brave souls…" he called "…enter my hall and make ready for tonight's endeavours, for they too will challenge your ability to remain upright as much as any skirmish!"

With the tension broken, the warriors laughed openly, albeit with an air of relief, and began moving into the hall, depositing their weapons and armour as they returned to their sleeping space as Woden, seeing one individual, in particular, continued.

"Let us hope that Waelfwulf makes it through to the last toast of the evening!" he teased.

Waelwulf, known to many as storyteller and keeper of words, had, on a previous night, been in full flow, enthusiastically reciting one of his most popular tales. The story involved golden swords that granted magical powers, great battles, and the happy marriage to a king's daughter, but on this occasion, he had barely set off on his quest when a particularly strong batch of mead arrived. Without realising it and keen to continue, he had drunk the horn dry in one long, noisy swig. There had been a brief moment of hesitation, as though collecting his thoughts, as his audience silently held their breath when, without notice, he muttered something that sounded to all present like "Oh mother!", after which he collapsed to the ground and snored heavily for the rest of the night.

The tears and laughter had continued well after the event, and everyone seemed keen to sample the brew that had floored one of the hardest drinkers in the Great Hall. Being reminded of it now reignited the laughter of that night and left those who had not yet heard the tale questioning those who had. Waelwulf, on the other hand, was less keen to have the story retold and stood looking sheepishly on as Woden continued.

"Come, Waelwulf. We salute your contribution to the chronicles. After all, too few tell of the sacrifice made to alcohol!"

Waelwulf's face finally broke into a smile before joining the others, laughing heartily, and once again, the tears of laughter flowed.

Leaving the warriors, who continued to rib Waelwulf, to their preparations, Woden and the three men withdrew to conclude their meeting.

“Kendra will meet us tomorrow before we break our fast. She wishes our encounter to take place by the ford in Haligsfeld.”

“Haligsfeld? The field in which our bodies lay? Is that not outside of this realm?”

“Do not worry, Renweard. Grimme and I know how to reach it.” Said Woden kindly.

“We shall assemble outside the great doors before day breaks and travel in one party.”

Renweard spoke again.

“My lord, forgive me, but may I speak freely?”

Woden nodded his approval, intrigued at Renweard’s candour.

“My lord, eight of us lay in death, and eight of us are now lacking that with which we set forth on this journey, yet only we two....” He gestured toward Abrecan “...are represented?”

Woden smiled and glanced at Grimme.

It was true that since the first disappearances, others of Renweard’s newly arrived party had shared the same unsettling experience. Shields, Swords; even the cauldrons with their contents of food; all had slowly evaporated away, often as the men looked on helplessly.

"My lord Renweard..." Renweard swelled at being addressed in such a noble fashion by one, himself, so noble "...it is for this very reason I called you and your men to serve here, in Valhalla."

He stood directly in front of Renweard and placed a hand on each shoulder and, speaking as a friend, continued.

"You are an honourable man, and you do your men a great service. I will have you bring all seven of your brothers to the field tomorrow. Together we shall see if Kendra truly can create a bridge between our worlds. We shall address these... seekers and set to bring about an end to this tragic episode."

Renweard nodded his agreement and gratitude.

"Besides: I have no wish to see you scowl our enemy to death!"

The men laughed again as the small group went their separate ways.

As they made to join the rest of their party, Abrecan started to speak.

"Do you think...?"

"Abrecan! Settle your mind and leave it till dawn. There is much drinking to be done here tonight!"

As if conjured by Renweard's words, Anfeald appeared in front of them. Blocking their path, he carried two over-full drinking horns which slopped mead clumsily onto the ground at their feet.

"It looks, my brothers, as though you might both be in need of these."

He offered them the drinking vessels, which they accepted gratefully.

"Anfeald, my friend, you truly do have the gift of foresight!"

Anfeald smiled, happy to have once again tended to his lord Renweard, who continued:

"Although next time, perhaps we could spare the ground spirits their mead shower!"

And laughing, they stepped over the puddle of alcohol and made their way into the sea of drinking, revelling warriors, taking their well-earned place among them.

Chapter 7: Kendra

The dawn was still a little way off as the ten men gathered in front of the Great Hall. Woden and Grimme, having arrived sometime earlier, stood with their back to the majestic building, looking out across the fields of Asgard. As they peacefully breathed in the cool morning air, they watched the Sun begin its slow ascent into the sky, as yet a slash of vivid orange bordered above and below by a thin line of purple cloud. Shadow remained for now, and detail was yet to emerge.

The Wandle's Ham eight appeared gingerly from the warm interior of their night's chamber. Behind them, thousands of sleeping, snoring warriors continued their slumber, all having celebrated the day's labours well into the mead-soaked night.

Woden greeted them, speaking softly.

"Renweard; Abrecan. Good morning." Then he turned to Renweard's party, addressing each in turn.

"Anfeald; Egeslic; Garberend; Eadig; Beadurof; Deogol. I greet you as Woden; I greet you as fellow warriors; I greet you as brothers."

The men looked at their leader: their *god* and their chests swelled with pride at having been addressed in such a way.

Woden continued.

"These are strange days. We have some knowledge of the events that have brought such trouble to your minds; our minds …" He gestured toward himself and Grimme.

"… but allow me to calm those minds and tell you that we do not think there is evil intent."

The men stirred; their curiosity roused.

"Huginn and Muninn have seen with their own eyes the seekers who would remove your remains in the old world, and they speak not of greed or destruction, but of care; of curiosity …" he paused, "…of respect."

The men seemed reassured by this, then Anfeald spoke.

"My Lord, we are grateful for your words and that you would trouble yourself with our plight, but…"

Woden listened as Anfeald continued.

"…My Lord Renweard has told us that we are to somehow commune with these seekers? How are we to have them listen?"

Woden smiled and responded kindly.

"Anfeald…"

He addressed the man but spoke to the rest of the party.

"… do not be fooled by a name, for though he may *mean* 'simple,' it does not imply 'foolish.'"

He turned again to Anfeald.

"We are to meet with Kendra; she will join us on Haligsfeld - yes, the field in which you lay in the old world…"

He had seen the question form in the minds and on the faces of the Wandle's Ham party.

"… she has ways of standing in both worlds at once, and I believe she alone will be able to find a way of bringing an end to this misery."

There was silence as the eight considered Woden's words. There was a time when Renweard himself would have doubted such a thing was possible, but in this place, such doubt was unfounded; anything was possible here.

"So then…"

Woden broke the mood cheerily, causing the men to start.

"… we must away to Haligsfeld. Kendra was most insistent on our timeliness."

With that, they set off, walking away from the Sun. The warmth on their backs was most welcome, but strangely, so too was the coolness of the early morning air, which flowed gently over their faces as they walked, easing their labour.

They carried no arms and no armour - as much as anything, because it had been reclaimed to the old world - but also because they were in the company of Woden, and there was none who could challenge him here in his own land. To walk unburdened came as a welcome change, especially when compared to the load they would normally carry in either this life or the last. Still, though, it felt somewhat unnatural.

"My Lord, I did not know that our field could exist in this world?"

Deogol spoke, suddenly breaking the silence and the concentration of the group.

"Haligsfeld, do you mean?"

"My Lord, yes."

"It does not."

"Then, my Lord, how can we…."

"How can we *stand* in Haligsfeld?" Woden interjected.

"Yes, my Lord."

"*We* will not. That is to be Kendra's endeavour and one which she bears without envy on my part!"

Deogol made to speak again, but a discrete shake from Grimme's head told him to wait and to let things unfold.

They continued on and, before long, found themselves in a large clearing alongside a small wood. The trees, though gently swaying in the morning breeze, seemed still to be sleeping and kept their secrets within the dark, damp interior, and the Sun, yet to arrive at their threshold, despite its steady progress, spread its warm, orange glow across the field.

A small stream, no more than a trickle, ran from within the wood and babbled gently off down the hillside. Beside it stood an old woman. She wore a loose-fitting, ankle-length dress and a large, flowing woollen cloak; a head scarf covered most of her long, grey hair. She was working with her hands, and at first, it was difficult to see what she was doing, but as they drew nearer, they could see that she was stripping the leaves and flowers from a large bunch of King Cup, her fingers stained orange and green by the plant, and throwing them gently into the stream. The Marigolds floated quietly away, and as they did so, Kendra's mouth moved silently as she uttered words to accompany the flowing water and its floral tribute. As the men approached, they chatted idly about everything and nothing, and although their voices were not raised, nevertheless, she suddenly held up an aged hand demanding silence. As one, they stopped and were silent; Even Woden did as Kendra instructed.

Some of the men looked at one another, amazed at the old woman's power and influence. Renweard looked at Grimme, who smiled knowingly.

"They are here… "

She said in a forced whisper.

"… they are here!"

The warrior party stood silently awaiting Kendra's next instruction, but none came. Instead, she began to speak in low, muted tones, as though her mouth were covered by an invisible veil that muffled and softened her words.

"Feorh m fêores dîgan fremian êower port…"

Renweard assumed these mutterings were incantations or invocations, such was the atmosphere, which now seemed to crackle gently around them. It had begun.

"… ûs of pro ic wilcumian unnon sê unorne fyrhđ!"

As she continued, a thin mist began to rise up out of the ground in front of her. The men of Renweard's party shifted uneasily and made to take a step backwards. Seeing this, Grimme gestured that they should remain still and quiet and to a man, they did as they were instructed; Grimme's composure bringing them calm, reminding them of whose presence they were in.

Woden himself remained still and silent, his good eye closed as though completely disconnected from his surroundings.

All the while, the mist cloud continued to build, expanding and swelling as it grew until it stood higher than the tallest man and wider than four shields held side-by-side, and although the grey, dense vapour swirled and billowed restlessly, it remained; contained within an unseen boundary.

As they looked on, Renweard realised that he had been in this place before. If only he could remember when. But then, how *could* he have been? He was in Asgard. Then it struck him. It appeared that Abrecan had been struck by the same thought as he whispered:

"*Haligsfeld*!"

"*BE STILL!*"

Kendra's forced whisper came to them across the field, but the prophetess continued. Slowly she raised both arms skyward, and it was then they felt it.

To a man, the eight sensed fluttering from within their chest. A movement that seemed at first like all the world was being pulled toward them to be swallowed up in some invisible maelstrom, yet at the same time as gentle as a butterfly's busy gambol, and then it moved outward and away as simultaneously, eight, small blue lights appeared through their chest wall and moved slowly into position, one above each grave.

The men could see them clearly now; eight large patches of dark soil arranged in a loose circle. This is where they had been laid after the last great battle. It seemed unreal to them: how a once great and heroic life could end in such corruption, and yet as they always knew they would be, they were here in Asgard among the fallen, called to do Woden's work.

The wind seemed to have increased now, along with the chill, when suddenly Kendra dropped her arms to her side. Her chin fell to her chest, and her eyes closed as though she were drawing herself up, gathering her inner strength.

The eight lights remained, shimmering noiselessly, and then, she inhaled deeply as she lifted her head. Slowly, she raised her right arm and pointed at the mist, her fingers gnarled with age and in a powerful voice, said.

"YOU MUST RETURN ALL OF IT!"

Her voice carried clearly through the now howling wind.

"THE EIGHT WHO LAY HERE HAVE NEED OF IT!"

"*Who is she talking to?*" Eadig whispered loudly.

"Be still! They'll hear you in the old world!" Renweard whispered back.

***

“Wh... who are you?” called Rab nervously through the wind.

“Who, me?” Colin replied

“No, her!”

Colin strained his eyes against the darkness to see what, or who, Rab was pointing toward.

Kendra shrieked, angered at the disrespect shown her by the term.

“HER? I AM KENDRA, PROPHETESS OF ASGARD; KEEPER OF THE BONES AND SEER OF ALL THINGS: THOSE THAT HAVE GONE BEFORE, AND THOSE THAT ARE YET TO BE!”

Rab spoke again, not really believing what he was seeing but not wishing to anger the old woman further.

“Kendra…?”

He looked questioningly at Colin, who returned the look, equally perplexed, albeit because of his friend’s strange behaviour, seeing nothing more than Rab apparently hallucinating.

“… I apologise; I didn’t mean to offend you. What must we return?”

He replied awkwardly as he tried to appease the angry woman in front of him.

"*What* do the eight need?"

Despite his question, it was clear to him that the woman was referring to the graves they had been excavating. Rab spoke again to the cold late-afternoon air, the tension in his voice palpable.

"This is a dream, right?"

Colin's reply was blunt and as cold as the air Rab was speaking to; he was at a loss to know what to do for his friend, who, in his opinion, was clearly having some sort of psychotic episode.

"If it is, you're the only one dreaming of it, Rab!"

He was just deciding whether to walk back to the 4x4 so that he could at least wait in the warm when he looked at his friend again.

I can't leave him here on his own. What the bloody hell am I gonna do with him? I'll have to just sit here with him till he snaps out of it. Come on, mate, snap out of it. Please!

When he spoke again, it was as a true friend, and as he took a seat on the ground nearby, he said:

"I'm here for you, Rab. I'm not going anywhere, bud."

Rab did not reply.

Kendra lowered her arm and allowed her shoulders to relax. She could see fear in Rab's face and decided that if he truly was an enlightened soul seeking knowledge, causing him to flee would not help her cause, so when she spoke again, it was with kindness.

"You are one of the seekers, yes? You are one who would look for the story of those who lay here? I hear your name on the breeze….Rab?"

Rab stared blankly back at Kendra, trying to make sense of what she had just asked. Seeing confusion shroud his face, she continued in an attempt to clarify.

"The eight who lay here…"

She gestured across the graves with an outstretched arm,

"…are the slain from a great battle in the west. Renweard; Abrecan; Eadig; Anfeald; Beadurof; Deogol; Egeslic and Garberend…"

The eight blue lights began to shimmer more vigorously as she spoke the names, and the whispers from each grew louder. Hearing this, Kendra turned and spat harsh, incomprehensible words over her shoulder. The whispers ceased immediately.

"…these eight were carried from the river and laid on their deathbed. Laid with them was everything they would need in the next life; in Valhalla."

Rab looked on, listening intently, waiting, but Kendra did not speak. Instead, she allowed her words to hang in the air while the man in the mist absorbed their meaning.

"Valhalla… *Valhalla*?"

Rab eventually broke the silence; a questioning look distorted his face. Kendra remained silent, her face alight with hope.

"As in, *the afterlife*, Valhalla?"

"Go on!" Kendra encouraged.

Colin looked up at Rab from his spot on the ground, and as he did so, he felt the blood drain from his face. *What did he just say?*

Rab continued.

"Are you trying to tell us that by taking the artefacts…"

It was Kendra's turn to look confused now.

"Ar-te-fass? What manner of…?"

Rab continued, modifying his terminology.

"… the weapons and belongings of… of the eight. Are you saying that if we remove them from here that they can't be used in… Valhalla?"

He gulped, not believing the words that had just passed his lips.

"HA!"

Kendra yelled, pointing excitedly at him as though he had just given the correct answer to an age-old riddle. The old woman was gone, for now, leaving an excited child in her place.

"YES! YES! That is it exactly!"

Rab finally moved from his spot, only a couple of paces, but as he did so, he and Colin exchanged a glance in the now fading light. Were it not for the intense cold that enveloped them both, keeping them grounded in the here and now, they would never have believed this was happening.

Colin slowly shook his head in disbelief. He'd hoped this was a sign that his friend had finally snapped out of it. Clearly, this was not the case, and he resigned himself to the fact that he was going to have to wait it out; he would have to sit and listen as Rab spoke to the cold night air; wait until he had finished his… conversation, after which he could get him somewhere warm and maybe even seek medical attention. For now, though, he sat and listened and tried to keep himself warm.

Rab, however, now fully able to move, his spell broken, pulled the collar of his fleece up around his neck, closed the zip tightly under his chin and walked slowly toward Kendra to sit on the ground close to where she stood.

"You see?"

Kendra asked, hopefully.

"You see *why* the belongings must be returned?"

Rab looked up from the empty grave he had been absent-mindedly studying. All that remained now of the carefully placed content was a small empty pit; the crumbs of dark, yellow sand showed no trace of the person it had once so gently held, nor offering any idea of how long it had held them.

He had always had the ability to stand in a place such as this and imagine how it might have been at the time of the burial. There were times when he could almost hear the voices across the centuries and feel their sorrow; he could imagine the act of burial: the effort of the body being placed in the earth; the smell of damp soil filling the nostrils and invading the senses, and every time he uncovered a grave, especially if there had been a skeleton, he would look on the face of the person within and imagine the hopes and fears and dreams they had once so longingly held on too. It seemed to Rab as though in that moment, so heavily saturated with emotion, that something had caused it to be permanently recorded in the earth, waiting for someone to come along and press replay.

He finally answered.

"I *do,* Kendra. But I don't know *how* I would do it."

Kendra seemed puzzled by Rab's response. The task was simple enough: bring the belongings back, lay them in their grave and replace the earth. Something in Rab's tone, though, told her otherwise; That, although he genuinely wanted to make it so, it was not as straightforward an undertaking as it seemed.

"Surely they can be laid in the place they were found? In the place put aside for them in their former life?"

Kendra pushed Rab for an answer but, in doing so, felt his frustration grow. *I must not lose him. We need his help*, she thought, and in an attempt to show understanding, she offered her support.

"I will make the incantations, Rab. It will be my duty to ferry the belongings home once they are returned to this place."

Momentarily shocked at hearing Kendra use his name, Rab tried to respond.

"I..."

It was no use; Rab was at a loss for a way to explain *his* situation. It was not that he didn't want to return the warriors' belongings - it seemed, actually, that it was the correct and proper thing to do. No, it was that they were now lying in plastic bags or wrapped in acid-free tissue paper and packed into cardboard boxes back at the archaeology unit waiting to be processed. *That part of it she must never know*, he thought. He had never liked the term: 'processed'. He always thought it sounded impersonal and completely removed humanity from the items that had once been such an important and treasured part of another person's life. Now, of course, they had names too. That *never* happened on any Anglo-Saxon site, let alone an early one. This was a period whose presence was particularly ephemeral, their earliest buildings being made of wood, and nothing *ever* written down; their deeds recorded only in poems and songs. Finally, though, Rab said softly.

"Kendra? The belongings that you speak of are no longer here in this place."

"Then where…?"

Being mindful of causing insult and recognising the need for tact, he continued.

“They are being… *studied* somewhere else. A place where they are safe, but they are not here.”

Kendra listened intently, her face reflecting the thoughts that were being processed by her mind.

“My problem is that the people who are studying them: my…”

He searched for a word that would mean something to Kendra.

“…my *leaders* will not believe me when I tell them of our conversation here today.”

He looked at Colin, his expression one of: *did that make sense?* Colin rebounded a look that said: *I still can’t see anyone!* And as Rab looked back at Kendra, where there had once been a powerful, confident woman, there now stood a frail, deflated old lady; the sorrow in her eyes so intense that it affected Rab physically, as a wave of the deepest, most profound sorrow swept over him.

“You must… you must try!” she said.

He did not reply. He knew that she was right: he must try. But where to start?

The silence that followed was deafening. Even the wind had dropped to a gentle breeze as though it, too, saw no need for drama.

Rab sat silently, watching as the prophetess turned and stared through empty, unseeing eyes at the eight small, blue lights which still hung over their respective graves.

"I have failed! …I have failed!"

Almost at once, he noticed that the eight small blue lights had begun to glow more intensely. They pulsated in a slow, synchronised rhythm while still maintaining their position over the pits, and each emitted a deep, deep hum that could be felt in the pit of his stomach; he began to feel nauseous, and there were the whispers again.

Rab rose suddenly to his feet, his head swimming and feeling quite unsteady as he did so. Colin, reacting to Rab's sudden movement, did likewise and, seeing his friend's discomfort moved to assist, offering an arm of support which Rab brushed away.

Kendra screamed at the lights.

"THERE *IS* NO WAY!"

As the whispers grew louder, Rab thought he could hear voices on the breeze, male voices.

"THERE *IS* NO WAY! WHAT WILL YOU HAVE ME DO?"

Kendra was still in deep, fiery conversation with the unseen presence behind her. She was becoming angrier and angrier, and more frustrated by the minute, and the hurt showed on her face. This was her sole purpose; This is what she had been chosen to do. To fail now at a time of such importance was unthinkable, and her mind was in turmoil at the thought of such ruin.

Although he could see only Kendra and the blue lights, Rab had long since come to the conclusion the latter were the spirits of the dead men. There could be no other explanation, given that they occupied the space above the graves, and they seemed to respond as though consciousness was present. It was in that sad, desperate moment that he made his decision, and Rab called out to her.

"Kendra!"

The protest continued uninterrupted as she became more animated.

"KENDRA!"

There was sudden calm; even the blue lights became still and remained silent as though they were holding their breath; Kendra turned to look at the archaeologist. The light in this world was now almost completely gone, whereas the light in Kendra's had fully arrived, and an intense orange glow backlit the visitor.

"I will do as you ask."

Kendra stared intently at him, her face frozen in surprise as new hope began to grow in her eyes.

"You can do this? You are certain of it?"

"No… "

He replied cautiously

"I'm not sure *how* I'll do it, but I will try."

"Words! Empty words!"

Kendra spat the words at him, doubting his sincerity, so in an attempt to demonstrate their good intent, he continued.

"Kendra. What you ask is… is difficult. There'll be loads… there will be many obstacles to… overcome."

He sought to use language that would make sense to Kendra.

"But I promise you; I will try. And if it's at all possible, I *will* return the artefacts… the belongings."

Kendra did not move, and for a moment, Rab thought she was waiting for him to continue. He was about to elaborate further when she turned her back to him. *Damn! I've blown it!* He thought. Instead, the eight blue lights began to whisper and vibrate as Kendra began speaking to them, which she did in the same muted tones she had used when she first met the man in the mist. This went on for some time until, again, she addressed the archaeologist.

"So be it…"

She said as she finally turned to face Rab once more.

"… but time is short, and Ragnorök is almost upon us!"

Rab sought to reassure her and reiterated.

"I *will* speak with my leaders, Kendra, and I *will* return the men's belongings!"

Kendra looked deep into the face of the man in front of her, her eyes boring into his. Rab felt a little uncomfortable with this but sensed that she was merely looking for truth, for sincerity.

"I like you!"

She said finally.

"I will trust you!"

The lights whispered noisily.

"I will *trust* him!" she insisted to the unseen audience.

The lights became quiet.

"We shall meet in this place as the light of the third day washes over the deathbeds. Then shall the men be reunited with their belongings."

Alarmed at such a short deadline, Rab said aloud.

"Three days!"

Almost at once, he sensed Kendra's annoyance at the interruption and sought to diffuse the situation.

"My apologies; In three days then."

It was then that Kendra realised; How could he know? Why should he?

"You do not know, seeker of knowledge? You do not know that our worlds are offset?"

Rab was confused, so Kendra continued.

"Do you not see that when in my world morn has come, in yours, the day begins to slumber?"

Now he thought about it, Rab had noticed the orange glow that emanated from behind Kendra but had assumed it was all part of the vision. It had never occurred to him that it might simply be breaking daylight. Seeing the realisation in Rab's eyes, Kendra spoke again, confident this time that he understood.

"It is this difference between our two worlds, Seeker, that will, with the *precise* incantation, carry the belongings from your hands back into those of the eight; As the storm brings with it the wind, such is this… distortion in time and place. Do you understand now, Seeker? It is this distortion that will pull the belongings back through the vortex that I will create."

He did, although that still only gave them three and a half days to find everything and bring it here for reburial.

Keeping his concerns well and truly to himself, Rab was curious to find out about something else and, while still nodding, an acknowledgement asked.

"Kendra, what will the eight do till then? What will they do without weapons?"

Kendra seemed delighted that Rab had shown interest beyond his own world.

"I am not permitted to tell you of that which is to come in our world…"

Rab felt a sense of deep disappointment which was replaced immediately with satisfaction as Kendra concluded.

"… but I will say that without their belongings, their part in the greatest feat imaginable would be diminished; you do them a great honour."

Forgetting that Colin had played no part in the conversation, Rab gestured toward his friend, causing Kendra to peer deeply out into the old world, though she saw nothing but Rab.

“We won’t let you down, Kendra. All of you. Tell them that please?”

Rab nodded toward the eight lights.

“They hear you, my friend. They have been listening to all that has been said. Now, go! Find your leader; find the belongings and meet us here again on the third morn.” Then to clarify, added, “The *eve* of your third day.”

Rab was about to speak again, he had another question when suddenly and from out of nowhere came a pulse of pressure that threatened to knock both he and Colin off their feet. They braced themselves against it, arms outstretched, instinctively trying to push back the wind, yet barely able to resist the unseen force, and their breath came in gasps as the tempest tried to force it back down their throat. As the shockwave diminished, they were finally able to open their eyes and adjust them to the now total darkness.

Kendra was gone.

So too, were the lights; They were alone on a cold, dark archaeological site.

Finally, Colin spoke.

“What the bloody hell was that?”

“My God, Col’!”

“Well?”

Rab seemed confused.

"Well, what? You saw…"

Colin felt a wave of anger sweep over him, that or cold fear, but relieved at having his friend return from wherever he had just been; he continued calmly.

"I saw you talking to the darkness, mate, nothing else."

"What do you mean?"

Rab was even more confused. *How could he not have seen that*?

Colin continued.

"Well, we were walking back across the site when you said you could see someone, a woman, I think, standing by your feature."

"Yeah, that's right. I was…"

"There was no one there, Rab; nothing, just the dark. Then you started talking to… Kendry?"

"Kendra; the prophetess…"

Rab corrected.

"Kendry; Kendra; whoever. The point is, I didn't see 'em mate."

Rab felt deflated; Had Colin *really* not seen anything? More to the point, he'd just taken on a massively important task, and he would definitely need Colin's help if he was to succeed in returning the men's belongings.

"We need to talk, Col…"

"I need a drink, Rab! And you, my friend, need to speak to someone!"

Rab felt insulted, his face flushed with anger.

"Like a psychiatrist, you mean? What, you think I'm losing it?"

Colin had not meant to offend his friend; He genuinely had not witnessed anything beyond his apparent breakdown in the middle of a field, and he'd stayed with him throughout to protect him.

"I'm just saying that *I-saw-nothing!"*

He emphasised each word to drive his point home.

"And I suppose that bloody hurricane just then was *nothing,* was it?"

Colin had to admit that he could not simply explain away the burst of high wind that had just hit them both but continued.

“I dunno what that was, mate, but I *saw* nothing. Now, if you’re telling me you did, I’ll take your word for it, but Rab, I’ve gotta be honest with you: you scared the ba’Jesus outta me just then!”

Rab remained silent, Colin’s words having fully hit home. He clearly *had* seen none of it; no lights, no Kendra, Nothing.

“I know what I saw, Col.”

“That’s as may be, but for now, we need to get you somewhere warm and think about what you need next.”

Rab’s anger flared again.

“Well, what I DON’T need is my head looking at!”

“Alright, alright. I just meant that it’s bloody cold out here; it’s been a long day, and we both need to talk about this some more…”

Rab felt the anger subside and calm take its place.

“Exactly! Kendra says that there are eight warriors, it’s their graves we’ve been….”

“But not tonight, Rab.” Colin interrupted. He didn’t have the strength for any more of this.

The men stood quietly together, Colin looking kindly into Rab’s eyes as best he could in this light.

"Oh, OK! No, you're right, Col. A drink, some hot food and a nice warm bed, yeah?"

"Yes, mate… for you anyway."

Rab looked puzzled.

"How do you mean?"

"Well, I've decided that as Her Majesty's finest can no longer spare the man-power to visit the site overnight, I'm gonna pitch a tent in the lee of those woods and stay here till we're finished."

Sites of this importance had always been prime targets for rogue metal detectorists - so-called "Night Hawks" - who use the cover of darkness to raid them and plunder them of anything of monetary value, destroying valuable archaeology in the process. The local constabulary had sent the occasional patrol car to sweep the area, which was almost as rare as the archaeology itself, their time being precious, but as the site was so far from the road and could not be observed directly, it had been deemed necessary to have a permanent presence there: Colin.

"Are you allowed to do that?"

"Yup. I spoke to Lucas back at the office; he spoke to the land owner, and they both agreed that it's probably the best way to protect the site. Well, s'all we've got anyway, so… there you are."

It was Rab's turn to be concerned for his friend's welfare.

"Will you be OK? If Night Hawks turn up, I mean? Maybe I could bring my tent; you know: to keep you company."

"You bloody won't! You need to get home and rest up; in fact, I don't wanna see you here in the morning..."

"But...!"

"No 'buts', you've got tomorrow off; I mean it!"

Seeing the protest grow and the words of reason forming in Rab's mind, he continued.

"Don't worry, I want you back the day after; You're not getting a free holiday out of this, alright?"

Strangely, despite the urgency of Kendra's request, Rab felt quite relieved. *A day off might help, actually*, he thought. *It'll give me time to think of a way to get Col on board with all of this anyway.*

With the argument settled, the two men walked back to the site hut, which they secured for the night by closing and bolting the steel shutters and locking the heavy doors before climbing wearily into the 4x4 and driving off-site: Rab away to his accommodation in the nearby pub, Colin to his home in the village a couple of miles away to prepare a tent, sleeping bag and other camping essentials which he now decided he'd set up the following day. He'd fully intended to do it tonight, but now that he was warm and dry, well, it would have to wait!

They pulled up outside The Crown Inn, where Rab had been staying for the past few weeks, and sat with the engine running.

"Home, sweet home, eh?" Colin ribbed.

It was normal for archaeologists to stay away when the site they were employed on was a significant distance from their home or base. Rab was used to it after all these years. The accommodation varied in quality - it was never five-star - and it could be quite boring in the evenings if you were the only one staying, but if there was a group of you, it could be the best fun ever. He climbed out from the warmth of the vehicle and gathered his work bag and the day's newspaper, something that might help break the monotony of the long dark evening ahead.

Well, that was fun, Colin thought as Rab slammed the car door closed and bid him goodnight.

Hopefully, that's an end to it.

Chapter 8: The Man in the Mist

The mist cloud through which Kendra had been in conversation with the old world closed violently. She had been talking to the shadowy figure within for several minutes when suddenly, as the decision to return the Wandle's Ham warriors' belongings had been made, Woden stirred from his frozen position. He had remained still and quiet for the whole encounter to the point where those present were uncertain as to whether he had heard any of it. Now though, he walked across and stood directly behind Kendra. It looked for a moment as though he was about to join the conversation when instead, he raised his arms high above his head and clapped his hands together; hard.

As he did so, a low rumble began to build from the west. As it built in intensity, the men of Renweard's party turned to see what new ill was about to befall them. They could feel its depth and power through the ground and in their gut and they prepared to meet the unseen menace when suddenly the trees began to pitch and sway as a powerful blast of wind rushed across Haligsfeld. It was so ferocious that only Woden himself remained standing as it abated; even Grimme had been forced down onto one knee. There was a bright, blinding flash of light; then all became still. The tempest had ceased as quickly as it had begun, and as the party began pulling themselves up off the ground, Kendra could be heard cursing loudly.

"I am Kendra! I am the Prophetess; the seer of all things…"

She said to herself as she struggled to her feet.

"And yet, Kendra: the prophetess, you were unable to foretell my displeasure!"

Woden spoke, an air of tension in his voice.

"Displeasure, my lord?"

Kendra looked at Woden contemptuously as she brushed herself down with her hands, busying herself in an attempt to buy time as she sought to decipher his words. She was an elder; a prophetess; and as such, Woden was a boy to her, despite his lofty status. Nevertheless, she afforded him the respect he was due.

"If you have a point to make, my lord Woden, make it plain…"

Woden cut her words aggressively short.

"The mortal was about to enquire further as to our purpose here. Could you not detect his curiosity?"

"I could, my lord Woden, but I was no more likely to expose the seclusion of Asgard than you were. Our negotiations had already concluded, and I was wont to leave his curiosity hanging on the wind so that it might indeed give him cause to return and, more importantly, return with the belongings of the eight."

Woden pondered the old woman's words. As she had spoken through the portal, he had spent the entire time probing the other side with his mind in an attempt to learn for himself what knowledge remained of *this* world and its culture back in the old; this was a rare opportunity indeed.

Many assumed that he already *had* full knowledge of it, but as the centuries had passed, his familiarity with the old world had faded, and it was as if a veil had been placed over his ears and eye; indeed, it had become necessary to *send* his ears and eyes: Huginn and Muninn, to gather any such information, but its breadth and depth were limited so that any wider, political or strategic view could not be determined. Grimme spoke for the first time in a long while.

"It would seem, my lord, as though Kendra has indeed had Asgard's security at heart."

"Go on…"

"That is to say: I, for one, felt that nothing was disclosed that could bring harm to our world; none that is not already upon us."

Woden nodded as he considered Grimme's sage words, then pointed matter-of-factly to the treeline and said:

"And the spy?"

All eyes turned to follow the direction of Woden's finger. As they looked, a figure, shrouded in the dark interior of the woods, moved furtively among the trees. All were at a loss to be able to identify the infiltrator in the woods; all but one: Renweard recognised him immediately; short and well built, but light on his feet, and an inquisitiveness that would surely bring down the wrath of the gods. It could only be Wulfgar.

"Wulfgar…?"

Woden demanded.

"Wulfgar of Deorham?"

"My lord, yes. It is he. I am certain."

Renweard hesitated, having spoken out of turn, expecting the worst as both the party of warriors and Kendra looked on in awe at the nerve of the man but also afeared as to his fate. They need not have worried. Woden suddenly roared with laughter as his company looked on nervously but soon realised he was genuinely charmed by the man and his audacity. *How foolish I have been,* he thought, *to imagine subterfuge among my own.*

He called Wulfgar to his side, who emerged sheepishly from inside the treeline, expecting the worst from Woden, whose punishment was fabled for being notoriously creative.

"Not today, Wulfgar; Not today."

He had seen fear on the man's face.

"Loki would be proud of you, my friend!"

Woden said as he pulled Wulfgar to his side in a one-armed embrace. Relieved, the company laughed openly, releasing the tension, and then Woden spoke directly to Kendra, who, until now, had retreated to the sideline.

"My dear lady. Can you forgive my paranoia?"

Ever the prophetess, Kendra replied.

"The paranoia? Yes, my lord; The performance? Never!"

Woden laughed again; a genuine, heartfelt laugh that was so contagious Kendra herself joined in it.

"Enough then, enough…" he choked back the tears of laughter "… I believe our work here is done for now. Let us break our fast in the great hall and celebrate Kendra's glorious endeavour. The beginning, my friends, of the end of your woes."

With that, the party moved off, walking away from the tree line, this time toward the glory of an Asgardian sunrise.

As they bathed in its light and warmth, some found it difficult to keep their eyes open, such was its intensity and instead closed them, walking blind but opening them again briefly to orient themselves and to check for obstacles that may lie in their path. One such was Renweard, who strode confidently among his men listening to their conversation.

"I think that is the last time we shall see the man in the mist," Eadig was saying. "I think he will keep our possessions for himself!"

Beadurof disagreed. "I do not think so, Eadig. I felt the presence of an honourable man; I believe he will be true to both Kendra and his word."

"We shall see. I will believe in him for now; we have no other choice." Anfeald said as he produced an apple of deep, garnet red from somewhere deep inside his tunic and bit into it enthusiastically, the juice exploding in all directions. The men laughed; Anfeald's appetite was as legendary as his fighting skill.

And so, they continued noisily on their way, mocking one another, teasing and laughing; all the while, laughing, such was there new found confidence that things would soon be as they should. But one of their numbers was no longer present. No one, not even Woden, had noticed the absence of one of their number and carried on, blissfully unaware.

Kendra had stayed behind at the stream where the portal had formed and where contact had just been made, watching the men disappear into the morning sunlight. She sat quietly by the edge of the water, deep in troubled thought. She had sensed something else as she talked with Rab; something unseen, as though another was present but unwilling to take part in the conversation. *Could it be the leader he had spoken of? Could they be the ones Rab needed to convince of their cause? I must speak to them directly,* she thought. *If they could not see me, or worse, did not believe me, that would be the only way I could convince them of the urgency of our need; The only way they would agree to help return the belongings of the eight.*

Her mind made up, she continued to watch as the eleven men of Asgard walked boisterously away. They walked taller now, she thought, and the darkness that had dogged them these many days had left their eyes and been replaced with the light of hope. So far, she had done her job well. *I shall return at dawn tomorrow. I will speak with the leader. I will make him see.*

With that, she began gathering flowers and herbs from the meadow, humming quietly as she did so.

***

The sun shone across the broad strip of exposed sandy soil creating an orange/brown glow that illuminated everything it touched: trees, vehicles, and even people; all were bathed in the glory of a cool autumn morning.

"Where's Rab Col?"

Angela walked across the site toward the feature she had been digging the previous day and which she hoped to have finished by lunchtime today. The grave had been fully excavated now and had yielded some amazing finds; They had been consistent with those found elsewhere on site, but her warrior had been of less high status, his grave containing no helmet, and the weapons, though beautiful in their own right and skilfully made, were nothing compared to the bejewelled example that had been found in one of the other graves.

"Mornin' Ange'. He was a bit peaky last night, so I dropped him off at the pub and told him to take today as sick leave."

"Oh no! nothing too serious, I hope? Was that why he wanted to speak to you last night?"

Colin was unsure what she meant but went with it anyway.

"Oh yeah, must have been." Then deflecting any further questions as to Rab's health, he continued.

"You nearly done here, Ange'? Only, we need to finish the rest of thc sitc now thc graves are almost done."

Angela secured several blank recording sheets to a clipboard as she replied.

"Yeah, pretty much; Just a bit of recording to finish up, and I'm there. Do you want to show me where to start next? I can move straight on to it then."

"Yeah, sure, they're over here."

They crossed the small, tinkling stream that bisected the site and walked a few hundred yards away from the area containing the graves to a clearing.

"Here you go, look down here. There are a couple of linears I'd like you to have a go at, which I doubt are anything more than boundary ditches for the cemetery, but in any case, they need recording. You OK with them?"

Angela studied the area, intuitively carrying out an assessment of the work that she would need to do.

"Looks pretty straightforward," she said. "I'll make a start as soon as I'm done over there, which should be around lunchtime. You never know; it might turn out to be a temporary village or something."

Colin laughed. "That's what I like about you, Ange': you've got such a vivid imagination!"

Although Angela had actually been serious about her suggestion, she took no offence, and they laughed as they walked back to the main area of the site when Colin added:

"If you think that's funny, you should see what I'm about to work on!"

"Sounds intriguing; What's that?" she asked.

"Site security…!"

He left his statement hanging in the air, and as Angela stopped dead in her tracks and stared after him, he walked away, leaving her wondering: *What on earth is he up to this time?* She shook her head dismissively as she prepared to conclude her excavation, sharpening a pencil with her trusty penknife.

Some minutes later, Colin opened the back of the 4x4, allowing the tailgate to crash noisily open, the sound resonating around the site, causing everyone to wonder what had happened. Six pairs of eyes flashed a look of alarm in the direction of the sound and came to rest on Colin as he wrestled a large olive-green cylindrical kitbag from the back of the truck and threw it unceremoniously into a wheelbarrow. This was followed by a small canvas holdall and a rubber mallet.

"What's he doing now?" Ian asked.

"Dunno," Angela replied. "He said something about site security?"

"Eh?"

"That's what he said: 'site security'. Next thing… this!"

She gestured with a nod towards Colin, who was now heading for the treeline, pushing the newly loaded wheelbarrow ahead of him. As they watched, he tipped the contents on to the ground before flipping the barrow on its back. He then began the laborious task of clearing the ground of obstructions, apparently in an attempt to make it more level. The larger rocks, he threw into a loose pile; fallen, dead branches from the nearby oak tree were also piled up; and a large clump of nettles was unceremoniously pulled from the ground by their roots, accompanied by the grumbles of a man wishing he'd bothered to put gloves on after all before tackling the latter. Then, standing the kitbag on end, he loosened the drawstring cord at its neck and upended it, depositing the contents onto the sandy soil; finally, the mystery was solved:

"A tent?"

"Well spotted! Yep, a tent and my accommodation for the next few nights." Said Colin, acknowledging his audience.

The team were agog as, one by one, they downed tools and sauntered across to Colin's new abode in-the-making.

"Are you *really* planning to stay here on site?" Ian asked. "Is that even allowed?"

"Rab asked the same question last night, and yeah, it's fine; I checked with Lucas, who checked with the land owner, and they basically said, 'go for it'."

The expression on the team's collective faces displayed a wide variety of emotions in response to this revelation which ranged from *fair enough* to *really?* Colin continued.

"They said it was alright to kip in the site hut if I wanted, but I figured that to get power and heating, I'd need to run the 'genny', which was more to likely *attract* attention, which, as you all know, is what I'm trying to avoid."

Angela looked horrified. "Sooner you than me! Won't you find it creepy? I mean: being on a cemetery on your own…at night…?"

"It ain't them in the ground that's gonna hurt me, Ange'; it's the living I'm more concerned about. Those Night Hawkers can be nasty buggers when they think they've been rumbled!"

There had been a few instances of violence over the years when Night Hawkers had been caught in the act, but more often than not, all that was found was evidence of their activities the day after, where hastily dug holes and clods of turf littered the landscape like an exaggerated mole attack.

This did nothing to ease Angela's concern. "I hadn't thought of that! That's even more reason not to stay, then, isn't it? What if you're attacked?"

"Oh, don't you worry about that; I've got it covered."

As he spoke, Colin reached into the apparently, empty tent bag and produced what was obviously a sheathed sword. There was a further mix of reactions as Colin drew it from its leather scabbard. Some were suitably impressed and greeted the shining blade with *woah!* And *wow!* Others, Angela included, looked horrified.

"This, ladies and gents, is my broken-back seax," Colin announced proudly.

Colin was part of an Anglo-Saxon living history group: '*Geoguth Bernicia'*. He spent most weekends during the summer at various historical sites around the country, those with Anglo-Saxon connections at least, with a group of like-minded individuals who brought to life the people of that most enigmatic of eras in an attempt to both entertain and educate.

Angela's fear deepened; even those who had been impressed when Colin had produced the weapon now doubted the wisdom of carrying a two-foot, sharpened blade around an archaeological site. Cal, an American university student, working with the unit for one season to gain experience in the field, voiced the concerns of the rest of the team.

"Jeez, Col! Are you sure that's a good idea? I mean, suppose you *don't* get arrested for 'possession' in a public place, and the Hawks turn up; you *use* that on one of the S.O.B.s, and you get to share cell time with them; and they ain't about to share their toothpaste with ya if ya catch ma'drift?"

Colin *had* considered all eventualities, but he'd decided, nevertheless, to go ahead with his plan.

"I know, I know. I'm not daft; I wasn't planning on patrolling the site with it; just, if they turn up, I thought I might... wave it about a bit."

He wielded the sword in an impressive figure-of-eight arc to emphasise his point.

"Who knows: If I wear my cloak and helmet, they might think they've seen a ghost and run screaming! Anyway, it's only for a couple of nights while we finish the last couple of graves."

The team laughed nervously as Ian attempted to offer his opinion.

"I'm still not convinced, Col, if you…"

Colin cut him off mid-sentence as he became more irritated by the protests.

"Look, guys, I get where you're coming from, I really do, but that's my plan, *alright*?"

They were not alright, but there seemed little point in arguing the toss any further; Colin was adamant, and his plan was going ahead whether they liked it or not. Ian changed tack and continued.

"*OK, OK*. I'll leave it. Do you need a hand with the tent?"

There was really little point to his question, as he'd already begun staking out the tent's inner lining, anchoring each corner with a plastic peg, and hammering it home with the rubber mallet.

"Do I have a choice?" Colin quipped.

"I guess not, especially if you want me to keep quiet about bloody Excalibur there!"

Colin accepted the offer of help graciously. He was, in fact, quite grateful for the assistance as it would make the task that much easier, and as the rest of the team dispersed back to continue working on the various pits, ditches and 'dark splodges', Colin and Ian assembled the tent amid an exchange of sword and sorcery-related jokes.

As the fly sheet went on and the last of the guy ropes were pegged and tightened, Ian had one last word of advice.

"Just be careful tonight, Col; seriously, mate!"

Hearing the sincerity in his voice, Colin, who had been about to launch another of his 'leave it' assaults, realised that Ian had only his best interests at heart. He released the sharp, preparatory breath he'd just taken in a long, drawn-out sigh, relaxing his shoulders as he did so, and nodding his agreement said resignedly.

"Yeah, OK, Ian; Tell you what: I'll keep the beast in its scabbard and lock it in the 4x4. I suppose if I *do* hear anything, I can always fetch it out then; maybe the hazard lights flashing when I unlock the truck will scare them off first, though, eh?"

Relieved that he'd finally made Colin see sense, Ian replied.

"Yes, mate; probably. Thank you!"

He reaffirmed his words with a nod and a look of sincerity which Colin acknowledged with a grateful smile.

"Right ya skiving sod; now bugger off and get on with some work!"

Knowing that Colin was both jesting and serious, he still had quite a bit to do. After all, he gathered himself up and started to make his way back across the site.

"Cheers, Ian!" Colin called after him.

Without looking back or breaking step, Ian raised a hand and waved an acknowledgement.

The rest of the day continued routinely without further surprise from either Colin or the archaeology. Angela had completed her excavation of the grave and moved on to the new feature, where she found evidence of a possible, brief period of occupation; she'd actually described it as "like someone had had an all-night barbeque", but beyond a few patches of charcoal here and there, and a half dozen small pits containing animal bone, there had been little else.

"I reckon…" Colin had said when he'd finally returned from his now, fully functioning campsite, "…that the funeral party for this lot…" he gestured to the eight, now empty graves "…had a bit of a send-off for 'em over here."

"My thoughts exactly," Angela said. "Date-wise, there's nothing to give us anything definite, so I suppose they could be from pretty much any period, although the fill is quite leached and washed out; even the charcoal looks a bit pale. The bone is quite well-preserved, mind you, especially for this soil; Pig mainly."

Aware of the fact that the content of archaeological features will weather over time, Angela had factored this into her theory of this area's potential use. Even underground, as water slowly filters through the soil over hundreds, or thousands, of years, it carries away nutrients and, therefore, the colour with it. In any case, this was useful information and added yet another dimension to the history of the site, another light beginning to shine on the so-called 'Dark Ages'.

Finally, as the day drew to a close, the team began the routine of gathering up and cleaning their tools, clearing any loose soil from their feature; and packing away anything they had used during the day. For most, that meant an extensive search of the vicinity, reclaiming loaned items - never loan anything overnight. You might be reassigned the next day! - and piling it all into a wheelbarrow before commencing the '*March of the Hi-vis Zombie*'; a coin phrased by Jules who, on a cold, foggy site covering many acres, had once been tasked with driving around to collect the workforce at day's end. As the team, who were always ready for its arrival, heard the approach of the truck, they had emerged wearily from the mist and murk, mud-spattered and seeking not brains for sustenance but the warmth and relative comfort of the 4x4 which would whisk them away to hot showers, hot food and a comfy bed. Today though, they were just a short walk from the site hut and the 'liberty' vehicle, and one by one, they began making their own way across to them.

“All done then, troops?” Colin was in the process of checking that the day’s paperwork was all in and filed and that any finds they had made were placed safely in the sample bucket, the time-honoured method of keeping everything together in one place before being taken to the main archaeological unit for processing.

There were a series of muted “yeah”s and “Mmm”s in response to Colin’s question, as those who were ready began loading first their equipment, then themselves into the 4x4. Those who still had a few last-minute tasks to attend to began hurriedly filing and securing their finds before doing likewise.

“Anything else you need us to do, Col?” asked Ian as he fumbled with the car keys, dropping them in the mud at his feet.

“You can clean them up if ya like; butter fingers!” Colin replied with a glance to the sky.

“Sorry…” Ian’s face shone red with embarrassment.

“… seriously though: is there anything? Do you need a hand before we head off?”

Colin genuinely appreciated the offer. "Nah, reckon I'm pretty-much sorted, thanks. You guys head off and have a good evening, yeah? And everyone…"

The team look looked towards Colin as they waited for him to make his announcement.

"…thanks for your efforts again today. We're almost there, yeah?"

He gave the 'thumbs up,' which the team took as their signal that Colin was ready for them to leave. No one was offended by the gentle shove; Colin was renowned for being a decent boss. He cared passionately about archaeology, but he was a champion of staff welfare, his mantra being 'if your staff are happy and feel valued, they'll bend over backwards to help you'. Stories of clashes with senior management and contractors were the stuff of legend. He had once refused to start work on a remote site until the proper facilities were in place: toilets, a heated site hut, hot water and so on. The panel van they had been asked to use as a site hut, and a five-gallon container of cold water had been firmly rejected.

With that, the team climbed aboard their transport and headed for home. They could already feel the effect of the truck's heater as they drove toward the gate - it had been left 'idling' so as to warm it up - and as they did so, Angela looked anxiously across to Colin, who was already walking back toward the site hut, presumably to lock it for the night

- apart from the toilet compartment of course. He looked positively excited at the prospect of a night under canvas, which did nothing to ease her concerns, and as she watched, Colin made his way across the site, humming quietly as he did so.

"Sooner him than me!" she said aloud.

"Huh? Oh, Col?... yeah, me too!" Cal replied, having realised to what Angela was referring.

"I hope he's OK…" she continued, "…I feel guilty leaving him out here on his own."

Ian glanced briefly at Angela through the rear-view mirror and could see the look of concern on her face.

"I'm sure he'll be fine, Ange', and in any case, it *was* his choice to stay?"

Angela looked back into the vehicle and at Ian's eyes which were now firmly back to watching the road.

"I know…" she said. "…it's just… oh, you know!"

"Yeah, we know, mate…"

Chapter 9: Comrades & Allies

Now that the others had finally left and the sound of the 4x4s engine could no longer be heard, Colin began readying himself for the night ahead. The light was already beginning to fade; the trees were no more than a silhouette against a pale amethyst sky, and he wanted everything to be done and dusted before dark if possible.

He finished the last of the paperwork, snapping the lever-arch file closed and placing it among those already stowed on the Formica worktop, using the microwave oven as a make-do bookend. Then he sat for a while, thinking, massaging his closed eyes and forehead with the palm of both hands as he did so. No deep thoughts came to him, and he simply allowed himself to drift lazily for a while as he let the day's labours evaporate slowly away.

Right then, he thought to himself, *best off to the tent, I suppose*. With that, he drank the remains of his luke-warm coffee before dropping the dirty mug into the sink. *I'll wash that up in the morning,* he thought, knowing full well he wouldn't. He scanned the work surfaces for the site keys but couldn't see them.

"Oh, blast! Where are the keys?" he said aloud.

No point in asking the night air, he thought, but after a brief search, the night air answered, and he spotted them poking out from under a newspaper which had been absent-mindedly thrown down after lunch. Scooping them up, he made for the door before stepping out into the cool night air. It was much colder now than he had expected, but being an experienced outdoors type, he had brought the warmest thermal version of everything, so he wasn't particularly phased by it.

And finally, with everything in *its* place, Colin decided he should now head for *his.* He pulled a black military-style torch from one of his many pockets and pressed the single rubber on/off button at one end. Then, twisting the lens to focus the beam, he made his way across to the tent. He had moved the second 4x4 earlier that day so that it was close by, and, as promised, he had secured the seax safely inside.

It was almost completely dark now; not even the silhouette of the trees was visible, so he busied himself, first by arranging the large stones he'd cleared earlier to form a fire pit, then by lighting a fire using the pieces of wood that had been strewn about his camp site. *Handy someone leaving that newspaper,* he thought. *I'd forgotten I'd need a summat to start the fire with.* He smiled to himself as he imagined the face of its owner, probably Cal, who liked to re-read yesterday's paper before starting the current edition. *He'll get over it,* he thought as the lifeless. Still, images of smiling politicians and advertisements promising fun and freedom if you bought their particular brand of motor vehicle turned black before popping back into life, reborn as bright, orange flame. The logs were alight soon after, and Colin sat staring into the fire from his fold-up chair, hypnotised by the flames as they flirted and danced with one another. He began to wonder about those who had done just this over the millennia; prehistoric tribes; Bronze Age; Iron Age, and of course, the Anglo-Saxons whose lives were slowly being revealed to them on this very site. Maybe they, too, had sat somewhere near here, eating; drinking; telling tales; or maybe they simply sat and stared into the fire, contemplating life's mysteries, of which, at that time, there must have been many.

He spent the next few hours this way, occasionally emerging from his trance to prepare a meal or visit the loo; In fact, had the Night Hawkers actually turned up, it was entirely possible that Colin would not have noticed; such was his rapture. Finally, though, tiredness overtook him, and he decided to call it a night; He was also acutely aware of the fact that he had a site to run the next day, so he slipped, fully dressed - apart from his boots - into his winter rated sleeping bag, and pulled the zipper close up under his chin. Soon after, he felt himself drifting off to sleep. *Must be more tired than I thought,* he mused, as his eyelids became heavier, and when finally, he was unable to keep his eyes open any longer, he felt the softness of sleep begin to cnvelop him and thought: *I'd really like to be able to talk to someone from this site; someone from way back; Just for a while.*

Then all was quiet, and the only sounds that could be heard were those of someone softly snoring and the rustle of leaves as the trees soughed gently overhead.

***

Abrecan belched loudly and was rewarded with an enthusiastic cheer from the rest of the war band. They had arrived back at Valhalla just as dawn had fully broken and were now engaged in consuming the morning's feast.

Renweard, however, sat off to one side, alone in his contemplation. He watched as the great hall's central fire licked the base of a great iron cauldron, itself suspended from a mighty oak beam by an enormous wrought iron chain. His eyes lazily traced the chain up toward the rafters, where it eventually disappeared among the smoke and firelight. As he watched, a cluster of bright orange sparks played back and forth on the fire's breath.

Suddenly, a soft, gentle voice broke the spell.

"My lord is not joining the feast?"

The words came to him almost as music. This was no warrior, no Thegn. He turned to face the direction from which the song had come.

"Beornia; forgive me, I was deep in thought."

A shock of plaited blonde hair fell forward as the slight features of the Valkyrie moved to place a tray of mead-filled glasses on the table in front of Renweard. His eyes were drawn to them as the movement of the liquid within caught the light of the fire before casting patterns of refracted light back onto the tray's polished surface.

"There is none required, my lord; you are well to be alone as you wish."

Renweard looked deep into the face of the woman. She reminded him of his wife: Wilena, albeit she was slightly taller and lean as for battle.

"And Wilena has red hair…"

"My lord?" Beornia frowned at the apparently random statement.

Reading her confusion, Renweard sighed and said:

"It would seem that I must *dine* on forgiveness this morning, lady Beornia; I was considering how alike my own lady is to you."

Beornia blushed and said:

"Now awful it is to be without…"

“Indeed…!” The pair fell silent as both now watched the dancing flame.

Abrecan, not content with his previous effort, felt he had more to give, and his second rendition resounded noisily about the great hall to the delight and approval of his comrades.

“Forgive the men, my lady; they have much to celebrate…”

Beornia had already heard the news of Kendra’s success in Haligsfeld. The eleven men had returned to Valhalla in such high spirits that everyone heard their arrival and were regaled with tales of mist and light and voices from the old world. It had been a long time since the telling of such a tale, and many faces looked on eagerly as the story unfolded.

“I heard your arrival, my lord, from Haligsfeld, and I am pleased for you all. Do you think the man in the mist will honour his word?”

This had been the very reason for Renweard’s long contemplation: would the one who calls himself Rab be true to his word? And if he were, would he then be able to convince the leaders?

“If only I could see the future, my lady. All we can do is put our faith in trust and hope….”

“And Kendra, my lord! I am sure that when she speaks to them again tomorrow, she will have a clearer view of their intent.”

Renweard was about to concur when he realised the error in her statement.

“My lady means ‘when Kendra speaks to them three days’ hence’?” he corrected.

“My lord, no; I am aware that Kendra herself has already spoken with Woden, who has granted her permission to visit the field alone tomorrow at eventide”.

A full day early? What has Kendra discovered? Renweard found himself drifting away with his thoughts when Beornia interrupted them again.

“That is what I learned, my lord. Does it displease you?”

She gathered empty glasses as she spoke, and for the first time, Renweard noticed her attire. She wore a pale green peplos: a simple dress worn by most women in the hall, which was held in at the waist by a chatelaine. But what had caught Renweard’s eye was the embellishment around its neckline. Embroidered in silver and gold thread was the depiction of a swan, its wings spread so that the tips reached each shoulder, its long, elegant neck forming a lose ‘S’ shape, and finally, the head, its beak of embroidered gold and garnet eye, came to rest beneath Beornia’s chin, nestling there as though each lovingly protected the other, and as she moved, light from the fire combined with the flowing fabric brought the majestic beast to life, its feathers fluttering in an unseen breeze.

Noticing Renweard's interest, Beornia spoke again.

"She is 'Ilfetu'; She is both the symbol of my status as Valkyrie and my spirit protector. We share this life and the death of those we bring to this place".

"Ilfetu…" he repeated the name, no more than a whisper. "Ilfetu…" he spoke again.

Renweard felt bewitched by its beauty and fought to draw his eyes away. He did so nevertheless, and immediately his thoughts returned to Kendra. Instantly, his mind cleared, and he knew at once what he needed to do. To be honest with himself, the *need* was not the true motivator; it was plain curiosity. *I must be present at the seeing,* he thought. *I must know what is said.*

Apologising as he went, Renweard stood up, stretched the stiffness from his back and shoulders and hurried across to the great doors of Valhalla before disappearing into the bright daylight. Beornia looked after him, but she was alone in so doing; the others continued the feast, blissfully unaware.

***

Two dark shadows made their way through fields bounded by hawthorn and beech. They walked silently so as not to disturb the night creatures: the owl, fox, badger and deer, whose turn it was now to inhabit this place. In the distance, the call of a stag rang out in the darkness.

"Eikthyrnir? Asked Renweard.

"Unlikely that old Thorny Oak himself is afoot," Kendra replied. "More likely one of the herd; there is many a hart and hind in these fields."

They continued on, in silence still, until they reached the same woodland clearing and stream they had visited previously. They could hear flowing water through the darkness, and though Renweard could not see it, Kendra made straight for its edge and stopped.

Suddenly, as though directed by an unseen hand, the clouds parted, allowing the near-full moon to illuminate the landscape. His eyes adjusted quickly to the newly revealed vista and Renweard at once found himself standing in almost exactly the same spot he had occupied a day or so earlier and right by the water's edge. In fact, two more paces would have had him drying his boots by the fire in the great hall.

"Kendra, I must ask: why? Why tonight? Why so soon?"

Kendra bid him be silent as she had already begun the seeing ceremony and was busy throwing flower petals into the stream. She had evidently gathered the marigolds on the previous visit in preparation for tonight; such was her haste.

"Kendra…?"

"BE STILL…!" she hissed.

Then, as before, she began the incantation.

"Feorh m fêores dîgan fremian êower port…"

The trees around them seemed to wake from their slumber.

"… ûs of pro ic wilcumian unnon sê unorne fyrhđ!"

A brief moment, devoid of all sound and still, still as the graves of the eight hung in the air, when suddenly a breeze came out of nowhere. It sang through the trees, making them pitch and sway and tugged at the clothes of the pair, forcing them hard against their skin, trailing behind them and flapping furiously. Then it was gone. In its place, the same eerie silence that had preceded it.

Renweard made to speak again, but as he drew breath, a faint mist began to rise up out of the ground. This time he recognised it and knew better than to interrupt Kendra now. As they watched, the same dense, grey vapour that had appeared to them before now swirled and billowed restlessly in front of them, and as before, it remained contained within an unseen boundary.

The moment arrived. Kendra slowly raised both arms above her head before dropping them suddenly to her side. As she did so, Renweard felt the same fluttering, wrenching sensation from within his chest as he had during the previous ceremony, and, as before, eight small, blue lights appeared, one above each grave in the field behind them and hovered there, noiselessly. Renweard knew at once what these represented, having felt their creation the night before. These were the immortal souls of him and his men. He knew this now, whereas last time, he merely suspected it. His was not a world of magic; he had no knowledge, less so, the experience of the dark ways. A deep, deep sadness washed over him, and he felt the need to cry out his anguish. He fought the emotion until it subsided, remaining still and impassive. The tension mounted as he waited for Kendra to speak into the mist when instead, she spoke to Renweard.

"I have no words!"

Confused, he replied.

"No words?

Kendra's frustration mounted.

"I have no words to bring them forth, to see into the mist!"

Her despair hung on the breeze, daring Renweard to question her words. He thought better of it and decided instead to offer his support and encouragement. *What words have I for this,* he pondered, already knowing the answer. Something happened then: a voice called to them through the mist.

"Hello!... Hello!... If this is some sort of trick…"

Renweard stared hard into the portal. He could just make out the faint outline of a man, a man brandishing a seax. Instinctively he reached for the handle of his sword, fearing an attack was imminent. Finding no sword, he prepared to fight hand-to-hand, a skill at which Renweard was unmatched.

He had struck an opponent so hard in one encounter that his sword blade had shattered, and then, surrounded by four fully armed warriors, he fought them with nothing more than a shield and an iron fist. Two fell at once under the onslaught of a well-aimed shield boss as it pushed the back of one man's head into the face of another; a third choked his last as the edge of the shield collapsed his windpipe; The fourth, no less a warrior than Renweard, threw down his weapons in an attempt to intimidate the great man. Instead, Renweard swelled at this honourable challenge and yelled a war cry so loud that men nearby assumed his wrath was aimed at them. He ran forward to meet his foe, tossing his own shield to one side as he did so. A clenched fist caught him squarely in the chest, bringing him to an abrupt halt, but he skilfully side-stepped the intended killing blow that followed, and dropping to one knee, he delivered a single, upward thrust of his iron fist to the man's solar plexus. His lungs emptied of air, the man clutched at his throat and chest, knowing that if he did not act now, it would very soon be over, but before he was able to do so, Renweard swept his feet away from under him, bringing him crashing to the ground. In mud, blood and spit, the man died, his eyes flickering shut like the last spark of the day's sun as she dipped below the horizon. *Sleep well, brother. We shall meet again in Valhalla, where we will feast together and tell wonderous stories of this day.*

A strange dialect brought him quickly back to the present.

"If you're Night Hawkers, I'll bloody 'ave you!"

***

Colin stood trembling in the cool dawn air, seax in hand. He had been in a deep sleep, dreaming of an oddly matched couple; a younger man and an old woman. She was telling the man that she… had no words and he… he was feeling deeply, deeply sad. Then he woke with a start.

Sitting bolt upright, he immediately found himself being forced to lay back down as the pitch of the tent's roof was pushed hard down into its interior, mere inches from his face. Outside, a gale was blowing in hard across the site, which caused the lightweight structure to flex, its sides billowing and bulging, each successive gust seemingly stronger than the last.

For some reason, Colin's sleep-weary brain had concluded that this was the work of Night Hawkers, so without stopping to don his boots, he scurried out of the tent, scooping up the keys to the 4x4 and ran to it, unlocking it with the key fob as he went. *I bloody knew this would 'appen!* He thought as he fought his way over to the car, *glad I brought the blade wimme.*

His seax had been laid on the back seat overnight, hidden beneath a spare hi-vis jacket that he'd found in the boot. He pulled open the car door, struggling against the wind as it tried to deny him access, and as he finally held it open, leaning with his back against it, dust, sweet wrappers, newspapers and anything else that wasn't secured flew violently about the cab caught in the micro-burst of the storm. He reached under the coat, grabbed the seax' handle and unsheathed the blade, he left the scabbard in the vehicle before turning to head out onto the site,

Almost at once, though, the wind dropped. The treetops, which had been pulled violently back and forth during the maelstrom, rustled gently once again as they settled back into place, and the dawn became still, albeit brooding, leaving Colin with a sense of unease. He stood motionless in the first light of dawn, breathing heavily, his breath misting in the air, and as he scanned the site for intruders, it was clear that he was alone, despite the fact that he was unable to shake the feeling he was not.

"Better have a walk round, I s'ppose," he said aloud to no one. "I'll never live this down if word gets out!"

He set off in the direction of the burials figuring that these would be the most likely target, and as he walked, he checked his pocket for the torch. *Blast! Must have left it in the tent.* He stopped, in two minds as to whether to go back and retrieve it, but decided to push on, his eyes having adjusted to the reduced light level now, and in any case, there was no point in announcing his arrival by flashing a torch around.

He moved stealthily on across the site, still convinced that there were others present, and trod carefully to avoid becoming swallowed up by one of the many holes that lay in wait for the unsuspecting; some of these were as deep as he was tall.

"I knew it! I bloody knew it!" he stopped short, peering straight ahead into the half-light. A few feet ahead of him, just by the graves, he could see a light: torchlight! *Right, I'm not having this,* he thought, and buoyed up by outrage and indignation, he ran forward, calling a warning.

"If you're Night Hawkers, I'll bloody 'ave you!"

And then he stopped dead in his tracks, mouth agape, hands trembling.

"What the…!"

In front of him, about two feet above the ground, hung eight pale blue lights, one above each grave. Each shimmered gently, emitting a soft, lowly hum, and just beyond, a grey mist rose silently up out of the ground.

"This is… it can't… what the…!"

As the mist grew, it too hung in the air, expanding as the grey, dense vapour swirled and billowed restlessly, yet it remained contained within an unseen boundary. Then he heard it; a whisper at first which grew until it became clear: someone was calling; he could hear a woman's voice!

"I seek the leader. I seek he who has sway over Rab," Kendra said.

Colin felt that he should be afraid. He'd certainly felt the adrenaline rush and experienced the ringing in his ears as he'd walked out to confront the Night Hawkers, but hearing the name of one of his best archaeologists and good friend being spoken from a cloud of mist was frankly too 'off the charts' to contemplate; there was no room for fear now as his mind whirled in a state of absolute confusion.

"You know Rab?" was the best he could manage.

"Only through our encounter in this place; through the portal which I have called into being. We spoke two nights ago and…" suddenly, Kendra was hit by a thought.

"You are the one in the shadow! The one who would not see!"

Elated, Kendra felt that fate had sent them all to this place and at this time. She turned and spoke to Renweard.

"Their leader has come. He is here. Fate has brought us to this juncture!"

Her joy was palpable on both sides of the portal; even the mist seemed to share in it as it moved excitedly within its invisible capsule.

"Surely, if fate has brought us here, then…"

She turned to face Colin through the mist, who had looked on in astonishment as the old lady spoke to her unseen companion. *This must be a dream,* he thought. I*t simply must be.* But all doubt was erased in a flash as Kendra spoke again.

"You *are* the one in the shadow! I spoke with Rab here, but two nights since and you…" she pointed at Colin "… were here with him!"

Colin thought for a moment, and then it came to him. *So, this is what Rab saw? Is this the breakdown I thought he was having?*

"You! You're the one Rab spoke to the other night?" he said finally.

"It would seem our leader *is* indeed among us!" Kendra said cheerfully. "We have great need of you; we have much to ask".

There could be no doubt; Rab had spoken of a Kendry… *no, wait:*

"Kendra?"

"He knows my name!" she said to the unseen bystander

"Yes, yes, I am she, prophetess to Valhalla and all within, and we are in desperate need of your help," she said urgently.

"What does a prophetess of Valhalla want with a mere mortal like me?" he asked warily.

"You believe?" she said.

"How could I not! Who on earth would go to such elaborate lengths for a hoax?"

"You should sit; *we* should sit," she said to both men.

"May we know your name, leader?" she asked as they eased themselves to the ground seeking a dry, comfortable spot.

"Wha…? oh, Colin. Colin Rhyll".

"Thank you, Colin Rhyll; we are grateful that you would speak with us at such a time."

"What *do* you want? *What* help do you need?"

Kendra spent the next few minutes enlightening Colin as to their predicament, though she was careful to approach each chapter at a slow, steady pace so that Colin could absorb the information and ask for clarification when he needed to, which he did often. Ragnorök, Woden, the ravens; all were revealed, and when she finally spoke of the eight and the loss of their possessions, the penny finally dropped.

"Good grief, that was you!" Colin uttered to himself, "To think I accused my ol' mate of losing the plot! So, let me get this straight; you want us to put the artefacts... the *possessions* back in the ground?"

Kendra nodded enthusiastically as he continued.

"But it has to be done by evening here on the third day?"

Kendra nodded again but corrected him, saying, "Yes, but since one day has already passed, we now have but two remaining!" she said nervously.

Colin frowned.

“No pressure then?”.

He thought a while longer, considering their options, speaking aloud as though hearing his thoughts might help clarify them.

“So, we’ve got two days; two and a half actually, to get the items from the unit in town, bring them back here and bury them. Sounds simple enough, but… do I *ask* for them and tell them why we need ‘em? No, we’d risk being turned down…”

He chuckled aloud to himself; Kendra winced, confused.

“… which we will be on the grounds of insanity, or do we just take them *without* asking? Could do *that,* I suppose, but then how the hell do I explain the sudden disappearance?”

He stroked his chin, deep in thought.

A look passed from Renweard to Kendra that asked, “what’s happening?” Kendra shrugged her shoulders and indicated that they should be patient. She was confident now that Colin would help. It was just a matter of how; it was important that he draws his own conclusions and decide on the manner of the possessions’ return.

Unexpectedly though, Colin shook his head and frowned deeply. Seeing this, Kendra felt the blood drain from her face as dread rise like a cowled, faceless demon from the pit of her stomach and into her chest. Her heart beat so fast and pounded so hard that she could hear each beat pulse in her head.

"Can't be done?" he said. "There's just no way we could get everything back here in time".

Kendra remained still, trying to come to terms with this turnaround of fate. How could this be? Where now was the hope that had swelled the chest and quickened the heart? But Colin wasn't finished. Just as the warmth of hope had all but diminished to be slowly replaced by the slow, insidious creep of despair, Colin spoke again.

"But I reckon there's another way we could get a set of weapons to your guys; tell me: do they have to be the exact same items that we took from the ground? Or can they be different weapons but of the same quality? Kendra…?"

Kendra had not moved, nor had her expression changed since Colin began talking. The ringing in her ears remained, the unshed tears held back only by the blinking of her eyes.

"Kendra?" Colin said again softly. This time she heard him.

"What…"

She cleared her throat, which had become tight and dry with contained emotion.

"What other way…" she whispered.

Colin looked at the seax, which had been held firmly in his hand for the entire encounter. This was a thing of beauty; No mass-produced replica from an on-line store. The weapon had been created by the master craftsman Bengt Nilsson at his smithy's workshop at Flottsund and had cost him about the same as the price of a small hatchback. Colin visited him there two years ago as he and some of his fellow Bernicians combined a trip to the burial mounds of Gamla Uppsala with a visit to collect his commissioned piece. They had all, to a person, fallen in love with the area. Grey stone and terracotta red buildings shared the same style of the slate roof and white-painted window surrounds. Bengt's workshop looked out over lake Ekoln, and on the day they had visited, the sun shone so brightly in a cloudless sky that it was impossible for the scene not to be burned into their collective memory. Then, as Bengt released his creation from the confines of its linen wrap, the small group of enthusiasts gasped. Colin wrapped his fingers deliberately round the birchwood handle and drew it slowly from its simple leather scabbard for the first time, and they gasped again. The silver-grey blade had been pattern welded in the age-old fashion whereby different thicknesses of iron were heated, twisted and forged together in a repeated process which formed the strongest blade possible but also allowed a degree of flexibility in the weapon. In each new blade, the resultant technique created a unique, permanently etched pattern which resembled that of Damascus silk. So valued was this technique that it was said that the smithies of old were looked on as magicians or alchemists.

Colin looked back at Kendra. It pained him, but he could see no other way.

"You see my blade?" he asked, holding the seax out to one side, admiring its beauty as he did each and every time he held it.

"I do; it is a fine weapon," Kendra replied.

"It is, and I have others like it; I have many friends… brothers in arms, who have weapons such as this, and more: spears, helms and shields…"

Kendra thought she could see where Colin's words were leading, and her admiration for the man in the mist began to grow.

"Are you saying…?"

"…if we were to bring *those* weapons here and bury them… it would have to be bloody deep mind… would they be acceptable? Would they be acceptable to the eight? Could they take our weapons into Valhalla?"

She had been correct in her assumption; he had indeed intended to make an offering of their own possessions, perhaps as a means of contrition. In any case, it was an honourable gesture.

"You would do this? For the eight?"

"For the eight and for you, Kendra. I can see how important this is to you and the men."

Kendra smiled openly as she felt her soul swell; Her tears, this time, those of joy.

"You are, indeed, and honourable man; However, I must ask..."

Colin was startled; a male voice had emerged from the mist, and as Kendra stepped to one side, he could see the figure of a man take her place in the portal. Ice blue eyes pierced the swirling grey cloud and bore into him from across the centuries, and long dark hair and a beard bordered an otherwise ordinary but caring face. He spoke again, his voice deep and heartfelt.

"I have listened to your words, and if you truly *can* do this, my warriors; my lord Woden; I… will forever be in your debt but forgive me, we must know: are all of your weapons as fine as this?" he gestured toward Colin's seax.

Before Colin could reply, Kendra's voice emerged from the mist.

"My lord Renweard, one of the eight, offers no insult, Colin."

At first, Colin had indeed felt a flash of insult; these were, after all, top-grade weapons made by master craftsmen, but on considering the man's words, it made perfect sense to ensure that should Renweard and his men take the Bernician weapons into battle, they would not fail on their first encounter. He smiled and spoke openly.

"No, that's fine; I completely get it: there'd be no point taking inferior weapons into battle."

Colin looked deep into Renweard's eyes and, although he felt more than a little intimidated, said.

"First of all, trust me when I tell you that these weapons will serve you well. They have been lovingly created by craftsmen with a passion for their art, and *none* will fail you; you have my word."

He nodded, seeking acknowledgement that Renweard had felt his sincerity.

"And secondly, no debt. I won't be doing this for gain. In any case, I *haven't* done it yet, so it best not to celebrate just now, eh?"

Renweard looked on but said nothing. Colin filled the void.

"All right, look; Time is short. You already mentioned that, so let me go and round up the others to try and get them on board." *That's gonna take some doing,* he thought.

"We'll meet you here in two days' time…"

"Two and a half!" Rab corrected.

"Alright, two and a half… but Kendra?" The prophetess lifted her eyes to meet Colin's.

"You'll need to do the ceremony. I mean, we can dig the hole and everything, but if there are any words that need sayin'…"

Renweard and Kendra glanced at one another, smiling at the sudden enthusiasm with which Colin was planning his return.

"We will *all* be present, Colin. The eight; Grimme; Woden himself. All will be present." then suddenly, she asked, "Are you unwell? …Colin?"

Colin had felt his head swim at the mention of 'Woden'. *What the bloody hell...* he thought. *Woden! The actual Woden? You're losing it, mate... you've probably just got what Rab had...* but as he regained his composure and looked up and back through the mist, he saw two faces staring at him, a look of great concern on each, and he knew: He knew that this was no dream; this was no hallucination brought on by a lack of sleep or illness; they needed him to do this; they needed them all.

"I'm OK. Really, I'm OK! See you in a couple of days then!"

Kendra frowned, "Couple?"

"Two and a half," Colin corrected himself.

Chapter 10: The Crown Inn

Rab sat at the breakfast table staring out through the mullioned bottle-glass window into a well-manicured but over-wintering garden. It was warm in the pub dining room, so warm that the window glass was beginning to mist up as more guests began to arrive, bleary-eyed, for breakfast. The pub was a popular stop-over for travelling business people and tourists alike, and of course, Rab's own archaeological unit used it for its staff whenever they needed them to work 'out of area'.

"Everything alright for you, Rab?"

The voice of Rhia, the pub landlady, intruded on his early morning torpor.

"Oh, hi, Rhia. Yes, thank you; Superb, as always."

He had always enjoyed the breakfast routine when he stayed here. The Crown Inn was one of the better B and Bs on the archaeology unit's books and was happy to start breakfast a little earlier than most. Despite the Landlord, Trevor apparently preferred a lie-in, which meant the team could have a leisurely breakfast before starting work. Unfortunately, word of this had gotten out, so it had more recently become popular with the travelling business community and work gangs, but it was still a nice place and a nice way to start your day.

Pleased that their venue had once again been delivered, she sauntered off toward the kitchen from where the aroma of bacon, eggs, toast and coffee was wafting, collecting empty plates; they were always empty and used cutlery as she went.

It was just about light outside now, and from Rab's position, he could see traffic moving along the road on which The Crown Inn stood. The building had occupied its position for over four hundred years, no doubt serving the weary traveller for all of that. The main oak timber frame accommodated a high central arch which would have been the entrance used by the horse-drawn carriages of the day and led to a courtyard that, in days long since passed. Passengers would alight and make their way inside to rest and sup ale by an enormous log fire while Hostlers tended the horses in purpose-built stables. On either side of the arch entrance, large cubes of stone, each around eighteen inches wide, stood guarding the corner of the building, each chipped and misshapen by the constant impact of iron-tyred carriage wheels; they had done their job well.

Rab finished his tea and replaced the cup in its saucer. As he reached for the teapot and a refill, the room was suddenly flooded with light as a large vehicle swerved off the main road and into the pub car park before coming to an abrupt halt directly under the window through which Rab had been admiring the dawn. Everyone in the room stopped in the middle of whatever it was they had been doing and stared, appalled at such a dangerous example of driving.

"Oh, good grief, no…" Rab whispered as he recognised the distinctive features of the 'Benny Hat' and its wearer as they alighted the vehicle and headed for the entrance of the pub.

"Is that Colin?"

Rhia stood in the doorway of the kitchen wiping a mug dry with an 'I heart NY' tea towel - a souvenir of last summer's holiday in the States.

"I'm afraid so; sorry! I'll have a word."

She continued wiping the mug as she said.

"Don't worry, I'll do it myself; looks like he's coming in."

Colin had stayed here himself in the past when he and his wife, Janine, had had a brief 'parting of the ways' as he'd put it, so he knew the staff here quite well.

The dining room door was held open with a large, heavy iron weight so that the main entrance could be seen from within, and as the outer door opened, the loud clack of its iron latch attracted the diner's attention; everyone turned to see the face of this disturber of the peace. Everyone, that is, apart from Rab, who continued to stare out through the window, his tranquillity shattered.

"Mornin' all!" Colin gestured a hand around the room and was met by disapproving grunts and glares. Having already seen Rab through the window from outside, he made straight for his table and, without stopping to ask, pulled out a chair and sat down. Rhia was on her way over to 'have a word' when Colin, seeing her, turned and called.

"Hello me ol' flower. Any chance of a cuppa?"

Rhia's face changed instantly from storm to sunlight as she struggled to conceal a smile. She had always liked Colin. In fact, when he'd stayed here before, the rest of the team had, incorrectly as it turned out, thought that Rhia had been the cause of his troubles with Janine. Rhia shook her head.

"You're a cheeky beggar Mister Rhyll, but as it's you…"

She turned on her heels and made her way back to the kitchen to make Colin's tea and as she went called over her shoulder

"… and watch how you drive into our courtyard next time, otherwise, your tea'll end up in your lap!"

Colin laughed, although he wasn't sure she didn't mean it.

"Ooh, I like her; spirited, I'd call her."

Rab smiled and replied.

"Dangerous, more like, especially if you insist on crashing into her pub like this!"

Colin looked into Rab's face expecting to see irritation but was instead met with a smile and a shaking head.

"I dunno how you do it…"

"That'll be my charm, boy."

They both laughed.

"Anyway, what's with the dramatic entrance? You looked like you'd seen a ghost or…"

Rab caught the sideways glance and the raised eyebrows just as Rhia arrived with Colin's tea.

"There you go, trouble…"

She said as she made room for the tray on Rab's breakfast table, placing a mug, teapot and a jug of milk among the various sauce bottles and condiment shakers like a game of culinary chess.

"… I've made you some toast as well; I know what you're like!"

Colin beamed as a fully laden toast rack was placed on the table along with a side plate and knife.

"Ooh, you're a darlin'! Thanks, Rhia. Got any strawberry jam, though? I don't like marmalade."

Exasperated, Rhia was about to reply when Rab stepped in, handing Colin a small plastic pot that contained various preserves, some of which was strawberry jam.

"It's alright, he can have mine; thanks, Rhia!"

Shaking her head, Rhia went about the business of seeing to the rest of her clients, inwardly admiring the man's pluck.

Colin, in the meantime, went about *his* business of buttering toast and leaned across the table for the butter. For the first time, Rab noticed a strong smell of woodsmoke and damp soil; It was coming from Colin.

"How was last night then? Catch any night hawkers?

Angela had messaged Rab the night before and told him of Colin's plan.

"I heard you'd taken to living on site now?"

Colin smiled and chuckled.

"It was fine, ta. Besides, it's only temporary." He took another swig of tea before continuing.

"No, no night hawkers…" he leaned in for effect, his face aglow with intrigue "… way better 'an that…"

There was a brief silence as Rab waited for him to enlarge on his last statement; none came. Instead, he continued spreading jam onto the thick slices of hot, white toast, which mixed with the melting butter and dripped messily onto the plate, making Rab feel hungry all over again. He closed his eyes in an attempt to erase the image and purge his gluttony.

"I saw the look on your face…"

Colin took another large bite and chewed contentedly.

"Oh yeah; what look was that then?" His eyes glistened mischievously.

Rab stared hard at his friend, looking for any kind of clue in his expression that might solve the great mystery; then the penny dropped. Hardly daring to ask for fear of reigniting the conflict of two days earlier, he nevertheless said.

"The sideways glance when I mentioned you'd seen a ghost; You've seen her, haven't you? You've met Kendra!"

Colin swallowed the last mouthful of toast before taking a long, deliberate drink of the hot, sweet tea. Then, carefully placing the mug back on the table, he turned to face Rab, hooking an elbow over the chair back as a support.

"I have Rab". He said softly. "Last night. Well, early hours of this morning, to be precise."

The silence was slightly longer this time. Colin knew he had a lot to tell Rab, but not here; he couldn't talk about it here. So, by an unspoken mutual agreement, they chose not to discuss the subject further until they were in the 4x4 and on their way to work. Instead, they finished breakfast - Colin somehow managing to blag an egg and bacon sandwich - while he brought Rab up to speed with what needed to be done on-site today and what had been achieved yesterday. Their excitement was barely contained, however, and without realising, both had finished the meal more quickly than they would normally, and while Rab made a brief visit to his room to brush his teeth and collect his work bag, Colin chatted to Rhia and Trevor as he finished yet another mug of tea.

Finally, with choruses of "see you later" and "nice to see you again" behind them, they were in the truck and on their way to work.

Rab was, inevitably, the first to speak.

"So, come on then; what happened?"

The drive to the site lasted about ten minutes, during which time Colin brought Rab up to speed with the previous night's visit. He listened as Colin told of mysterious grey clouds, voices in the mist and tiny blue lights. All of this was familiar to him, except for the part relating to the male warrior. He had only spoken with Kendra.

"I can't believe you met Renweard as well. I mean, I saw the eight lights, which I found out later are the souls of the men, but I never actually met any of them."

Despite having been afforded this great honour, Colin felt no sense of satisfaction nor any pride or conceit. Instead, he felt horribly guilty; he had, after all, doubted his friend for having seen exactly what he was now describing. Rab continued, babbling with excitement.

"And you've actually agreed to give up all of your replica weapons and shields and what-not? I can't believe it. I'm really impressed; it's so generous of you all… what?"

Colin's expression had changed, just as the Bernician's contribution was mentioned.

"Yeah, about that…"

Rab recognised the change in Colin's demeanour instantly. He had seen it many times, usually when he needed someone to relocate to a different site or re-excavate a feature that had been badly dug. A mix of necessity, tempered with a reluctance to offend, it resembled pain and showed as such in his expression.

"… I haven't actually seen anyone to ask 'em yet. To be honest, I'm not actually sure how I'm gonna manage that; they all live so far apart, see? Not miles away, but…"

Rab did see; he saw that given they had a little under twenty-four hours before the weapons needed to be buried, they had almost no time to contact everyone, collect the items and get them to the site. Always assuming, of course, that everyone would be willing to part with their most treasured - not to mention expensive - possessions. Then a thought hit him.

"Hang on; what's the date today?"

He pushed back his sleeve to uncover his watch and peered at the tiny date window.

"I think you're saved; It's the twenty-eighth today."

It took a few moments for Colin to recognise the significance of the date, but when he finally did, his expression changed from the gloomy forest of confusion to bright, sunny meadows of joy.

"Our monthly meeting! Tonight is our monthly meeting! Well, of all the... I can't believe it!"

It seemed that luck might, indeed, be on their side.

Geoguth Bernicia, Colin's living history group, met on the twenty-eighth of each month. During the summer, they conducted club business in the evening as they camped at various historic sites around the country. It was a much less formal event then, and in some ways, seemed more relevant as they sat around a camp fire eating and drinking and always dressed in the clothes of the Anglo-Saxon period. It somehow felt quite natural. During the winter, though, there were very few such events, and they met instead at The Crown Inn, the same pub that was Rab's accommodation for the week.

"You'll still need to contact everyone, though, Col; otherwise, they won't know to bring their weapons!"

Colin seemed doubtful, and his face reflected it.

"Mmm … I dunno. I'm not sure I should ask them to bring their weapons along tonight; might seem a bit… presumptuous?"

Rab hadn't thought of that and agreed wholeheartedly.

"Yeah, good point. What if you were to drop them a group message - you're all on the group's social media page, yeah?"

Colin nodded.

"In which case, maybe send them a message saying something like: *I need to ask you all a massive favour, one that requires great sacrifice,* and break it to them when they get there. Hopefully they'll be curious enough so that when you tell them about Kendra and the eight…"

Their next potential obstacle had just revealed itself.

Colin's expression changed again; He was back in the gloomy forest.

"This is mental; What am I supposed to say: oh, hello, guys! Fancy burying thousands of pounds worth of your most treasured possessions in a field? Yes, that's right…" he continued his sarcastic tone, "…because a cloud BLOODY ASKED US TOO!"

It was a fair point, and as usual, Colin made it rather well, if a little overly dramatically. But what else could they do? Rab waited for the dust from Colin's outburst to settle before saying.

"I think you've pretty much hit the nail on the head, Col. I mean, I wouldn't put it *quite* like that, but essentially, yeah: guys, can Asgard have your weapons, please?"

The tension broke instantly, and they both laughed aloud, and as ridiculous as it sounded, that was what Colin decided he would do. They chatted a while longer until they were happy with their idea, which Colin now recapped.

"Right, the plan is: I'll send the message in a bit and ask everyone to confirm they can make tonight's meeting; I *won't* ask them to bring anything, but when they get there, I'll tell them what's happened and why Kendra is asking for the weapons. I doubt anyone will believe us, but if I can just persuade them to come to the site at six o'clock tomorrow evening…"

"With their weapons!" Rab added.

"… with their weapons, I reckon Kendra and the eight will do the rest."

The plan was as good as they might have hoped for. In any case, they were short of both time and options. Both Colin and Rab recognised this, and both knew that it would take nothing short of a miracle to pull it off.

They were a few minutes late arriving on site and the rest of the team, having already arrived, were in the process of changing into their work boots, drinking tea from a flask or, in Cal's case, snoring in the back of the second works vehicle with a newspaper draped over his face.

"Morning, troops!" Colin called as he climbed down out of the truck. "How are we all?"

Angela fixed him with a worried look and, as she shrugged herself into her hi-vis coat, said sharply.

"We were a bit worried, Col; More than a bit, actually! We expected you to be sitting next to a camp fire by your tent…"

Rab interjected.

"Tent? I thought you'd slept in the site hut!"

"Embarrassed," Colin said.

"Oh yeah; forgot to mention that. Sorry!"

Angela continued, barely pausing to draw breath.

"… only the site was deserted, and we thought something might have happened, and the truck had been nicked or something!"

Not for the first time today, Colin felt a pang of guilt and, realising he had been a little selfish, said calmly.

"All right, all right. I'm sorry, Ange'. Something *did* happen …"

A look of alarm returned to Angela's face.

"… not like that; I just had to nip off and see Rab first thing. It's all fine, trust me!"

Angela was not sure she *did* trust him but relaxed anyway.

"I'm sorry, I didn't think; I honestly thought we'd be back before you guys arrived… I'm OK; no harm done, yeah?"

She smiled and nodded.

"OK, but *please* don't do that again. Are you planning to stay tonight?"

Colin stole a sideways glance at Rab, who busied himself by pretending to organise his toolkit in preparation for the day ahead, also pretending not to listen.

"I am, just for tonight, though. Reckon we'll be done here tomorrow; what do you reckon, Rab?"

Hearing his name mentioned, Rab replied casually.

"Wha…? Oh, yeah, definitely by the morning; it'll be all over by then… hopefully!"

Having no reason to suspect a hidden, double meaning, Angela seemed satisfied with Colin's answer.

"Good…" she said, "… because I'm staying too!"

Then, leaving the two men stunned by the announcement, Angela turned and walked off across the site to start her day.

"Well, that was unexpected!" Colin said absent-mindedly.

"Yeah; a lot of that going about at the moment!"

Both men shook their heads and laughed, still managing to find humour in the absurdity of it all.

"Best I get that message out, Rab. You ready to make a start?"

He most definitely was; He'd only been signed off from work for one day since the evening on which he'd met Kendra, but it had felt like a lifetime. There was very little to do in his room at the B&B, and he felt uncomfortable going out lest he was seen - he was supposed to be ill after all - so he'd spent the day sleeping, reading and watching daytime television. The day ground painfully on, and he was quite relieved when he was finally able to climb into bed and switch off the light, and despite the lazy day he'd just had, he was amazed to wake the following morning having dropped straight off to sleep. Responding to Colin's question, he said.

"Yes, mate, Absolutely. You go and get that group message sorted; I'll have a word with Ange to see what needs doing?"

Colin was more than happy for Angela to delegate work to the team; he trusted her abilities as much as he did Rab's, and he was frankly relieved that he could finally get on with the task at hand, so leaving the two of them discussing the next stage of the site's excavation, he headed over to his tent.

He'd left in a bit of a rush this morning, waiting only as long as he needed, or excitement would allow, before setting out to find Rab. In his haste, he had left his belongings unattended, and the tent flaps wide open. Luckily though, it hadn't rained, so the interior of the tent remained dry.

Perhaps more importantly, he'd had the foresight to take his seax with him. After the events of that morning, he'd re-sheathed and re-wrapped it, and making absolutely sure there was no one around to witness it, placed it securely on the back seat of the 4x4 where it now lay, awaiting its next call to arms.

He moved his fold-up chair into a patch of sunlight and, once he'd made sure it was fully open and stable, sat down. *These are actually quite comfortable,* he thought as he reminisced over last night's bonfire and the hours he'd spent watching the flames.

"Didn't know if you'd fancy a cuppa, Col?"

It was Ian who offered the handle of a well-filled enamel mug to Colin.

"Three sugars, isn't it? That's what you've got anyway."

Colin was never disappointed to receive a cup of tea. *Strong and sweet,* he always said, *just like me!*

"Thanks, mate; you're a diamond."

Ian didn't linger; It was clear that Colin had other things on his mind; he would normally have been scratching around on site before anyone else had arrived, so there was clearly something afoot. Not wishing to pry, he set off across the site to the feature he'd been assigned by Angela and prepared to excavate.

Colin settled deep into his chair and, having taken a sip of hot sweet tea, placed the mug on the ground next to him. Then, to the accompaniment of ripping Velcro, he retrieved his mobile phone from the top left pocket of his gilet and searched the menu for his contacts. The living history group were stored under the heading '*GeoBern,*' which he selected and began to type his message to the group:

Hi everyone. I'm really looking forward to our meeting tonight and to seeing everyone. It seems like ages! I have a massive favour to ask of everyone tonight, and I mean MASSIVE, so if at all possible, can we all try and make it, please? I'm not exaggerating when I say that if you're willing to take part, this WILL be life-changing! See you later. Col.

Being 'old school,' Colin read the message back to himself to check the grammar, then absent-mindedly mumbling said, "If that doesn't get their attention, nothing will." He pressed 'send', and a second later, the phoned bleeped and flashed up a 'tick' icon confirming the message had indeed been sent.

"Nothing I can do now but wait," he said to himself, and reaching down, he scooped up the mug and began drinking the contents.

To say that time dragged for Colin and Rab was an understatement. They had busied themselves with the day's work which was interesting enough, but inevitably, their minds were never far away from the subject of Asgard or Kendra for long, though neither spoke of them.

Every so often, Colin's phone would announce the arrival of another message, and each time, Rab's head and shoulders would appear above ground from his feature like a bizarrely dressed meercat, his face hopeful of another Bernician confirmation which Colin would either confirm with a thumbs up or shake his head if the message was related to something else. So far, of the twenty-six people who had been contacted, nineteen had replied, and all were interested and were 'definitely coming'.

At lunchtime, they gathered at Colin's tent instead of the usual crush in the site hut, and one-by-one they arrived with various mugs, bags, lunch boxes and heated ready meals and proceeded to eat, drink and have the conversations that only archaeologists seem to have.... Colin sat listening when suddenly it occurred to him that this was not unlike the fireside conversations of the Bernicians in camp. In fact, it may well be that gatherings held here, some fifteen hundred years ago, were just like this: talking, eating, reminiscing. All very human activities.

"Predictable things, people," he said aloud.

"What's that, Col?" Ange was seated nearby.

"Eh? Oh, I was just thinking how scenes like this must have played out hundreds of times over the years, especially with the Anglo-Saxons, y'know?"

"Thousands; tens of thousands, I reckon," she replied, seeing his point and sharing in its wonder.

"Reckon, you're right, gal. Anyway, look…"

He said, suddenly remembering Angela's comment about sharing his campsite,

"… what's all this about stopping on-site tonight?"

Angela was glad Colin had brought this up, as she'd been so busy herself that she'd almost forgotten.

"Oh right, yeah. Well, strangely enough, my tent was still in the boot of my car - don't ask - and I thought, well, you know… You might be glad of some company".

Her tone was so cheerful and matter-of-fact that Colin didn't have the heart to deny her the opportunity to help. The only problem, of course, was how the Hell was he going to explain everything to her? Company being the one thing he most definitely would not be lacking.

"Maybe it'll explain itself?" Rab had volunteered later as they finally began finishing up for the day.

"I mean, seeing Kendra through the mist did it for you!"

Colin couldn't deny that he'd been a total sceptic until he'd seen Kendra for himself. He really had been worried for Rab's mental health, but having now met and spoken to the people through the mist, he knew that this was as real as it gets; either that or they were both barking mad!

And so, they found themselves, the working day done; Angela's tent pitched a few feet from Colin's, though not too close as Colin was also renowned for having a painfully loud snore, and everyone heading off-site to their respective homes, including Rab who was being dropped off at the pub by the other of the two vehicles.

"See you both later then," he said through the open back window of the 4x4.

"Can't wait!" Angela replied.

When Colin had explained that he had a meeting of the Bernicians at The Crown Inn that evening, Angela had been fascinated and begged to be invited along. Of course, Colin had no intention of leaving her alone in a field in the dark, so after feigning club secrecy akin to that of the Masons and citing strange initiation ceremonies, he finally 'agreed' that she should come.

The Sun, now almost fully set, settled low on the horizon, itself nothing more than a thick black line accented by the lacey tops of the gently swaying trees, as once again the site fell silent and the 4x4 headed toward civilisation carrying its occupants to well-earned rest and sustenance. The two remaining archaeologists began organising the evening meal, and before long, a fire burned steadily in the pit that Colin had used the previous evening, occasionally flaring with the wind as it began heating the heavy iron pot that Colin had suspended by its carrying handle from a road iron: a long steel stake with a crook at one end used to create temporary barriers which they'd borrowed from the tool store. As it swung gently in the breeze, its contents bubbled noisily, wafting the aroma of a freshly prepared stew across to its eagerly waiting recipients.

"Beats the Pot Noodle I had last night, Ange'!"

"Oh, really? … I knew you wouldn't be eating properly!"

Without taking his eyes off the fire, Colin smiled warmly.

"Well, I am tonight".

"Yes, you are…" she said, "… yes, you are!"

Chapter 11: Wassail, Bernicians!

The monthly meeting of Colin's living history group: *Geoguth Bernicia,* was scheduled to start at 8 p.m., and as was usually the case, some of the group had arrived early to claim a quiet corner of the pub, which would invariably become less so, to make a start on the evening's "refreshments". The room they favoured was at the back of the pub and had its own entrance meaning they could come and go without having to interrupt the rest of the ale-buying public or diners and was of a reasonable size; large enough, anyway, to accommodate the twenty or thirty individuals who normally attended, although the ceilings, being low and oak-beamed, provided a particular challenge to the taller members of the group who were required to duck as they moved through it. Some had, in fact, taken to wearing their Anglo-Saxon helmet to and from the bar, much to the merriment of the bar staff, albeit to the bewilderment of their fellow customers.

As Rab was a guest staying at The Crown, he decided that he'd wait until Colin and Angela arrived before heading down to the bar, as he didn't know the members of the group particularly well and didn't want to be seen as gate crashing. Instead, he ate early, at around six thirty, then lay on his bed reading, planning to remain there till he heard Colin arrive.

Sometime later, he awoke with a start as a loud 'WASSAIL!' followed by the boisterous throng of voices invaded his room. Heart and head pounding together, he sat bolt upright on the bed, momentarily disorientated. The copy of the monthly archaeology magazine he'd been reading lay crumpled on the floor, and the room was now completely dark, save for the light that washed in from the pub sign, which was just beneath his window, giving the room an eerie, sulphurous glow. He flopped wearily back onto the bed and listened to the sounds coming from the bar downstairs as his mind tuned slowly back into the world, and his heart rate settled back into something like a normal rate. Despite having slept, he felt completely drained and would happily have laid there all night had it not been for his promise to Colin that he would be at the meeting tonight.

"It's crucial that you're there, Rab; I'll need all the help I can get!"

Rab had no intention of letting down an old friend, nor Kendra and the eight, who were relying on them both to deliver on their word.

He rolled slowly onto his side and peered at the digital clock on the bedside cabinet.

"Ten past eight; better make a move, I suppose," he muttered to the room.

Just then, there was a gentle tap at the door. Sitting up slowly, he called.

“Yeah, it’s open!”

Nothing happened, and then the tap came again. Sighing heavily, he stood up and took the two or three short steps to the door and, twisting the lock, opened it.

“Oh, hi Ange’. I didn’t expect to see you here!”

Noticing the look of surprise on Rab’s face, Angela took a step back from the door to stand a little way into the corridor; she seemed slightly embarrassed.

“Oh…well, I hope it’s OK, only I felt a bit like a spare part down there.” She smiled awkwardly.

“No, of course, I don’t mind; why would I?”

He stepped back and beckoned her into the room.

“Come in; I just need to brush my teeth, and I’m ready.”

She hesitated briefly before entering the room, then walked straight across to the window where to one side stood a student’s writing table. It resembled a small bookcase, albeit with a drop-down writing surface, and just in front of it was a captain’s swivel chair.

“This is nice.” She said, looking around the room. “I didn’t realise this place was so old.”

“’eah, iffs an ol’ courchin’n I vink” Rab said through a mouthful of toothbrush and frothing toothpaste. Angela looked up from thumbing through the archaeology magazine she’d found on the floor and, doubting her own ears, said.

“Sorry? I didn’t catch that!”

Rab rinsed and wiped his mouth, feeling much refreshed for having brushed his teeth.

“Sorry. I was just saying that I think it’s an old coaching inn.”

Angela laughed. “Oh… Haunted?”

It was Rab’s turn to laugh. “Oh, you have *no* idea!” he said mysteriously. “Shall we?” He gestured with a hand toward the door.

As they left, Rab snapped the door shut behind him and checked that it was locked by firmly pushing against it. They made their way along the narrow, gloomy corridor; through a set of fire doors and down the stairs that lead to the main entrance hallway. As they descended, the sounds from the bar grew louder and louder before finally exploding in their ears as they walked through into the room at the back of the pub where the Bernicians had set up their temporary camp.

Two things came as a surprise to Rab as he stood by the doorway scanning the room and its occupants: first, no one was in Anglo-Saxon clothing. He wasn’t sure why he thought they *would* be, but that was the image he'd created in his mind. In fact, everyone was dressed in, well… *normal* clothes. There was everything from bikers in jeans and leathers to one individual who wore mustard-coloured chinos and a tweed jacket. Had it not been for his long grey hair and a plaited, beaded beard, Rab would have assumed that he was in entirely the wrong place. His second surprise was the number of empty pint glasses that covered almost every square inch of the tabletop. There were maybe twelve people in the room who could only have been there for an hour at most, yet there was almost three times that number of empty glasses, and refills were just on their way from the bar. Angela had clearly had the same thought.

"Good grief; they might not *look* much like Anglo-Saxons, but you could be forgiven for thinking you'd just walked into a mead hall!"

Rab laughed aloud, somehow catching the attention of Colin, who was leaning against the bar chatting to Trevor, the landlord. Calling out across the noise, he said.

"RAB! THERE YOU ARE, YOU OL' BUGGER! I SEE MY ENVOY FOUND YOU?"

Rab didn't yet have a head for shouting. He was still a little sleep weary, so instead, he gave the thumbs up, then gestured, "Drink?" by tipping the invisible contents of an equally invisible glass into his mouth. As if communicating by some internationally recognised drinkers code, Colin held his newly replenished pint glass up so that Rab could see it, indicating that he was "all sorted, thanks!"

"Drink Ange'?" but she too already had a pint put by on a table nearby and so politely declined.

"Cheap round!" He said as he made his way over to Trevor at the bar and ordered a cider. Trevor's retort made Rab chuckle in agreement: "Not for that lot, it ain't! I'll make the equivalent of a whole weekend's takings from these guys tonight!" he said happily "…if I haven't already!"

Rab spent the next half hour sipping his drink and checking his watch. They really did need to make a start soon; time was tight enough as it was. It was almost a quarter to nine before it was decided that everyone who was going to come was there and that they should push on with proceedings. In all, there were now twenty-one Bernicians, which by Colin's calculations, gave them a fifty/fifty chance of success.

"I'm feeling pretty good about this, Rab!" he'd said as the room was called to order.

A lot of Rab's assumptions were being contradicted tonight; for example, he'd always assumed that Colin was the one in charge of the living historians, but to his complete surprise, when the time came to start the meeting, it was the man in the yellow chinos and tweed jacket who stood up and walked to the head of the table. There came a sudden, sharp rapping that cut high above the noise in the room as he beat the bottom of an empty beer glass on the heavy wooden table. Gradually the noise faded and finally stopped as the last whisper and Shhh! died away.

"Thank you, ladies and gentlemen, thank you."

"No; thank you, Red Baron!" called a heckler from the back of the room, which erupted once more with laughter.

Jon Richardson was co-founder of *Geoguth Bernicia* and was well respected for his extensive knowledge of all things Anglo-Saxon and, in particular, the *migration period.* This referred to the time in the early fifth century when so-called 'barbarian tribes' such as the Saxons, Friesians and Jutes, began moving into countries like Britain to fill the apparent void as the Roman Empire, overstretched and weakened by attacks on its borders, recalled both its military and citizenry to defend Rome; there were few who had studied the period more extensively. Unfortunately for Jon, though, his name was apparently so similar to 'Von Richthofen' (though he'd never seen it himself) that for some of the members, it was impossible to resist and he had affectionately become known as 'The Red Baron'. He took it in the spirit it was intended, despite his austere appearance.

"Yes, yes, thank you, jester!" he replied. "But if we could get down to group business now? Thank you." The room became quiet once more, and in the unmistakable slow, matter-of-fact tone of an academic, he addressed the room.

"Now, I know that Colin has an important request to make of us; that was really quite apparent in the manner of his text message earlier this morning, but I'm sure he won't mind waiting a short while before taking to take the stage?"

He nodded toward Colin, seeking confirmation but received none. This could not have been further from the truth; In fact, Colin was standing so close to Jon that he might have been mistaken for his shadow, such was his eagerness to speak to the room. His expression somehow reminded Angela of her mum's Golden Retriever, Roxy, who would sit, waiting expectantly for her ball to be thrown, just one more time. She could keep it up for hours - if you let her! From their vantage point by the bar, both Rab and Angela could see Colin's look of anticipation turn quickly to one of frustration as Jon opened a file and produced an agenda of some fifteen pages, which he began to arrange, by category, on the table in front of him. Rab leaned in and whispered to Angela.

"Those…" he said, nodding toward what looked like half a ream of A4 paper "…are going to end up either on the floor or out through the window!"

Angela giggled and replied: "Or worse!"

They *both* giggled like naughty school children, which inevitably attracted a raised eyebrow from Jon, who had turned to peer at them from over the top of his half-moon glasses before turning back to the Bernicians and continuing

"So, if we *could* just start by going over the minutes of the last meeting…"

Colin emitted a faint but audible whimper that caused everyone in the room to turn and look in his direction. Surprised by the sudden attention, Colin shook his head dismissively and said, "Oh, sorry, just err… clearing my throat."

All but Jon could see that this was clearly not the case, and all but Jon continued to look toward Colin. Unchallenged and completely oblivious, Jon continued.

"Mmm…, yes, the minutes of the last meeting. So, the first point is clothing. It was noted that several members are travelling to events in Anglo-Saxon clothing, which is fine, but apparently, some of you are also wearing the small domestic knife, which, as you all know, is illegal in a public place…"

He droned on in a similar fashion, addressing small points of order which, frankly, could have been resolved via email for a further five minutes. Colin, meanwhile, continued to wait eagerly off to one side, but it was clear, again to all but Jon, that everyone *else* in the room was as eager to discover what the life-changing opportunity Colin had messaged them about was as Colin was to relay it to them.

Fifteen minutes later and not yet half way through the stack of papers, a feeling not unlike claustrophobia began to smother and suffocate her as finally, Angela could take no more. She could see that the only person in the room who was remotely interested in what Jon was saying was Jon himself, and everyone, including Colin, was too polite to ask him to stop.

"That's it!" she said aloud, slipping from her bar stool.

To the sheer amazement of everyone in the room, they watched, open-mouthed, as she made her way purposefully across to where Jon was standing. She moved in alongside him, pausing briefly before leaning in and placing the palm of one hand on the pile of papers. Then, while shielding her mouth with the other, she whispered something unheard directly into his ear. As she spoke, Jon remained completely still, both palms resting on the table in front of him, listening intently. His eyes settled briefly on the Bernician immediately in front of him, making her feel uncomfortable, and causing her to turn to avoid unwanted attention. Yet his gaze did not rest there; Instead, his glazed eyes stared off into the distance seeing nothing but a kaleidoscope of blurred shape and colour. Everybody in the room leaned forward instinctively in an attempt to hear what was being said, but Angela somehow managed to maintain discretion, and her words were audible only to the one for which they were intended.

For a while, nobody spoke or moved; it was as though somebody had pressed life's 'pause' button. Soon after, though, the conversation began in whispers, starting at the back of the room, which then crept slowly forward like an incoming tide before breaking in waves as full, excited conversation. Spell broken; Jon blinked several times before clearing his throat. Slowly he turned to face Angela, who, despite the expectations of the room, did not wilt under his glare. Instead, she maintained her position, hand still firmly on the pile of papers, denying access, and returned Jon's look with an expression that read: *"You know I'm right!"* Seeing the apparent stand-off, the room fell silent once more as everyone appeared to be holding their breath. There followed the briefest hesitation, then quite unexpectedly, Jon's face broke into a smile: a genuine "eyes and all" smile. The room exhaled, relieved.

"D'you know? I believe you're right, m'gal!"

Angela smiled, her appreciation for Jon having seen sense. The twenty-one Bernicians, however, remained silent, apparently in awe of the stranger in their midst. Most knew that she was one of Colin's work colleagues, but beyond that, nothing. One or two of the younger members of the group had decided that perhaps it was time to put that right. "I wonder whether she'd join the group?" one mused optimistically, regretting it straight away as the group he sat with began teasing him. "Look out!" one called "...Joe's smitten!"

"Colin!" Jon called as he beckoned him over from the corner he'd retreated into since the meeting had begun.

"Colin, you have a truly loyal friend in this young lady," he said, gesturing toward Angela. "Will you accept the apology of an old fool who wanted no more than to clear the agenda of minutiae so as to provide you with a clear, uncluttered platform from which to speak?"

Angela felt a little guilty now; *what a lovely apology*, she thought, from someone who hadn't realised they were causing so much tension and who thought that they were, in fact, helping a friend and colleague by simply clearing the decks.

Angela made to speak, but Colin beat her to it, feeling humbled at such a heartfelt apology.

“You know: you never cease to amaze me, Jon. I should have known you weren’t just hoggin’ the floor. I’m the one who should apologise!”

They shook hands in the midst of a room filled with delighted, albeit confounded, people, most of whom had thought there would be some kind of reprisal, instead of which, all was well; all was very well, in fact.

“Think nothing of it, old boy; order is restored, eh?”

“Thank you, Jon!” Colin said humbly as he made his way over to the head of the table and prepared to speak.

He stood and waited for what felt like an age as he watched the Bernician’s retake their seats once more; one individual returning from yet another sortie to the bar bearing a circular, tin tray laden with glasses of all shapes and sizes - mainly pints - containing liquid of various shades, from clear to brown and amber. Opening his mouth to call order, he stopped short as suddenly the banter was interrupted by the familiar ‘glass-on-wood’ rapping that signalled a new speaker was about to commence, and as Jon placed the empty glass back on the table in front of him, Colin gestured that Rab should join him.

As the noise died away, he looked out over a small sea of faces, all eager with anticipation at what the next few minutes might reveal; There had been a flurry of text messages between some of the members throughout the day as they tried to guess what might be proposed. All were way off the mark:

I reckon he's got us another gig at Uppsala, one suggested.

More likely, a residency at West Stow! Another replied.

Sutton Hoo for me! Stated someone else.

They could not have known that what they were about to hear would stretch not only their imagination but also alter their opinion of Colin; his credibility; maybe even his sanity, and that what he was about to propose was, if not the stuff of science fiction, the stuff of legend. Whatever they thought, they would never see their world in the same way ever again.

Colin pulled himself up to full height and drew a deep, calming breath that filled his lungs.

"Oh crikey… now I'm here…!"

As he spoke, Colin peered nervously around the room. His eyes passed quickly over a dark, unoccupied corner off to one side of the bar where, for a fleeting moment, he saw the face of an old, grey-haired lady who smiled encouragingly at him from out of the gloom. Colin recognised her instantly as his heart skipped a beat; It was

Kendra! She remained briefly as an afterimage, like a recently extinguished light, and was gone.

Sensing that Colin's mettle was being over-tested, Rab leaned in and whispered.

"It's OK, mate; we've got you! Remember: you're doing it for Kendra and the eight!"

Colin turned slowly to look at Rab, still tingling, spellbound by the experience, and whispered:

"She was just here, Rab!"

Rab was confused. "Who was Col? Who was just here?"

"Kendra!" he said distantly.

But before Rab could reply, Colin had turned back to face the room, leaving his friend stunned at the revelation. He took great comfort from the visitation and, of course, from his friends, and remembering once again why he had called the Bernicians here tonight, he began.

"OK… right. Well, first up, let me thank Jon for stepping aside so that I can get on with my piece…"

Jon nodded graciously from his seat in the corner where he sat with a pint of real ale, himself equally intrigued by what Colin needed to say, and, more to the point, why it was so important that he needed to say it now.

“…and also, to my work colleagues - *my friends…”* he corrected “…In some ways, their presence is going to be of greater importance; no offence Jon…” none was taken “…because, well, because what I need to tell you is frankly, going to sound bloody ridiculous at first!”

He swallowed hard and, taking another deep breath, continued, his chest and neck pounding.

“Both Rab and myself have been paid a visit…” he chose his words carefully “…not from a venue or another living history group as I hear some of you thought, but… well, from a lady called Kendra…” the room waited “…*Kendra* lives in…” He hesitated “…lives in Asgard… *THE* Asgard!”

Nobody in the room reacted. Instead, to a person, they sat open-mouthed, expecting this to be one of Colin’s practical jokes, for which he was well known. Finally, though, a voice from the back of the room asked the question that was on everybody’s lips.

“*Asgard*? As in: Woden; Valhalla; Valkyries? *That* Asgard?”

Sensing their scepticism but not blaming them for it, Colin replied slowly.

“Yes, Dave; *that* Asgard, and, well… they need our help.”

“Woden needs *our* help!” said another.

This was not going well, although, to be fair, it was going pretty much as they'd expected: Just how *do* you convince a room full of people that Asgard is real? That Woden actually *does* exist and isn't just a character played by a well-known actor in a movie franchise? Colin and Rab had asked these questions, and many more like them, over and again and had eventually decided that tackling the subject head-on: by simply saying what needed to be said was the only way around it.

Colin seemed lost for an answer, and sensing that he needed assistance, Rab moved in beside him. He placed a hand of support on Colin's shoulder, then, leaving his beer glass on the table, he turned to speak to the room.

"I think most of you know me?" he began. "If not, I'm Rab: Colin's friend and work colleague…" he paused before continuing. "… look… all we ask is that you hear us out while we try and explain all this, but guys… you *really* will need an open mind; this is *not* going to be your average request!"

A voice that sounded as though they might just be winning the room over said, "Go on; we're listening." Rab seemed to have captured the room's attention… for now, so, seizing the opportunity, he spoke again.

"Colin and I were both visited, on separate occasions, by Kendra…"

So far, so good; He galloped on, hoping to deliver the information in one 'hit' before being interrupted again.

"…she *is* a prophetess of Asgard and has been charged, by Woden, with replacing the weapons that Colin, myself, and the rest of the archaeological team removed from eight graves just up the road from here…"

A murmur began gently circling the room.

"… Apparently, as the weapons, and other possessions, reappear in this world, our world, they *disappear* from Asgard, meaning that the warriors, to whom those items belong, are unarmed and unable to take part in…" *here we go*, he thought "…in Ragnorök…"

Colin had shared the exact same thought.

"…so, we suggested, and this is where it gets tricky, that some of you might be able to help… by allowing us to bury *your* weapons… tomorrow. Tomorrow evening to be precise!" He rattled the last sentence off like an automatic weapon.

There was stunned silence. No movement, no exchanged glances, nothing.

At once, the room exploded in uproar; the silence shattered violently as questions were fired at the two men from every and all directions. One individual stood up and glared at Colin before making his way out into the night and driving away. *One down!* Colin thought as their eyes met and clashed across the room. The commotion continued noisily at this level without let-up so that finally, Trevor, who was beginning to receive complaints from the other guests, began ringing the barbell loudly in order to get their attention, his vocal attempts having failed miserably. It worked almost instantly.

The furore died down, and finally, with order restored, he spoke firmly to the assembled group.

"There are *other* guests trying to have a quiet drink and a civilised meal in the other bars! Or had you not noticed? Now, as much as I enjoy your company and value your custom if you can't keep it down in here, I'm going to have to ask you to leave! Do you understand?"

They absolutely did, and a wave of softly spoken apologies washed gently across the room.

"OK. In which case, feel free to carry on *quietly*! But if you disturb the other guests again, you'll be asked to leave; Alright?"

Again, the room nodded in quiet agreement as Jon, having organised the evening's event, ushered Trevor out of the room, a hand on his shoulder as a friendly gesture, promising to keep the room in order while apologising profusely the whole time.

Colin had taken a seat at the outbreak of bedlam, as had Rab and Angela, who were both now trying to persuade Colin that it would be better if he continued the conversation from this point, him being a group member.

"There is no point, guys; this lot thinks I've lost the plot. Maybe they're right; I'm not sure myself anymore!"

He looked deflated, older even, as he sat slumped in his chair, beer glass held limply in one hand, looking as though it might slip from it and smash on the flagstone floor at any moment. Angela, who was always prepared to go on a little faith, especially where her friends were concerned, was as confused, if not more so, than everybody else in the room. She had not been present at either of Kendra's visits, and neither Rab nor Colin had seen fit to mention it to her, so she could not be expected to fully grasp the situation, let alone defend it. It did, however, provide an answer for some of the strange behaviour that Colin and Rab had displayed over the past few days: Colin's sudden desire to spend his nights camping on-site for one; she never really *had* bought into his 'site security' explanation. Whatever the explanation, she was here to support them, so she made her way over to where Colin was sitting and interrupted what looked like a pretty deep conversation with Rab.

"Look, you two; I haven't got the foggiest idea of what you're up to, but it looks to me that whatever it is, you need to talk to these guys and quick; You're losing them!"

They looked up together and turned to face the room. The sea of faces that had greeted Colin earlier was still there, but where before they had displayed enthusiasm and anticipation, they were now questioning; critical.

"You're right, Ange', not to mention the time that's been wasted tonight so far." He looked at Rab and said

"In for a penny, eh?" then took his place at the head of the table once more.

Nobody spoke and nobody challenged; in fact, it was as much as some people could do to look at him as they felt embarrassed on his behalf, fearing they were witnessing some kind of a break down; a situation Colin was all too familiar with, having suspected the same of Rab. Now though, the entire room sat quietly and patiently waiting for him to continue. When he finally did, he did so carefully, treading slowly through each sentence as though trying to avoid stepping on the broken pieces of the previous conversation.

"Right then… look… I know how this sounds, trust me I do, but me and my mate Rab here really *have* both had the same experience, albeit on two separate occasions, and although I was there for the first: the one Rab saw, *I didn't* see anything."

Angela sensed that he was regaining their trust as they listened intently once again.

"...To be completely honest with you, I pretty much accused Rab of what you're likely accusing us of right now, and who can blame you? But... well, there you are..."

He let his words hang for a moment, hoping that somehow it might allow them to be fully absorbed before deciding to continue. As he made to do so, a disembodied voice fired a question at him from the back of the room. It was difficult to see the person, and they, sensing this, moved into the light; it was Jon.

"Colin; Rab; First, let me say that I admire your courage. We are, are we not, a diverse gathering of souls? We *Bernicians*? And are we not sisters and brothers who share a singular passion? And when called to arms, do we not *form* our impenetrable shield wall to protect our kin?"

Angela thought she could see where this was leading. Of all the people here tonight, Jon was, in her opinion, the least likely to have come on board with what Colin and Rab were proposing. Yet here he was: their clan leader, calling his warriors to arms; bidding them to stand together; to unite and answer Asgard's call for aid. He continued as the room listened. Angela was not only correct, but she too could now see that her friends meant every word:

"I am more than a little curious to know how we few, gathered here tonight, might be called on to assist our brethren-in-arms; how we mortals might become key players in the last, great battle."

He paused for effect, and seeing this, Rab seized the opportunity and spoke again.

"It cannot be overstated, Jon… everyone…"

He acknowledged the room.

"We archaeologists have, inadvertently, been responsible for stripping these eight warriors of their weapons and their personal belongings, just at the point when they need them most, and while none of *you* bears any responsibility for that, it was to you, the *Bernicians*, we felt we could turn for help."

The room seemed to buzz gently as the implications of what had been proposed started to become clear. If this *was* true, and they: Geoguth Bernicia, could in some small way be responsible for rearming part of the Asgardian army, they would be permanently and intimately connected to a people whose lives they had studied for so long and from across so many unyielding centuries, that perhaps they too could become part of legend; part of one of the great, heroic tales.

Rab allowed the group to chat excitedly among themselves before making the big ask.

"So, will you help us? Will you help the eight warriors of Asgard?"

The room began to buzz more energetically now. Small groups of Bernicians talked among themselves, occasionally leaning across to speak with neighbouring tables; some nodding, others shaking their heads.

Clearly, though, not everybody in the room believed this was anything other than fantasy and were even less enthusiastic if it meant having to give up their prized replica weapons, which could cost upwards of an average month's wages. A small group stood up and started heading toward the door. Seeing this, Jon called out across the noise.

"LADIES, GENTLEMAN; thank you."

The group that was about to leave stopped and waited for Jon to continue.

"I have a proposal, if I may?" He looked to Colin and Rab for permission to proceed. They, of course, agreed, intrigued by this latest turn of events.

"Clearly, some of you have already signed up for this, which is admirable, and for that, we thank you; others, however, remain sceptical and are yet to be convinced. Might I, therefore, propose the following..."

He walked forward, removing a chair from his path and continued on in among the group of dissenters.

"I think we would all agree that if indeed, Woden, Kendra and Valhalla are found to be more than plain myth or legend, we would surely wish, not just to be able to play a part in it, but for our names to be written into that same legend and for the glory would almost certainly follow...?"

The tide had most definitely turned in their favour now, as most of the Bernicians seemed to be won over. Even those who doubted the credibility of the story seemed prepared to hear Jon out; such was the drama of his performance.

"…therefore, shall we agree that we will *all* gather tomorrow…"

He threw a glance, nodding at those who had been about to leave.

"… at the site of the graves…?"

Then looking to Colin and Rab for confirmation, they nodded together, Colin adding, "At six P.M.!"

"… at six P.M., and in full… I think we should no longer refer to our clothing as mere 'kit'; let us from now on refer to it as 'full dress' and with as many weapons as we can muster. Perhaps then we can give our brothers in Asgard a selection from which to choose…" he continued, anticipating a question from one of the doubters, raising his voice almost imperceptibly "…if however, this is nothing more than fantasy, we shall have lost nothing more than a few hours of our time at which point we can…" he paused, looking for the right words "…discuss the matter with Colin at a later date!"

The entire room, even the sceptics, seemed happy with the compromise. Afterall, if, as Jon said, this was nothing more than an elaborate hoax, all they would have lost was sleep. If, however, it was a genuine call for help from Asgard, they would forever be in favour with none other than the pagan gods themselves, not to mention the eight warriors.

So, with complete agreement and in high spirits, the group began to disperse and head for home, with all but four of the attendees agreeing to be at the reburial ceremony the following evening. As they left The Crown, conversations were had, and plans were made as to what each would bring with them and arrangements made for how they were going to get to the site.

"I think we've cracked it, Rab!"

Rab placed a hand on Jon's shoulder and said:

"Thanks, in no small part, to this man!"

Jon beamed.

"Glad I could help, old boy! Glad I could help. Now, I must away; there is much to attend to."

He, too, then headed out of the door and home, leaving the three: Colin, Rab and Angela, alone for the first time that evening.

"That went well!" Colin said after a while.

"Eventually!" Angela said, "You boys do know how to stir up a wasp's nest!"

There was a brief pause, and both Rab and Colin knew what was coming.

"Why…"

"Would you have believed us?" Rab anticipated.

Another pause as Angela considered her response.

"I might have… well… I… oh, probably not!" she concluded, feeling slightly deflated.

Rab raised his eyebrows, feigning offence. Angela smiled.

"We wanted to Ange', we really did…" Colin's voice tailed off, then, remembering how the evening had started with Angela's interruption of Jon's minutes said.

"What did you say to Jon, by the way? To get him to stop talking, I mean?"

Angela laughed.

“That, my brothers in arms, will be *our* little secret: Jon and me! See you in the morning!”

With that, she turned and walked to the 4x4 that she and Colin had arrived in.

“Looks like I’m off too then, boy!”

Colin said with a chuckle. Then without warning, he pulled Rab to him in a friendly embrace and said

“Thanks for being here tonight, Rab; I couldn’t have done it without you, bud!”

Rab was taken aback. He’d never seen an open display of affection from Colin; not like that; not ever, and he felt both humbled and privileged at having been the recipient.

“You’re welcome, mate.”

He said, stunned, as Colin disengaged and walked out of the door to ferry himself and Angela back to the site.

Chapter 12: The Gathering

Despite the fact that, without a doubt, tonight would be *the* most momentous event in any of their lives, even when taking their encounters with Kendra and Renweard into account, the day passed relatively quickly for Colin, Rab and Angela. It had largely been a case of finishing those excavations that they'd found at the last minute, as was almost always the case on most archaeological sites; removing the fencing; back-filling some of the deeper holes, and generally clearing the area in an attempt to remove any trace of the team ever having been there - which was actually not possible. Even so, the site had been signed off by the county archaeologist as having been investigated and recorded satisfactorily and could now be handed back to the contractor, who would no doubt begin construction of the new houses that were planned for the area.

What was of most concern to Colin, among these, was the need to back-fill a fair number of their excavations, including those of the eight graves which would be needed in tonight's ceremony.

"I'm in a bit of a fix, Rab, to be honest." He'd confessed at morning tea break over coffee and doughnuts. This had become something of a tradition over the years on the sites that Colin ran: On the last day, or as close to it as possible, he would arrive with a few bags of the sugary treats and the means with which to make "proper coffee" as he called it. Inevitably the archaeologists who worked for the company were well accustomed to this and were keen to be selected to work with Colin, not least because of this ritual.

"I mean, if we can't bury the weapons in their original grave, where *can* we do it?"

There was further, intense discussion during the break, yet when the time came to return to work half an hour later, they were still no nearer to a solution. All three had offered up ideas that, one after the other, had been rejected: wrong place; too shallow; not enough time. The latter rang true for all of them. There was still so much to do to conclude this excavation, and they all still had so much paperwork to finish that their minds struggled to focus on all but the most pressing issues of the moment. Finally, it was Angela who suggested they might be able to back-fill the graves as planned but open up a large, single pit nearby, which could be used for the ceremony.

"You said that the original graves would be too shallow anyway, Col', so why not wait till everybody leaves this afternoon and make a *new* pit with the digger; before it goes off hire?"

Colin listened intently and then said, "Go on…"

“Well, you’ve got a permit to operate the digger, yeah? So that’s covered; we’re mostly done now apart from Rab, so maybe you could stand the team down straight after lunch…”

Colin’s face registered both surprise and panic simultaneously, which Angela was quick to diffuse.

“…don’t worry, most of the teams have finished already; they’re just waiting for the nod from you now and trying to look busy in the meantime.”

His face relaxed into a smile. “Crafty buggers! Mind you, you’ve all worked so hard this week, so I’m not complaining. Maybe I’ll have a walk round in a minute then, and if everyone *is* done, they can head off as soon as they’re ready. Is the site tidy now, then, Ange’?”

Angela knew Colin would see sense. This was yet another trait he was renowned for.

“Pretty much. See what you think while you’re doing your rounds.”

“Yeah, sounds like a plan. Cheers, gal’!”

With that, he quickly rinsed his mug and, having thrown the wrapper from a sandwich that Rhia had sent from the Crown Inn - “Ooh, she’s a diamond!” he’d said as Rab presented him with it - he started to make his way around the site checking in with Ian, Cal and Bernie, all of whom confirmed that they had indeed finished everything that had been set for them and that even the site hut and Portaloo had been cleared of two months-worth of muddy boots and wet archaeologists.

It was fast approaching twelve-thirty, and happy with what he'd seen, Colin decided that once they'd made one last check of the site, they could call it a day. He was about to relay this to the team when he heard Rab calling and, on looking across to where his friend was working, saw him gesturing frantically, pointing toward the site hut. Shifting his gaze, he instantly recognised the company vehicle with its "Western Archaeological Services" logo emblazoned along the side.

He'd never liked the acronym created by the company name, feeling that W.A.S. implied has-been or redundant. The company bosses, however, saw it as a nod toward the past and were really quite proud of what they felt to be a 'clever play-on-words.'

"Oh, that's torn it!" He said to himself as he made his way across the site. The team, who had been in the process of packing away their tools and equipment, were conveniently within a few feet of each other, so Colin made a bee-line for them and, as he passed, called, "Make yourselves look busy, guys; Lucas has just turned up. He must have smelt the bloody coffee and doughnuts; Sorry, gang!"

He walked away to grumbles of "Typical" and "Trust Lu'!" and made his way quickly to the site hut.

"This is all looking neat and tidy, Col'. You almost done here then?" Lucas said as they shook hands.

Lucas O'Donnell was another of those *'nice blokes to work for*, but he was also senior management and, as such, had responsibilities beyond that of staff welfare; If he could save the contractors and, therefore, W.A.S. money, he absolutely would and sending staff home early to vacate a site was an easy way of doing it. Besides which, he knew there would be doughnuts today, so a site visit was inevitable. His presence today, though, represented a major spanner-in-the-works; he was not known for making short visits.

"Hi, Lu'! Yeah, almost; the gang are just tidying up the loose ends, you know: a bit of paperwork and some sampling. Should have 'em done by mid-afternoon."

Lucas looked surprised. He glanced around the inside of the site hut, noting as he did so the files were neatly boxed and everything squared away for transport.

"Really?" he said. "Looks like you're all but done to me!"

Inwardly chastising himself for not anticipating this spur-of-the-moment visit, Colin attempted to distract his manager.

"Doughnut?" he said as he offered up the remains of a bag of jam-filled bakes.

"Doughnuts? You guys know how to live!" he said in mock surprise. "Are there any custard-filled Col'? You know I'm a sucker for a custard doughnut!"

Colin was all *too* aware; on his last visit, Lucas had devoured all but one of them, and today, unfortunately, he had not managed to hide them in time, and so, with great reluctance, he handed the bag containing the last two to his manager.

"Oh, only two left? Can't let these beauties go to waste." He said as he ate the first in three mouthfuls. Colin marvelled at how Lucas always managed to avoid covering himself with sugar. The rest of the team would sit and eat slowly and carefully, leaning slightly forward, sometimes with a hand beneath their chin so as to catch any potential fallout and therefore avoid becoming wasp bait, and yet still they left the site hut with a liberal dusting of sugar and the tell-tale red or yellow blob on either their chin or chest, often both in Cal's case, that indicated their preference: jam or custard.

“No, you tuck in, fella!” Colin said encouragingly, “There’s plenty left”. Then, wishing to get to the point of Lucas’s visit but equally wishing he would leave so that they could prepare for tonight, he asked, “So what brings you here today then, Lu’?”

True to form, and with not a grain of sugar anywhere about his person, Lucas finished the second doughnut and, after one last exaggerated swallow, said, “Oh, I’m just on my way to the new site up the road here. Jeb’s running it, and he wants me to take a look at something or other before he makes his final decision on where to start; you know how he likes a bit of moral support?”

Jeb Harris did indeed like to have someone in authority cast an eye over his plan of work before committing spade to soil, and as a result, he would often call Lucas in just to “make sure”. It could be a little annoying, especially as there were so many sites to manage, but he was such a gentle soul; it was as though part of an old hippy lived in him, and nobody minded, really, especially if there were sugary treats to be had en-route!

“That he does, yeah.” They both laughed. “Mind you, I wouldn’t hang about here too long if that’s the case. You know his walkabouts can be quite lengthy, and if you want to get back to the office before four…”

Lucas clearly hadn't considered this. He went deep into thought as he sipped the coffee Colin had made for him long before he'd even asked for it.

"Mmm… I hadn't thought about that… maybe I should scuttle along there now before lunch. I could see the site while the team are in the hut out of the way, so to speak."

It's working, Colin thought to himself while trying to conceal his joy, adding, "It's almost lunchtime too, as you say, so he might let you get away quite quickly…"

Lucas could not see Colin's point.

"…he'll be wanting *his* lunch too!" and the penny dropped.

"Oh…, of course; you're a genius, Colin! I think I'll get over there now in that case. Is there anything you need me for here? Anything you want me to look at before I go?"

There genuinely was nothing new to look at as Lucas had visited only two days ago with the county archaeologist, and as much as Colin liked the man, he just wanted him to leave.

"No, not really, Lu'…" he said, feeling slightly guilty at his manipulation of an old work mate "…I mean, you're welcome to take a look, but there's nothing new since you were here a few days ago. You get along mate; they have fish and chips on a Friday… you never know!" he added temptingly, further adding to his guilt.

"Well, if you're sure…?"

He was, In fact. Colin had never been *more* sure. He, Rab and Angela needed to be making preparations for this evening, and Lucas could not feature in that, so as they talked, Colin slowly walked towards Lucas's truck, surreptitiously leading him away from the site.

"Anyway, nice to see you mate!" he was saying. "You'll have to swing by another day; when you've got more time, y'know?"

Lucas climbed into the driving seat and pushed the key into the ignition as he replied, "I will; I will." Then, as he started the engine, he had a sudden thought. He was about to ask Colin a question that had been slow-burning at the back of his mind since he'd arrived, and it had just reoccurred to him. Colin never learned what the question was. As soon as he saw it forming on Lucas's face, he closed the car door and called, "Take care, fella!" before turning and walking away. At that moment, the thought evaporated in Lucas's mind and was gone, so shaking his head, he drove slowly away through the gate and was gone.

Colin had only walked a few paces when a voice behind him said, "You sly old sod!" it was Angela.

"Dunno what you mean!" Colin replied with a wry smile.

"You know very well what I mean! That was a masterclass on how to hoodwink your boss. You couldn't have been more underhand if you'd tried!"

Colin was pleased to have been recognised for the talent he possessed, but even so, he still felt a little guilty.

"Well, thanks for the praise, but if I'm honest, I didn't enjoy getting shot of poor ol' Lu' like that; we go back a long way, and he's been really good to me in the past." A look of remorse swept briefly across his face, then was gone. "Anyway, had to be done; we've got so much to do!"

"That we have!" Angela agreed, but for now, at least, the coast was clear.

Colin made his way back to the team, who had been 'working' in the background as he and Lucas had spoken. Ian had slowly scraped a thin layer of sandy soil from the section he'd finished - two days ago - to reveal the multiple layers of stratigraphy. The differing shades of soil now stood out clearly from one another, and, had Lucas visited his trench, it would have been an impressive distraction. The others had employed similar subterfuge, all of which was now hastily abandoned as Colin approached.

"Sorry about that, guys; couldn't be helped. Are you all done now, yeah?"

To a person, they confirmed that they were indeed completely finished and whether they'd wanted to or not, there was very little else they could do; real or otherwise.

"Right then, gather up your bits and pieces and Ian, are you happy to drive back to the unit?"

Ian nodded. "Yeah, absolutely. What about Lucas, though? Won't he think it a bit odd that we're all *suddenly* finished here?"

Colin laughed. "Don't you worry about Lu'; he'll be up the road with Jeb 'til at least three, by which time you'll have *just finished*, get it?" he said, gesturing speech marks with his fingers.

They absolutely 'got it', and without further question, they swiftly loaded the 4x4 with their tools and personal gear, and within fifteen minutes, they too were gone, and the site fell silent.

Colin made his way across the site to the hut where Rab and Angela had already gathered. As he approached, each caught the other's eye, and as all three stood in the sunshine, grinning at one another like fools, he said, "Lunch first?"

***

Despite the fact that they now had around five hours before the arrival of the Bernicians, lunch was a brief affair. None of them hurried their food, and all made sure that they'd had a hot drink, yet within thirty minutes, they had eaten, washed up and tidied the hut.

"Looks like we're ready to crack on then?" Colin said.

Angela was in full agreement. "Definitely! I'd much rather be ready too early and hang about afterwards than have a last-minute panic!"

"Right then…" he said, "…and we're all agreed on the location of the pit?" They were; It had been decided that they would position it so that it was as far away from the new houses as possible, thereby reducing the chance of it being disturbed in the future by someone establishing a vegetable plot or some other garden feature.

The contractors plan made provision for a small estate of a dozen houses, and the area the archaeologists had chosen to rebury the possessions of the eight lay well off to one side, away from any construction, and within that part of the site where Angela had earlier discovered the temporary residences and evidence of feasting. It was also quite close to a slope that led down to woodland, so it was even less likely to have been built on.

And so, with everyone in agreement, Colin made his way across to the mechanical digger. These were a common feature on modern archaeological sites where, ironically, time was often against the team. It was not uncommon for archaeologists to be working in one area as contractors worked in another that they'd recently been vacated. In fact, it often felt as though you were being chased across the site, and unless you were working on a site with research funding, rescue or commercial archaeology: where the site was excavated before being built on, moved at a frightening pace.

Climbing into the cab, Colin made himself comfortable before firing up the engine. He'd driven many different versions of these massive machines over the years and felt quite at home in this, his lofty perch. He lifted the digger's enormous bucket so that it was clear of the ground, then selected forward drive and released the handbrake. The great steel beast rumbled forward, resembling some kind of lumbering steel dinosaur, its broad tracks and wheels chirruping noisily as it came, yet despite its twenty-ton weight, it barely left a mark on the ground behind it.

Meanwhile, Angela and Rab waited for him at the reburial site. They had marked it out roughly by scratching lines with a road iron, not wishing to draw attention to it later on by marking it out with coloured spray paint as would otherwise be the norm.

The ground vibrated ominously as Colin approached, the noise and smell of his machine's diesel engine filling the air, and once he was in position, he operated the levers so that the enormous machine pivoted on its extended arm and bucket, causing it to look as though it were dancing The Twist, and he began to dig. Rab always found this moment exciting; as the digger cut new ground, the unmistakable aroma of freshly disturbed soil filled the air, the promise of new discovery just a few scrapes of the bucket away, and although they had already cleared the area of archaeology, it was felt that they should keep a watch in case anything they may have missed was uncovered. They continued down for the next ten minutes; two people watching, one digging, occasionally stopping to check on potential archaeology, which, in every instance, proved to be nothing more than a large stone or a tree root. On this rare occasion, they were relieved to find nothing as, had they done so, it would need to have been recorded fully and accurately, just as they had been doing for the past few days.

The great diesel dinosaur steadily ate its way deep into the damp, dark earth until, finally, it was done, and a pit, two metres wide by three metres long, lay open in front of them. Colin switched off the engine and climbed down from the cab to stand alongside Angela and Rab.

"Think that'll do!" he said.

"Think you're right, Col'," Rab replied as he hopped down into the pit, and although he was around five feet, nine in height, he stood shoulder deep in the hole, looking up at the others.

"*Do* you think it's deep enough?" Angela asked, "Only, I would hate for this to have to happen again."

"I reckon so, Ange'…" Colin replied earnestly, "…It's deeper than anyone is likely to go in the future, and given that we're at a point where the ground breaks away down-hill it's really unlikely they'll build anything here; landscaping at most, I reckon, and that'll be what? Two feet deep, maximum?"

Colin's reasoning made complete sense. They were indeed in a completely unusable area at the edge of the site, which, they remembered, was why it had been chosen in the first place.

"Yeah, you're right; it's perfect! I just hope Kendra will be happy with it." Angela said.

The words hit home, bringing the reality of the situation back into sharp focus. *What if Kendra hated the location? What if, after all this, they* had *to use the original graves?*

All three chose not to voice these shared concerns and stood silently for a while, staring down into the newly excavated pit before going about the business of making the area ready for the evening's ceremony.

Using the mechanical digger, Colin levelled the ground in the immediate area of the pit so that the Bernicians could stand, en-masse, and move safely about, as it would be almost dark by the time they started to arrive. The loose soil excavated from the pit had been piled up to the side where the ground started to drop away so that, hopefully, nobody would make a downhill tumble in the gloom, and finally, a series of small fire pits were created about one metre from the edge of the pit to both lights it, and warm the participants. They were ready.

***

"They should start to arrive soon," Rab said as he checked his watch for the umpteenth time.

"You said that two minutes ago, Rab. They'll be here, mate; stop worrying." Colin said matter-of-factly.

But Rab *was* worried. *What if nobody came? What if, after all this preparation and with all the expectations, there were only three people here tonight? What if...* Angela could see Rab's torment, uplit by the flickering fire that had so efficiently cooked their evening meal, thrashing back and forth across his face as worried eyes sought, as yet, unnecessary solutions to problems that, so far, did not exist.

"Rab?" she spoke softly so as to calm his anxiety "...they *will* come; Colin's right."

Rab sighed, relaxing his shoulders in the process.

"You're right, I know. It's just..." but before he could finish his sentence, he was interrupted by the sound of revving car engines, at least three, possibly four, and the accompanying rise and fall of flashing headlights as they bounced their way across the uneven site car park.

"There you are! What did I tell you?" Colin said elatedly. "I knew they wouldn't let us down!" Inwardly though, he too had harboured doubts, but these now evaporated and were gone.

Jumping excitedly to their feet, the three made their way the short distance from the campsite to the car park to meet and greet their guests, arriving amid the clamour of a small army as they alighted their respective vehicles. Familiar faces smiled widely, renewing the acquaintances of the previous evening as they unloaded cars and vans of well-wrapped cloth bundles and wooden boxes, and all to the sound of car doors clunking heavily shut and van doors sliding effortlessly open; it was as non-medieval as it possibly could be. All the same, it was to the accompaniment of eager, excited voices.

In all, twenty-eight people had decided that this was an event they just had to witness; even some of those who had been completely sceptical the night before had seen fit to attend, if only out of morbid curiosity or to see two people make complete fools of themselves.

"Jon; Lynn; Graeme. So many of you!" Colin was overwhelmed.

"Of course, old boy; You didn't think we'd miss out on this: the opportunity to help *Asgard,* did you!" Jon was the first of many to shake hands with Colin.

Colin shrugged, accepting Jon's logic. "I reckon not!"

Jon continued. "So, what will you have us do? This is your endeavour, after all."

Colin looked toward Rab and beckoned him over. As he arrived, Colin placed an arm around his shoulder, pulling him in and said with a nod. "Mine *and* Rab's!"

A forced yet delicate cough drifted in from behind Rab, catching their attention. It was Angela. "Oh, bugger…" Colin exclaimed as he turned to look "…Ange' is right, though; the night belongs to all of us, really; *I* wouldn't be here if it weren't for Rab and… none of us would be here if it weren't for Ange' and you so, well… there you are!" A pregnant pause hung quietly on the air until finally, the sea of solemn, pensive faces could hold on to the laughter no longer, and like a series of small, breaching dams, it burst out into the night, leaving Colin bemused as he looked around him saying "What? What did I say?"

Finally, when all was calm, and order had returned, they set about finalising their plan for the evening, and while Rab and Angela lit the fires around the burial pit, Colin addressed the Bernicians.

"Right then; first up: thank you all so much for being here tonight. There's no point in trying to explain too much cos', well, it's not like anything you'll have seen before, frankly. What I *will* say, though, is that, well... you're all amazing and generous and again, just... thank you so, so much!" The group remained silent, listening intently, although all openly welcomed the acknowledgement of their upcoming sacrifice. Colin continued. "In a nutshell, there are eight warriors who are in need of a sword; a spear; a shield and if at all possible, a helmet each. Anything after that: small knives, chainmail and so forth, will be a bonus, so what I thought is, if you all gather up whatever you've brought with you, I've laid out a tarpaulin..." He gestured to where a large waterproof sheet had been laid and secured on the ground with tent pegs. "...if we could go over one-by-one and lay our weapons on the sheet by category as it were: shield, sword, and so on, we'll have a clear picture of what we have to offer the Asgardians; does that make sense? You'll see that I've already laid my kit out, so maybe use that as a starting point?" The entire group nodded in agreement. "let's get to it then, yeah?" and with one final thumbs-up from Colin as their cue, they made their way as one organised unit over to the tarpaulin where they began laying out their offerings alongside Colin's.

As he queued with the others, Jon turned to Colin and said, "Lucky you had your kit with you already, Colin?"

Colin smiled wryly as he replied, “You’re not wrong there, Jon… not wrong at all!”

To see this taking place was an awe-inspiring sight, not least because the Bernicians, as agreed, had all come dressed in their finest Anglo-Saxon clothing. Woollen tunics, finished at collar and cuff with two-tone coloured braid, were held in at the waist by leather belts from which hung pouches and small knives of various shapes and sizes; woollen cloaks kept the cool night air at bay, fastened to one side by the broken circle of a penannular brooch; the ladies present wore linen dresses over which a richly decorated and tablet-woven coat of wool was worn, and a few wore hats, although most relied on long locks of dark hair to keep their heads warm. It was as though Asgard had already arrived.

Across by the burial pit, Rab and Angela began to walk back from the fires that now illuminated that part of the site. They had worked, screwing up newspaper and placing it between the kindling before setting it alight with matches, building a fire from the ground up. As they had done so, they could hear the hubbub of the Bernicians drift across the site to them on the night air, and, just as neither had given little in the way of thought to its cause, neither was prepared for the sight which now presented itself to them and as they turned, they were stopped dead in their tracks by the vision in front of them. Lit by a circle of roaring fires was a scene of industrious, everyday Anglo-Saxon life which unfolded in front of them as people came and went, depositing weapons and household items onto a sheet on the ground before moving aside to allow someone else to do likewise, and as each stepped away from their precious offering, they were guided by an unknown member of the group to stand alongside the burial pit which lay waiting silently, its vast, ominous mouth yawning up out of the ground, ready to receive one last glittering meal.

To one side, Colin and Jon were taking stock of the cache that now lay as an offering on the groundsheet. There were at least a dozen swords, including Colin's beloved Seax; around the same number of Ashwood shafted spears; nine shields and six helmets. But the Bernicians had gone beyond generosity; Alongside the weapons and armour were offerings of two sets of full chainmail; eight drinking horns, two of which were adorned with gilt brass fittings; battle horns; small knives; leather shoes and perhaps the most incredible of all, Jon had presented his beloved replica of a seventh-century lyre, complete with its sheepskin bag.

"This is beyond anything I could have imagined, Jon, and your lyre; are you absolutely sure?"

Jon had never seen Colin move like this, ever in charge of his emotions, always a smile and a joke ready to play on his lips; he now stood looking over the weapons cache with a tear in his eye and a quiver in his voice.

“Absolutely, dear boy; we are ever at your service; Bernicians, one and all, eh?”

“I dunno what to say…”

Angela and Rab joined them and stood on either side of Colin. They, too, were lost for words. Jon, however, knew exactly the right ones for the occasion:

“Then say nothing, dear boy; say nothing. Kendra will no doubt join us presently, and she will have word enough for us all.”

Chapter 13: The Offering

The night's fast was long since broken, and the sun had already climbed high into the sky as Woden, Grimme, and the Wandle's Ham eight approached Haligsfeld, where Kendra sat waiting by the stream. Woden spoke first, and despite his great standing, he expected her response to be less than charitable.

"Forgive the lateness of our arrival, my lady prophetess; there was much to attend to before we could leave Valhalla: Some of my army fear that they too might now suffer the same fate as the eight, and I would have their minds at ease before we could away."

He spoke the truth; Many of his warriors, having seen the fate of Renweard and the other's weapons, had grown nervous over the past few days and, as such, had sent representatives from their respective clans to petition Woden for assurances. The exchange had been frank but respectful, eating and drinking as they debated, and Woden had, for now at least, calmed their fears.

Kendra looked up from her spot beside the stream where she had been sitting for the past two hours. She had, at first, been infuriated at the tardiness of the men, but she too had much to attend to before the ceremony could begin and had spent some of that time gathering the plants: marigold and, this time, sprigs of Yew which would be required for the return of the possessions, before coming to rest at the water's edge, her mind becoming calm as she relaxed by the gently tinkling stream.

"It is well, my lord..." she said calmly "...my hands have not been idle, and all preparation has been made in your absence."

Woden relaxed both mentally and visibly. He could sense, though, that there was something else, something of which Kendra chose not to speak. It unsettled him to the point where he felt the need to ask her of it, but knowing there would *be* no point in speaking of it here, he chose instead to focus on the job at hand.

The men stood a while, hypnotised by the sound and vision of running water, the atmosphere a heady mix of both anxiety and anticipation, and some considered their fate while others pondered the arrival of their soon-to-be-acquired weaponry.

There had been much discussion in the Great Hall last night as they ate and drank, and while the rest of the army spent the evening much as they always did: in song and verse and with copious amounts of drinking and merriment, the eight felt less inclined to do so and sat quietly, deep in thought, this though occasionally interrupted by bursts of raucous laughter and cheering nearby as another story resolved or punchline was delivered. Abrecan spoke first.

"*Can* it be done, my lord? *Can* the prophetess deliver our belongings to us as she claims?"

Renweard looked kindly at his comrade and brother and smiled kindly, dwelling on his thoughts briefly before replying.

"I believe she can, Abrecan; she has not failed us this far, and I see no reason to doubt her now." He sensed, though, that there was more to be said, as some of the others looked as though they, too, had doubts.

"My lord…" Eadig now joined the conversation, having spoken not a single word since the Sun had dipped below the horizon. "…I do not doubt Kendra; she is, after all, chosen of our lord Woden…"

"But you entertain doubt, Eadig? I see a troubled brow besets my brother." Renweard offered.

Eadig and Renweard had grown up together in the same village and had become men and warriors, sharing the same rites and initiation ceremony when they were just twelve years old and when Eadig's parents were killed in a raid on their village and his sister taken a slave, it was Renweard's family who took him in to raise him as their own. It was fitting, therefore, that they should now serve in this place together. Eadig drew himself up for his reply.

"I doubt the seeker, my Lord..." he said frankly "...perhaps not his sincerity, but his means; can he *really* do as he says he will?" All eyes settled expectantly on Renweard. This was the question that had lingered in the minds of many of those present. All had witnessed the conversation between Kendra and the seeker, the second visit, as yet, unknown to them, and all agreed that he was an honourable man, but he seemed to doubt himself; otherwise, why would he need to speak to a higher office? Why could he not simply return their possessions without assistance from elsewhere?

Renweard listened intently, allowing all to voice their concerns before, as the conversation began to descend into chaos, raising a hand calling for silence. The men became still at his bidding and listened intently, knowing that it would be foolhardy to do otherwise.

"All that you say is sound and true, and it is well that you would voice your concerns to me; such is our bond. But there is something that you are, as yet, unaware of..." he gathered his cloak around him and leaned forward into the centre of the circle so as to keep his words from the ears of those nearby. "...not two days since Kendra and I met with the leader of the seeker..." Renweard could see that he had their attention, as to a man, they too now leaned forward, straining their ears against the surrounding throng. "As we departed Haligsfeld, after that first meet, Kendra remained. She had sensed something: a presence in the mist that did not make itself known at the time, and so she made to return on the following morn." He took a long, slow drink of sweet amber liquid from his horn before continuing. "I learned of this from Beornia…"

"The Valkyrie?" Egeslic asked incredulously through a forced whisper. "…the same…" confirmed Renweard, "…and I insisted that I be permitted to join Kendra; It was well that I did; Her instinct served her well, as no sooner was the portal opened than a voice came to us from the old world…"

"The seeker's lord…!" Abrecan mused.

"The seeker's lord!" Renweard confirmed. "So, you see, my brothers, we have the means. He, at least, is certain that he can deliver us the weapons. There is but one rub, however…" he paused before delivering the news that he knew would not go over well. "…these will not be our own weapons."

The men spoke at once and together so that Renweard was unable to clearly determine what each was saying, although, in truth, he did not need the words. Each became agitated and argued fiercely as each demanded an explanation. Renweard raised a hand to call the men to order. This time it had no effect. He raised both hands, calling for silence; still, the clamour continued.

“BE STILL!” he called, standing abruptly, casting aside his cloak. It floated as though carried by water before coming to rest on the ground behind him, where it lay still and silent, seemingly cowering at its master’s feet. “I *will* tell you of that which is planned, but I need you to hear me!”

Aside from the mayhem in the rest of the hall, which had continued unchecked, the seven became still, sinking back into their place by the fire, waiting for their lord to speak again.

“The seeker lord goes by the name ‘Colin.’ He is one of a small band of warriors who possess such weapons as those we have lost back to the old world, and believe me when I tell you that they are of *such* quality, should our great lord and host take it upon himself to wield one of them…” he gestured toward Woden “…it would sit within his hand like an old friend and exist quietly alongside those which are already in this place. It is a great honour these men and women bestow on us; such is the esteem with which their possessions are held.”

Renweard’s word was more than enough for his men. He had always been an honourable and trustworthy lord, putting the needs of his people before that of his own, and they would not do him the dishonour of doubting that word now.

"My lord?"

Renweard returned blearily to the present to find ten expectant faces peering at him, all of whom seemed to be waiting for him to answer.

"Mmm... my apologies; you have need of me?"

Grimme chortled, "My lord Woden wishes to know whether you are ready? ... to join us for the ceremony...?"

Renweard straightened and inhaled slowly through his nostrils, filling his lungs to capacity while at the same time noting the look of amusement on Woden's face, who stood tall at the rear of the group beside Kendra.

"...unless you have some other place to be?"

Renweard saw the mischief for which Grimme was so well known dance across his face and laughed in apology, exhaling into his now rapidly relaxing frame.

"Forgive me, my lord, Grimme; I am more than ready, having fully returned to the present!" he confirmed.

The group allowed itself a chuckle at Renweard's expense, though none was meant as an insult which, indeed, the man himself recognised.

With that, the eight, bidden by Kendra, took their place in the area that had once been occupied by their graves. Woden and Grimme stood back to allow Kendra room to do her work, and amid the tension and anxiety of a band of proud yet uncertain warriors, the ceremony began.

As was usual, Kendra began by dropping the marigold petals she'd harvested earlier gently into the stream, which floated swiftly away. The water was faster and the stream higher today due to the previous night's rain, and the gathering watched expectantly as the deep orange raft dipped and turned, meandering playfully along its glimmering course.

"Feorh m fêores dîgan fremian êower port..."

The incantation began, spoken softly at first, Kendra's words seemingly uttered through a tone of underlying menace. Yet the men felt calm, comforted.

"... ûs of pro ic wilcumian unnon sê unorne fyrhđ!"

But something was different; something hung in the air like an unseen presence, something old and nameless that only two of those present had ever witnessed, and many years had since passed.

All could see the mist cloud beginning to form, expanding as it always did, rising up out of the ground. They watched once more as the dense, grey vapour swirled and billowed restlessly, as ever, contained within an unseen boundary, and as Kendra stripped the sprigs of Yew, dropping the needles and the red, berry-like arils into the stream to follow in the path of the marigold petals, it began.

At first, it was nothing more than a hum, but low and dangerous. Gradually though, it increased in intensity until almost all present felt an unbearable pressure that tightened the chest and gripped the throat, pulsing deeply, becoming heavier and heavier, and all the while, the men inhaled deeply, gulping and gasping for air. A great wind blew in, lifting cloak and bough, causing the men to brace hard against it lest they be levelled like newly felled trees, and for what seemed like an eternity, their struggle continued; sight, hearing, and strength fading as the phenomenon fed, their resolve no match for this demon.

It continued, building in intensity as each of them became more and more disoriented, their vision phasing in and out of focus, making them restless and uneasy, wishing only to run. None did, for they knew that to move now might not only jeopardise the entire ceremony but would also bring upon them great dishonour. Instead, they stood their ground and endured.

The portal assumed its familiar form, settling serenely in front of them, and despite the seemingly unending turmoil, Woden stepped forward to stand in front of it, fighting the wind as he did so, his cloak horizontal, wrestling the tempest, invisible fingers clutching at their master's shoulders in an attempt to hold fast. With a nod from Kendra, he held both arms outstretched as he tipped his head back, staring up into the sky, before swinging them effortlessly forward to bring his palms forcefully together.

An explosion, the likes of which *nobody* present had ever witnessed, not least its creator, lit Haligsfeld with an intensity so penetrating that Woden himself was convinced he saw briefly with *both* eyes. There was no sound; none whatsoever, as briefly they existed in a vacuum until, without warning, the final assault arrived as a shock wave; an eruption of light which none withstood, throwing God, Lord, and Warrior alike to the ground, the dignity of none being spared, as they pitched and tumbled with the rest of the wind-borne detritus.

Finally, the tumult subsided, allowing their vision and senses to return slowly to normal. They lay for a while on the sandy earth, breathing heavily, pushing small clouds of dust up from the ground in front of them, wondering… hoping that the onslaught was finally over. They waited only a short while before climbing cautiously to their feet, wary in case there was yet more to follow. There was not, and as the dust settled and the surrounding trees shivered noisily back into shape, they rose up to stand tall, dusting themselves down, preparing for what might come next.

"Is anybody injured?" Grimme called as he dabbed the blood away from the corner of his mouth with the back of his hand. "Does anybody need assistance?" To a man, all were safe and uninjured. Then looking at Kendra, he called, "My lady! Are you without harm?" She had not been spared the effects of the turmoil and had suffered the same fate as the men; he had seen her fall and flail in the commotion, but he noticed that despite her dishevelled appearance, she looked remarkably calm as she stared wide-eyed at something which held her gaze.

Renweard gasped involuntarily. His men swung round defensively to see what had so unsettled their lord, but they, too, now stood motionless, stunned by what presented itself to them. Woden and Grimme looked on in wonder at the vision as it shimmered silently; they, too, were both astounded and gript. The cloud, no longer grey, no longer swirling, hung like a pool of crystal-clear water in the air and had become mirror-like, yet was now a deep, royal purple befitting the status of those present.

But what held Kendra, Woden, Grimme, and the Wandle's Ham eight; what bewitched them all, was not its enigmatic beauty, not even the way in which it defied their divine learning. It was the thirty-one astonished, speechless faces that stared back at them through the mist. The connection had been made.

***

Rab, Angela, Colin, and the rest of Geoguth Bernicia had waited… and waited. For over an hour and a half, they stood by the eight graves as the circle of log fires crackled and spat, watching as the deep, orange flames flirted with the evening breeze. The enthusiasm and excitement with which they had started the evening's venture, however, had slowly given way, first to polite anticipation, followed by mild frustration, before finally deteriorating into outright exasperation.

"What the bloody hell are we doing here!" one of the sceptics who had attended the previous evening called out. "I knew this was a load of old twaddle!" Embarrassed, Colin said nothing. There were a few low-key grumbles from some of the rest of the group, but none which were audible, as no one really wanted to offend Colin; even though, as the heckler had pointed out, this was starting to look like a '*load of old twaddle.*'

Rab leaned in so as to whisper to Colin. "Where the hell *are* they, Col'? They've never been late before now!"

"Tell me about it! I dunno, boy. Bloody bad timing, though, eh?"

In an effort to support his friend, Jon spoke directly to the group, "Ladies; Gentlemen; A little patience, I feel? This is, after all, the supernatural with which we deal and, as such, dictates its own timetable." He spoke convincingly, but he, too, was secretly starting to wonder whether he had been wrong to believe Colin's tale. In any case, he likewise acknowledged a nod of gratitude from him. The protests faded at Jon's words, and there was relative silence as the entire group, to Rab's amazement, continued to wait. Colin, meanwhile, simply assumed that although some, or most, felt that this was a waste of their time and effort and that they'd been duped by a master of his art. Those who did feel that way nevertheless decided that by leaving now, they might miss out on something, so, regardless, they stood, and they waited in silence.

Jon was the first to notice it; at first, it was nothing more than a low hum which caused him to feel as though he needed to equalise the pressure in his ears. As he pinched both nostrils closed and blew against the restriction, he noticed that others were doing the same as they began to look anxiously about at one another. The noise continued to build in intensity until everyone was fully aware of it and blinking furiously. They shook their heads to clear themselves of the light-headedness. The air became turbulent and confused as Jon called out over the noise to Colin, "IS THIS IT? HAS IT BEGUN?" Colin was as unsettled as everyone else. "I DUNNO, JON; I'VE NEVER SEEN IT LIKE THIS BEFORE!" They walked across the grave circle toward one another, carefully avoiding the flames which now leapt and writhed, apparently reaching out from their pit in an attempt to grab them as the breeze, too, increased in strength. “YOU MEAN IT ISN’T ALWAYS LIKE THIS?” Jon asked, arriving unmolested. “NO, THIS IS BRAND NEW; LIKE I SAID: I’VE NEVER SEEN IT LIKE THIS BEFORE!” Colin seemed worried, albeit accepting of the maelstrom that now began to envelop them.

Jon made to speak again, but no words came; there was, in fact, no sound whatsoever. Instead, a blinding flash of the most intense light imaginable seared the retinas of all present, followed instantaneously by a shock wave that threw everybody violently back onto the ground. “OH MY GOD! THEY’VE DONE IT! THEY’VE ACTUALLY DONE IT! THAT WAS A NUCLEAR DETONATION; I’M SURE OF IT!” Jon said aloud, his voice lost in the turbulence of the prevailing squall, and convinced that the end of all things was upon them, he curled up into a tight ball and waited for it to arrive.

It was as though the earth took, and held, a deep breath before exhaling violently as anything that was not either tied down or secured flew back and forth in the confusion. Bernician and archaeologist clung on to one another, and as the world came to an end around them; some cried; some screamed, but most just lay quietly on the ground and waited for the end. Finally, though, the air became still, and light levels returned to normal, although it would take several more minutes before their eyes could readjust to the now total darkness. One by one, the archaeologists and Bernicians lifted themselves cautiously from the ground as calm returned to the site. Realising that Armageddon had not, in fact, been unleashed, Jon's thoughts turned to the welfare of the group. "Is everyone OK?" he called out. "Is anyone injured?" By a small miracle, everyone had come through the ordeal largely unscathed, and with the exception of a few minor scrapes and bruises, they were all fine, if a little shaken. Relieved, he looked around him, taking a head-count but immediately noticed that one individual was missing; he called to him. "COLIN!" there was no reply. "Has anybody seen Colin?" He scanned the site in a full three-hundred-and-sixty-degree arc, but there was no sign of him. "I can't see him. I CAN'T SEE HIM!" He was becoming increasingly concerned as the entire group now joined in the search for their host.

Then they heard it.

"Someone, *please* gimme a hand out of here, will ya!" Colin's voice called from out of the darkness. "*HELLO*!" he called gain more forcefully. As one, they stopped searching and stood completely still in an attempt to focus on the direction of the sound; nothing. Worried eyes scoured the site, and torch beams probed the darkness; still nothing.

Angela, though, searching the area around the new burial pit, thought she heard something and turning to face the direction from which it came, she called nervously, "Colin?" there was a brief pause before. "Yes, it's me! Can you give me a hand up out of this bloody 'ole!" Laughing but relieved, the group rushed over to the pit and stared down into it. Thankfully, some had had the foresight to bring torches with them, which they shone down into the abyss. Lying face up in the bottom was a soil-spattered, dust-covered Colin, recognisable only from his gilet and the colourful language that now emanated from the pit. There was uproar as the tension was completely shattered by laughter. "Oh my, Colin; you do know how to make an entrance!" Jon quipped, relieved to see that his old friend was OK. Colin's utterances continued as he was helped, unceremoniously, from his hole in the ground, and some tried to assist further by dusting him down. "I can do it! I can do it!" he protested loudly.

Their merriment was short-lived and rudely interrupted, however. "LOOK!" someone was calling. "LOOK AT THIS!" they called again excitedly. It was Rab. The group instinctively rushed en masse to render aid, only to find him pointing excitedly at a scene of the most surreal beauty. A shimmering wall of light resembling a mirror of amethyst hung silently in the air. It was as high as it was broad, which Colin mentally calculated - in the 'feet-on-the-ground kind of way he often displayed - that it must be at least twenty feet square; he'd never fully taken to metres! They moved closer and peered warily, deep into its heart, where a series of shapeless objects seemed to shamble and stir nervously from within. Slowly, the mist cleared, and finally, they saw them; Their eyes now fully adjusted to the dark, they stared open-mouthed as from within the mirror, a group of ten men and one elderly woman, battered and weather-beaten, stared back at them; they too, seemingly dumbfounded by the scene they now found themselves looking in upon.

For a while, nobody moved. Instead, each party beheld the presence of the other regarding each other across time. Kendra spoke first, having recognised both Rab and Colin at once. "You came… you came! And with so many!" she said, seemingly overwhelmed by the gesture of such generosity. "That we did, Kendra…" Colin said proudly, and despite Rab having been the first point of contact, what seemed like weeks ago now, he took it upon himself to address her on their behalf. "These are the men and women of Geoguth Bernicia." To the Bernician's surprise, the Asgard warriors stirred in disapproval. Confused at first, Colin quickly realised that the Bernicians in the sixth and seventh centuries would have been the sworn enemy of these Wessex men, so to avoid further consternation, he quickly clarified, "this is merely a title by which we identify ourselves; none of us here are true Bernicians, and in any case, those rivalries are long behind us in our time."

"If you don't count chucking-out time in Newcastle," somebody whispered from the back of the group.

The Asgardians relaxed, apparently happy with Colin's explanation as the introductions continued.

"Kendra, may I introduce Angela…" feeling somewhat self-conscious and completely at a loss for what to do or say, Angela, bowed, then half-curtsied. Kendra smiled kindly.

"Ah, child. You are a messenger, yes? A messenger for the gods!" still unsure of the best way to respond, Angela replied, "Yes, ma'am… Kendra… sorry!"

It was Colin's turn to cover a smile; He was so glad to have had Angela on board with this, and as if to promote her importance to Kendra, he added, "Without Angela, Kendra, there would *be* no meeting tonight! It was Angela who paved the way for us!" Angela blushed, thankful that she was able to conceal her embarrassment in the darkness.

"Then she has my blessing…" a voice boomed out of the portal. It was Woden. "…look to me, child." He insisted.

Angela looked through the portal and slowly up into the one good eye of the immortal Asgardian. He was more human than she had imagined, her expectations no doubt coloured by years of movie imagery, and despite his status, she sensed a kind, caring, individual.

He considered her for a moment before saying, "I sense there is yet more to your tale; I feel that we Asgardians and you: our Angel, have more than one path to tread together."

Overwhelmed and unable to contain herself any longer, Angela felt the tears she had been holding back escape and run warmly down both cheeks as a wave of pure emotion broke over her.

Something happened then that Kendra herself had not thought possible: A hand emerged slowly from the portal, Woden's hand, and both parties gasped as it softly cradled one side of Angela's head before gently wiping the tears aside with a sweep of a thumb. "Be still, little one; be still." Both sides of the portal looked on as the hand was withdrawn and Kendra, regaining her composure, spoke again.

"My lord Woden, Colin, and Rab are the architects of tonight's gathering; it is they who have brought together this body of souls who have so generously agreed to rearm the eight with their own possessions."

Woden spoke again, "Then we shall forever be in your debt; tell me, seekers: what would a fitting tribute be to you? To the men and women of Bernicia? What will you have Asgard do to repay such a debt?" Colin remembered the brief conversation he'd had with Renweard on the night of that first meeting. He sought Renweard's face in the crowd and fixed his gaze with that of the great warrior he reiterated.

“There is no debt, my lord; all that we require is that our fellow warriors, who were stripped of their possessions by the hands of some here tonight, be made whole again; so that they too can join in the great battle which is to come.” Renweard smiled through ice-blue eyes and nodded his approval as Woden responded.

“So be it! You are, indeed, an honourable clan and shall be revered as such throughout my halls. Kendra!” The prophetess readied herself for Woden’s command. “I believe it is time.”

“My lord, yes…” she said, and then to the Bernicians, “…you have the weapons?” Colin stepped to one side, allowing, for the first time that night, an unobscured view of the sheet on which their weapons lay, waiting to be claimed by their new owners.

To his surprise, it had remained largely unmoved by the wind that had torn through the rest of the site. This was the moment the men of Asgard had been most anxious to exorcise: Would the Bernician weapons be of sufficient number and quality so that they could indeed do battle in Asgard? They were not disappointed.

A dozen swords, the same number of spears, nine shields, and six helmets lay around and, among other, precious items, including a mystery object contained within a sheepskin bag.

“Is that a lyre?” Eadig had spotted the sheepskin bag, which lay inconspicuously among drinking horns, glassware, and jewellery.

“Is there a lyre within that bag?” he asked again, pointing excitedly. Jon was unable to contain himself as pride swelled in him. “It is that, my brother. Do you play?” Eadig was beside himself with joy. “That I do; when I have the means!” Jon walked forward and lifted the bag carefully from its place on the tarpaulin, and offered it up to the portal. “Then once more, you have the means, my friend; please, accept this as my gift to you!”

Kendra stepped forward, once more taking control of proceedings, concerned that someone might attempt to transfer an item directly through the portal, which would have had grave consequences, not least for that which was transferred.

“You have excelled yourselves; all of you. Your generosity is more than any of us could ever have wished for.” As she spoke, she cast her eyes about the site behind the Bernicians, searching for the eight graves into which the goods were due to be deposited. She could not see them and, becoming suspicious, said, “I see not the graves, Colin; I see not those places into which your offerings must be placed!”

Colin felt a wave of panic rise in him, which he controlled with a nervous clearing of the throat. As he began to speak, he sensed both Rab and Angela shift uneasily at his side; Kendra sensed it too.

"Well, we hit a bit of a snag… a small problem Kendra."

Once more, the Asgardians shifted uneasily as Abrecan uttered, "They cannot help us after all!" Colin heard him through the portal.

"No, you're wrong!" he said firmly. "We said we would help, and we bloody well will; you just need to trust us!"

Kendra sensed his annoyance; *all* sensed his annoyance; those on the Bernician side of the portal more so. It took a lot to rile Colin, and he was clearly riled at this insult.

Kendra once more diffused the tension. "No one doubts you, Colin. We are merely concerned that we have no means by which to rebury the possessions; without the deathbeds, we will be unable to transfer your generous offering into our world."

Colin had, of course, anticipated this and began to explain their predicament. "The problem we have is that where the eight graves … the eight death beds currently lie, there will soon be enormous stone structures; their foundations will cut deep into the earth…" he chose his words bearing in mind their lack of modern buildings knowledge siting some with which the Asgardians might be familiar "… these will be similar to the ones left behind when the Romans departed …"

Kendra spat disgust into the soil

"… and if we bury the possessions there, they will be disturbed again very soon, and we … you, will be back to square one … back to where we started … without weapons." He clarified.

Kendra considered his words staring hard at the ground for what seemed like an age before asking, "What is it you propose? You have an alternative?"

Colin smiled, relieved. *At least she's open to compromise,* he thought before continuing, "I do; we've chosen a spot across by where those fires are now burning …" he said, pointing to the new pit.

Kendra cast her eye into the field, recognising it instantly.

"The temporary village!" she turned to Renweard. "This is where your kin celebrated your delivery into Valhalla, the point from which you were carried to us by the Valkyries."

Angela leaned in toward Rab and whispered, "*told you!*"

Rab did not react. He was too engrossed in the conversation that was unfolding in front of him, keen to know whether it would be resolved as they hoped. Kendra turned back to Colin, her face rapt with curiosity.

"Continue," she invited with a casual wave of her hand.

"Well, we've prepared a pit large enough to accommodate all the possessions we've brought here tonight. It's far enough away from where the stone buildings will be constructed, and it's right on the edge of the field, where no more will ever be built. We hoped that if we placed everything there, you could transfer it to Asgard … in one journey".

Colin finished speaking and waited nervously for Kendra to respond; *would she use the new pit? We're stuffed if not; there's no Plan B,* he thought. But Kendra did not answer straight away, choosing instead to remain silent as she considered the Bernician's proposal.

A few long minutes passed, and as both sides of the portal waited, the tension increased as Kendra scratched her chin and muttered to herself as she paced to and fro, wrestling with her decision before. Just as she opened her mouth to speak, Woden interjected.

As they had waited, that which had unsettled him as he spoke with Kendra by the stream; that which she had chosen not to make known, had become clear to him and the thought of it triggered a wave of foreboding that spread up and through his body like a wave of ice water.

"Before you give your answer, prophetess, I would speak with you … at once!"

"My lord …" she said, knowing full well that Woden had read her intent "… I am all too aware of the consequences, but what choice do we have?"

Woden remained resolute. "At once, Kendra!"

Kendra knew better than to challenge him now. His bearing told her that he was exerting his divine authority, and though she had known him from a boy; teaching him the ways of the gods, sometimes punishing the wrongdoings of the child, he stood now before her as her lord and master and as such, she yielded to Woden's command without further argument.

"Grimme! Renweard! Join us, please!" he ordered.

Chapter 14: The Deliberation

The four leaders had been gone for over half an hour, and as the portal had been sealed to everything but sight - Woden deciding that cross-cultural exchanges should be strictly supervised - the Bernicians had decided that now would be a good time to get a brew going, and to the delight and bewilderment of the seven remaining Asgardian warriors, they had begun by producing the paraphernalia of that noblest of arts: tea making.

"Do you think there could be a problem, Colin?" Jon asked as he sat back in the collapsible camp chair, a cup of his preferred Earl Grey held in cupped hands so as to warm them.

Even on 'active duty,' Jon insisted on this particular beverage stating that 'Anything else just would not do!' and always drank it from a china cup and saucer with a slice of lemon, which in his opinion, was the 'civilised' way to do things, despite being clad in early mediaeval attire.

"Could be Jon, although we're stuffed if there is; I haven't got a clue what we're gonna do if they insist on using the original graves."

Jon frowned wistfully and cast an eye over the eight pits which, until just over a week ago, had held the earthly remains of the same men who now stood and watched the strange behaviour of their brethren from the future.

Even in this poor light, he could see that it would be a mistake to place the items back there; They were shallow, maybe a foot deep, and slap, bang in the middle of the new housing development; if the earth-moving equipment didn't, unearth them - probably quite violently, and certainly without regard - then the subsequent gardening activities of the proud, new owners probably would, destroying them once and for all, and this great endeavour would have been for nothing. No, they could not be returned there.

"Let us hope, then, that our hosts are able to find a way to resolve the issue. Afterall, if *our* offerings are destroyed, there are no more to be had; we have, you might say, 'exhausted our supply!'"

Colin decided not to dwell on Jon's ominous contemplation, as pertinent as it was, deciding instead to keep an open mind and a positive attitude, although Jon did have a point.

"Fingers crossed then, eh?" he said nervously.

"Indeed," Jon replied.

***

"What are they doing now?" Eadig asked as he attempted to see through the wall of men that clustered around the portal, each trying to guess what strange item the Bernicians would produce next.

"They're boiling water in a … a … I don't know!"

"Let me see …" Eadig insisted as he finally pushed his way to the front "… it can't be that complicated!"

Apparently, it was; As they watched, one of the Bernicians, an older woman dressed in the attire of one of the Ides - a well-respected lady of the village - took a handful of small, flat white pouches and dropped them into a strangely shaped pot.

From their various vantage points, they agreed to a man that it appeared to be made from fired clay, probably using the same method from which their own cooking pots were formed.

"Except…" as Egeslic pointed out, "… this has a small drinking horn attached to one side and a hand grip on the other!"

"Maybe that's where you drink from?" Garberend suggested. They marvelled at the idea.

After a while, the same woman lifted another strange vessel, similar in size and shape to the first, albeit fashioned in iron, from its position over the fire and poured boiling water into the pot containing the small bags. She then stirred the contents for a few seconds with a spoon before leaving it to stand.

"I'm confused..." Abrecan announced after a few minutes, "...is it some kind of warming device? It does seem colder on that side!"

The others nodded, conceding that he might have a point.

"Wait! She's stirring the pot again!" Anfeald said excitedly as though all might now be revealed. There was a collective gasp as the clear, boiling water that had entered the pot now exited through the small horn to be collected in a series of smaller ceramic drinking vessels. It was brown!

"Alchemy?" suggested Abrecan.

"No, this is a different magic...!" Eadig mused.

"a potion, then? A potion to..." Deogol did not finish his sentence; none of them were any the wiser as to what it was they were witnessing.

Finally, some of the Bernician's, having added a fine white granular powder - "It glistens!" Abrecan insisted - and what they all recognised as milk, stirred the mixture enthusiastically with spoons and began drinking.

"Is that it…?" it was Garberend "…all that for a drink! Give me a horn-full of mead, not the hot brown slurry of the old world."

Beadurof, himself known to have produced many a fine brew of mead, including that which had been responsible for the intoxication of Waelwulf at the now legendary story-telling, protested, "The Mead does not make itself, Garberend; it is a long and precise process!" but the defence of his art went unnoticed as it always did; the men more interested in drinking the Mead than its origins.

The warriors laughed heartily as their merriment continued until, out of nowhere, someone asked the question that they had all been avoiding; the activities of the Bernician clan having been a useful and welcome distraction.

It was Eadig, and his words put an end to all and any high-spiritedness.

"Is there a problem, do you think? With the Bernician's offerings?"

No one answered; no one *had* an answer; in any case, there was no need.

"I think we are about to find out!" Deogol said.

Their heads turned toward the sound of footsteps as Woden, and the others returned, all bar one bearing an expression of grave concern; Kendra was smiling.

***

Having summoned Kendra and Renweard to a private meeting, the three of them, accompanied by Grimme: ever Woden's counsel and voice of reason, moved away from the portal, Kendra casting a casual hand over its glimmering surface as she did so. At once, all sound from the old world ceased as she sealed it to all but sight.

They walked a short distance to where an ancient oak spread its vast canopy, casting shade around its considerable girth and providing food, shelter, and security to countless small animals and insects as it had done for more than half a millennium.

From here, they were able to see both the warriors and the portal but still be suitably distant so that Egeslic and the rest of the men could not approach unnoticed in order to eavesdrop; Egeslic, ever the maker of mischief.

Anticipating Woden's objections, Kendra spoke first.

"My lord, I know what it is you would say!"

His eyebrows raised in an arc as Woden replied inquiringly, "You do? Then you will also know that I cannot allow this; Kendra, you are needed here!"

Renweard and Grimme listened in silence as the two great minds before them continued their debate. They could have no knowledge of the plan Kendra was on the verge of revealing to them, so instead, they waited, their part in the conversation, for now at least, redundant.

"I can see no other way…" she protested "… the death beds are soon to be obliterated, devoured by great iron beasts, to be lost forever beneath the relentless advance of progress." She paused for effect. "But, if we do it my way, my lord, we shall have the Bernician weapons; Renweard and his men shall once more bear arms, and you, my lord Woden, shall have an ally: ears and eyes on the other side… in the old world."

Grimme was the first of the two onlookers to grasp the significance of the words Kendra had just spoken. At first, he remained still, allowing them to find their mark, to fully absorb their meaning, but as the enormity of their significance hit home, he asked.

"Are we to understand, my lady, that you propose… an exchange? The Bernician weapons for our prophetess?"

Renweard started, shocked at the revelation, and shifted uneasily in his position by the enormous tree. *It cannot be! Asgard must not lose its most powerful communicator! How, then, could our two worlds be connected? Surely, there was none in Asgard to replace such a revered lady?* His mind reeled at the endless possibilities of their world without Kendra.

In the short time he had dwelled within the Great Hall of Valhalla, he had seen how important she was; how everyone, God, Valkyrie, and warrior alike, looked to her for counsel, and all respected her knowledge of the spirit world and the wyrd: that which is yet to come into being.

He agreed with Woden; this must not be allowed to happen.

Kendra expected Woden to respond but sensed that, for now at least, the great man seemed to be holding something back and so remained silent on the matter. Instead, seizing the opportunity, she answered Grimme's question.

"You are a wise and noble man, my lord Grimme, and yes… it is that which I propose; do you object?"

Grimme's response was instant. "I do, my lady! What will Valhalla… Asgard, do in your stead? You must realise that your counsel is held in high regard and that without it, we would be exposed and vulnerable to all that is not of this world?"

Kendra smiled on Grimme, knowing that which he could not. Indeed no one, not even the mighty Woden himself, could know the full implications of what she was about to reveal, but before she did so, she turned and addressed the warrior of Wandle's Ham.

“My lord Renweard, you have not voiced an opinion. What would you have me do?”

Renweard was momentarily caught off guard, having unexpectantly heard his name spoken amid such an important and decisive conversation as this, but recovering quickly, he said.

“It is not my place to offer counsel on this most weighty matter, but…”

“…but you are about to!” Kendra teased. Renweard smiled patiently.

“… but I cannot agree to a plan which leaves Asgard without its prophetess for the sake of we, eight. We cannot, surely, be worthy of such sacrifice?”

Kendra smiled but did not answer. She watched the faces of the three men as their eyes bore into her, each pleading their case that she should not make this sacrifice.

She turned and looked toward the portal where the seven warriors who had accompanied Renweard into this world now huddled around it, jostling for position, laughing, joking, and making merry. Finally, she spoke.

“My most noble lords; Look to your men.” She gestured with an outstretched arm toward the Wandle’s Ham warriors.

"For these souls, I would gladly make the sacrifice, and there have been others before who have suffered a similar fate…"

"A few…" Woden interrupted, "…and over many, many years!"

"What my lord Woden says is true…" Kendra replied, "… but if my sources are correct, and I have no reason to doubt their word, it would seem that what we have seen so far is only the beginning."

To maintain privacy, she turned so that her back was to the portalas though to show her face to anyone, but the three leaders might prematurely alert them to the approaching danger, such was the news that she was about to deliver. She drew herself up with a deep intake of breath and spoke.

"They believe, as do I, that a great number of Asgardians are about to meet the same fate as the eight; that a period of great learning is underway, and that, in their quest for knowledge, a great many of our men and women will be disturbed from their death beds and in so doing, they will be stripped of their possessions in Asgard and Folkvangr."

The three leaders of men were stunned into silence. Woden bore an expression of stern contemplation as he decided whether Kendra's words held true. He had no reason to doubt his prophetess; it was she, after all, who had created the conduit between their words; she who had brought their two great peoples together, and his messengers: Hugin and Muninn, had increasingly brought news of his kin being disturbed in their earthly resting place. But this? How could it be?

Grimme had no reason to doubt Kendra either. Even if he had done so, he had no means with which to counter her assertions, so decided instead that what she had spoken must be true. The thought terrified him.

Renweard, however, had a question.

"Who are the 'sources' of which you speak? Do we know them? Can *we* speak with them?"

Woden shook his head, inspired once again by Renweard's perception and quick thinking. If he was not worthy of God-hood, then no one was. But of *course,* we must speak with Kendra's sources; and *before* any decision is made. His mind suddenly free from doubt, Woden said,

"My lord Renweard is correct…"

Renweard swelled with pride that he should be so honoured.

"…Kendra, I insist that we speak with your sources; who are they?"

Expecting this, she replied.

"You already have my lord Woden; my sources are, in fact, well known to you all!"

"Then who…?"

The three men were none-the-wiser, so Kendra stepped aside, revealing a clear, uninterrupted view of the portal. There she stood and looked silently toward it, waiting for the veil to be lifted from their eyes.

"Of course!" Woden was the first to see the answer.

"Your source; it's the seekers! Rab, Colin, and Angela are your source!"

Now it had been spoken aloud, it was obvious. Of course, they were the source; who else could know that other graves were about to be disturbed, their contents removed for study?

"I am glad that the knowledge has come to you, my lord…" Kendra said, genuinely relieved that it had not taken as long as she had anticipated, "…but there is more you should know; More I would have you know before we can decide on a plan."

With that, Kendra relayed the information that had recently been passed to her via Colin, which had led her to decide on her current course of action.

Angela had been attending a job interview at the main offices of Western Archaeological Services just two days ago. She was hoping to secure a full-time post in Finds Processing: that part of the team responsible for the cleaning, identification, conservation, and storage of every last find to be lifted from out of the ground. She had decided to apply, as much as anything, so that she could work indoors, especially in winter, but also because it would mean job security; like most field archaeologists, she was employed on a three-monthly 'rolling' contract, and when the work dried up, so did your income.

It was during her tour of the unit and the various departments within that she was made aware of an impending upsurge in the workload; part of a 'could you cope in such a busy environment?' assessment.

She had been shown plans for a further six trial evaluations, all of which were within an area steeped in Anglo-Saxon history and some very close to other sites which had yielded, among other things, two substantial hoards and a further four full excavations; one of which was the site that Andrew had been on his way to inspect when he'd popped in for a doughnut. Work was due to start on these within the next few days; in fact, she, Rab, and Colin had already been assigned to one of them. With her recent experience, she had recognised the significance of this and had told Colin, who had, in turn, spoken with Kendra.

"This is unbelievable! If what you say is true, my army will be without tooth and claw at a time when there is much to bite and maul!"

Kendra spoke again, but this time she had words that would soothe her lord's mind.

"It is for this reason that I must away into the old world, although I would say that there is a small chance the new pit will suffice and that the transfer will work without the need of my sacrifice…"

She held the attention of the three men as hope now returned to their faces.

"…but know this…" she sighed "… If I am spared and do *not* travel to the old world, it is likely that the onslaught will proceed unchecked. Colin, Rab, and Angela have agreed that they will try to halt the advance, but in truth, it is likely they can do no more than slow it."

The hope that had started to grow in the faces of Woden, Grimme, and Renweard dwindled and was gone, as they now, at last, fully understood the implications of Kendra's words:

If she stayed, Asgard was lost, while if they lost Kendra, there was, at least, some hope for Asgard in that she might be able to prevent the discovery and removal of the long-dead warriors from their resting places.

“Will you be able to open a portal from the old-world Kendra?” it was Renweard. “…from the other side?”

Woden and Grimme looked from Renweard, deep into the old woman’s face, anticipating her answer. Kendra did not look at Renweard as she answered, fixing her eyes instead on a beetle that scurried past on the ground. *Scamper little one*, she thought, *we must all hurry along our way into the wyrd.*

“I do not know; there *is* no way of knowing until I am on the other side and make the incantations; only then will it become clear.”

There was silence as each, lost in their own thoughts, struggled with the inevitability of the situation. Eventually, though, each of them came to the same conclusion: there was no other way, and to prevent the emptying of the graves and the depletion of the Asgardian army, Kendra must pass through the portal and join forces with the Seekers.

It was decided.

Chapter 15: The Decree

Seven worried faces greeted Kendra and the three lords as they returned to the portal. Renweard's men had clearly been deep in conversation, voicing their concerns, as all conversation ceased the moment they'd arrived.

"You look troubled, my brothers…" Woden said, sensing their unease

"…but there is no need to fear; we four have reached a decision that will best suit us all - Asgardian and Bernician alike."

Despite having complete respect for Woden, the men were not convinced.

He, Grimme, and Renweard clearly knew something that was not to their liking; the men could see it lurking beneath their expressions; calm yet troubled; an underlying truth waiting to burst forth, and they could hear it in Woden's tone.

Only Kendra seemed at ease with whatever decision had been made, her face relaxed… calm, in complete contrast to the others; something was clearly amiss.

Abrecan spoke first.

"My lords; my Lady Kendra; please forgive me; I sense that there are those among you who are troubled by some unknown ill. Forgive my impertinence, but is there a problem with the Bernician offerings?"

Neither Woden nor Grimme, Renweard, or Kendra were offended by Abrecan's frankness. He was known by all as a gentle soul and a man of great fortitude, kind and caring with his family at home in Wandle's Ham, yet ferocious and unyielding on the battlefield.

"You have earned our candour Abrecan, and our respect..." Woden said as he addressed the man who stood before him, awaiting an answer.

"...we have discussed that which concerns you, and despite a few..." he chose his next word carefully "...misgivings, we have devised a plan which we are certain will see us through these troubled times."

Placing a hand on Abrecan's shoulder, he continued.

"It would not, however, be appropriate for me to divulge our plan to each clan or warrior separately. Rather, I shall speak to Asgardian and Bernician together as one clan, one army."

Woden smiled; a warm, open smile that rose up from his heart to light the whole of his face.

Abrecan and the others felt its sincerity and respectfully submitted to their lords will.

"Let us, then, be reconnected with our brothers and sisters in the old world!" Woden said as he gestured to Kendra to re-establish the portal.

As Kendra moved toward the gateway to carry out Woden's bidding, Renweard approached his men, calling them to him with a gesture of both hands.

"My brothers, stand with me; stand with me at this most glorious of times, that we might, together, learn of our fate."

The men moved toward their leader and, as was the case in life, formed a loose circle with Renweard at its heart. Then they turned to face the portal, and they waited together.

Across on the other side of the portal, the Bernicians had also seen the return of Kendra and the three leaders.

They had waited anxiously as their evening gave way to the complete darkness of an autumn night, the chill creeping stealthily in under cloak and coat alike, causing the wearer to pull it in tight around them, instantly rewarded with the warmth of a woollen hug.

"LOOK!" Angela called as she saw the seven warriors greet their kinsmen. As one, the Bernicians stopped what they were doing; all conversation ceased abruptly, and all eyes turned to the portal.

Through the amethyst haze, they saw the four leaders return from their meeting in Asgard to be greeted by the seven who had remained.

"What d'you think they're saying?" it was Rab.

Colin replied. "Dunno mate; they've obviously made a decision about our kit, but there's something else; something… I dunno; some of 'em look worried."

They had been out of sight the entire time and had been so for around half an hour. Needless to say, the Bernicians were relieved to see them return, albeit that some of the Asgardians wore a look of concern that had troubled Colin.

Jon agreed. "I'm afraid you may be right, dear boy; there does appear to be an air of vexation among the men, although Kendra seems fairly relaxed so…"

"Mmm… Looks like we're about to find out…" Colin interrupted as he pointed to the portal; something was happening there on the other side.

He couldn't help thinking, as he watched the scene unfold in front of him, that the portal resembled a bizarrely misshapen cinema screen, such was the light that spilled from it into the dark autumn night. There was no sound - *like a silent movie,* he thought - yet still, it managed to convey its message from Asgard as the players 'acted' out a scene of greeting and reunion.

The Asgardians spoke briefly, kind words it appeared if the men's bearing was anything to go by; Woden comforting one man in particular before Renweard gathered his men to him, and Woden gestured Kendra toward the portal.

At his command, Kendra, once again, cast a hand casually over the glimmering, pale violet surface of the portal.

Voices whispered softly as a gentle, almost imperceptible breeze passed through the gateway between the two worlds, lifting nothing more than a few strands of loose, untethered hair, gently caressing the face of the onlooker, then all was completely still.

The opening of the portal felt to Rab like the moment your hearing fully returns as you come into land after a long flight, and despite having been able to hear everything in *this* world, the absence of sound from the other felt eerie; unnatural, and he was glad that the connection had been re-established.

Seeing, and now hearing, movement in Asgard, he walked swiftly across to where Colin and Jon were still sitting in their folding camp chairs and spoke.

"Looks like we're about to receive the verdict, guys. You ready?"

They were indeed ready. Jon having already emptied his cup of its third refill of Earl Grey before placing it safely in the tea-for-one picnic basket it inhabited when not in use.

Unusually for Jon, though, he had decided that it could wait until later to be washed; such was the importance of the impending announcement.

Colin, being Colin, simply finished his coffee and 'screwed' the base of his mug into the soft soil at the side of his chair so that it remained upright, then joined the others as they, too, began to gather at the portal.

On both sides, the men and women whose future now rested with the decision that had been made in Asgard stood and regarded one another; two worlds, two time periods; one family.

What felt like an age passed between them, as brother eyed brother, sister, warrior, Lord and God alike; seeking clues in the eyes of those who stood opposite them across the void; to know if they, too, felt the unbearable tension that gripped and suffocated all those present. Finally, the wait was over; Woden stepped forward and prepared to speak.

"My people; hear me!" he said, addressing Asgardian and Bernician as one community.

Bodies and feet on both sides of the portal shifted and shuffled anxiously in anticipation.

"There has been much to discuss, and much rests on the outcome of our discussion. We have therefore taken longer than we would have hoped to reach our decision, and I apologise to you all for having to stand the long wait and for having to bear the tension that I now see on the face of each and every one of you."

Nobody spoke, but there was a collective ripple of appreciation that their ordeal had at least been acknowledged and was now finally being addressed.

Woden continued, moving straight to the point.

"I will not hide the fact from you that there is some concern regarding the new hollow: None of the eight have lain there…" he gestured to the men, "…and there have been no incantations to summon the Valkyrie; it is, therefore… unholy and, potentially, invisible to Asgard, and as a result, it may not yield sufficient spiritual energy to fully enable the transfer of the Bernician weapons…"

The assembly murmured nervously so that Woden raised a hand to quell the alarm before continuing.

"…we have, however, decided that as the original death beds are in such a position that places them directly in the path of destruction, we have no alternative but to use it, and I would thank you for your initiative and for its construction."

"Well, that's summat anyway!" Colin said, relieved.

"Mmm… It sounds to me, though, that there may be a '*but*' to follow." Jon replied, sensing there was more to come. He was correct.

Woden continued, "This solution does, however, carry with it a certain… risk."

"*As I suspected.*" Whispered Jon.

Woden stepped to one side, inviting Kendra to join him as he did so, indicating that she should now address the gathering.

"I believe Kendra is best placed to explain the reasons behind our decision since it is she who must take that risk and is set to lose most by it, should we succeed."

Woden held out a cloak- swathed arm, indicating that he was ready for Kendra to speak.

Dutifully, she stepped forward feeling suddenly weary, as though the efforts of the past hour had taken their toll and were starting to draw on her physical reserves. She felt the need for rest; for peace.

Taking her place before the gathering, she slowly peeled back the headdress that had protected her against the heat of the morning sun, the two worlds being offset temporally, which, having reached its zenith in Asgard, now beat down on them relentlessly. Yet as she bathed in its glow, she did not feel its warmth.

Ever the prophetess, ever the counsel and steadying hand; she stood before the gathering and eyed each and every face in front of her, acknowledging each person individually, offering hope and understanding with nothing more than a kind eye and a warm smile.

To some, the moment was unbearable, such was the tension that ensnared and smothered them, and as they tried piteously to return Kendra's smile, they could not help but feel that these might be her last moments in either world; as though she had been condemned to death. Then, as the tears came, Kendra spoke to both night and day simultaneously.

"It may be that when the incantation is made, and the transfer begins, there will be enough power in my words to carry the Bernician gift across the divide into Asgard without incident. This is my lord Woden's wish …"

For a moment, hope began to return to the assembly as they breathed easily again, having - literally, in some cases - collectively held their breath.

"…However, it may be that words alone will not suffice. If this is to be, it has been decided that I will make the journey and cross into the old world. From there, I will be able to use one final incantation to usher the weapons through the portal and into the hands of their new masters." She gestured with a hand to the eight.

At first, the crowd did not react. Most just stared, open-mouthed; their expression froze as though petrified.

Certainly, those on the Bernician side could not have grasped the significance of the phrase *'one final incantation.'* To Colin, Rab, and everyone else, it merely implied additional or supplementary; a kind of spiritual shove.

To the Asgardians, however, it meant exactly what it said: final, no more; irrevocable. If Kendra did this, they would lose her forever.

The voices of protest rang out in Asgard, leaving the Bernicians wondering what point they had missed.

"What the hell is going on?" Colin asked against the background noise. "Did I miss summat?"

Angela had no such misapprehension; she sensed in Kendra's words a finality, an inevitability, suggesting that Kendra herself knew there could be but one outcome. In fact, it felt to Angela that Kendra wished for it to be so.

"She wants to leave Asgard!"

"Eh?" Colin said, convinced he'd misheard her.

"She wants to leave Asgard; the new pit is giving her the reason to do it," Angela said, reaffirming her previous statement.

"What on earth makes you think that, Ange'? I mean, she's pretty important there. What would they do if she left?"

Angela sighed. "What will *she* do if she doesn't?"

Colin, try as he might, could not see what the advantage would be to Kendra were she to leave Asgard, especially as it meant having to live among them in the old world.

"Well, for a start, where would she live?" he said, gesturing around him with his hands to reinforce his point. "Then there's the small question of how she'd make a living, and that's *before* we look at how she would adapt to life on this side of the portal; she'd stand out a mile!"

Jon joined the conversation. "I must say, Colin, I feel inclined to side with Angela on this occasion…" he said as he huddled inside his long, woollen cloak for warmth. "…consider for a moment her long years of service to Woden and the Asgardians. In all those years, which may run into many hundreds, Kendra will have used her knowledge of all things natural, and perhaps more importantly, she will have used the incantations that we have witnessed tonight countless times."

Colin was still none-the-wiser. He waited for Jon to make his point, but when none came, he asked, "And…?"

Clearly, Jon had not made himself as clear as he'd hoped, so he continued.

"Well, let's think about it for a moment; every time Kendra uses her powers, every time she speaks one of, what must be a number of incantations, she uses a little more of her own precious life force."

Jon held the attention of the entire Bernician group now, who had gathered silently around him, Angela and Colin, their faces emerging out from the dark like those in a Joseph Wright painting, lit though, by bonfires rather than candles, which still burned fiercely around them. He continued.

"…with the passing of time, she has become more and more weary, weakened by the constant demand on her abilities; until tonight…" he paused for effect "…where she finds herself presented with an opportunity; an opportunity to break those bonds and live a mortal life; a finite life."

He turned toward the portal where Kendra stood, silent and alone. Seemingly, the heated discussion that now fully engrossed the Asgardians concerning *her* proposal and *her* future did not seem to warrant *her* inclusion.

"I believe that Kendra…" he turned back to Colin and the others "…wishes to be allowed to die!"

No sooner had the words left his mouth than Kendra's eyes flashed in Jon's direction and held him in her gaze.

They seemed to have somehow taken on the light of the Bernician bonfires as, despite the fact that she stood in Asgard and in full sun, they burned with an intensity that seared through the portal to settle on the man who had seemingly discovered her true intent, and although Jon had expected a reaction from his audience, he had not anticipated what he now saw on each of their faces.

Colin, Angela, Rab, and the others had suddenly taken on a look of alarm. For the briefest moment, Jon froze as he felt the hairs on the back of his neck lift and tingle, his breathing coming in short, shallow gasps. But the intensity with which Kendra's gaze held him stirred him, and whether he would want to or not, he turned to face her.

"I think she heard you mate!" Colin said carefully.

"I believe she did at that!" Jon replied, his voice dry with nerves, unsure as to whether he had endeared or offended their host. They were soon to find out.

Kendra closed her eyes and drew a long, deep breath that seemed to move the very air around and between them as a breeze gently shifted once more between the two worlds.

"YOU WILL ALL NOW LISTEN TO *ME*!" she roared over the melee, her voice booming, almost masculine.

The silence was as complete as it was instantaneous, and everyone turned toward the prophetess.

Some had witnessed the assertive side of Kendra's character before; certainly, those in Asgard, even Woden himself, were well acquainted with Kendra's authority and the regard in which she was held. She was not to be displeased nor angered.

The Bernicians, with the exception of Rab, had not witnessed anything like it; they stood in complete obeyance of the command.

"My people..." she said kindly, her voice returning to normal, once again casting a compassionate eye over the entire gathering to ensure that both sides of the portal understood they were, indeed, one people and of the same house.

"...you have talked long, and the hour is late. Our path was chosen for us by wyrd; by fate, and as such, your discussions, as noble as their intent may be, serve no purpose."

Jon stepped forward as though to ask a question, but Kendra quickly held up a hand, indicating that she had more to say.

"There are some among you..." she looked directly at Jon "...who believe that this... unrest is of my making;

perhaps even to my liking." she raised a finger as Jon once again made to speak. "I will not lie to you. There have been times; many times, when I have wished for nothing more than to relinquish my role among you; There have been times where, having carried the great weight of Asgard's inestimable problems for over a millennium…" her eyes rested longingly on the eight, empty graves "… I have wished for the cool, quiet embrace of the earth…"

Somewhere in the old world, a Bernician wept openly.

"…but let it be known, as Woden is my witness, that my duty to you all remains unaltered; whether I would serve from Asgard or from the old world; I serve you still! There will be no further debate, no more discussion of whether or why. We must do this; we *will* do this; IT IS DECIDED!"

Her shoulders dropped as though having made her speech, there was little strength left for anything else, so she stepped to one side and then sat heavily on the ground, an old lady once more.

"Reckon that about seals it then!" Colin whispered to Angela.

"Mmm… Reckon, you're right!" she replied quietly.

Woden, having remained silent throughout the entire event, stepped forward. It was clear to him now that

Kendra's motives and desires were both one and the same, her only wish being to serve the people as she always had.

He felt great sorrow at the prospect of losing such a venerable soul as this to the old world; he would miss her friendship and counsel, and he swallowed hard his emotions. Kendra was cherished and beloved by all and a formidable opponent both in debate and in battle; respected by friend and foe alike. But having discussed their options at length under the old oak, he knew that it must be so; it must be allowed, and Kendra's wishes must be respected.

Nobody moved as Woden made to speak. His first words, though, were with regard to the great lady who sat at his feet.

"My lord Renweard! If you please, you will see to the comfort of my lady." His voice atremble.

Gesturing that Anfeald and Deogol should assist him, Renweard moved to where the prophetess sat, exhausted and spent, and with great gentleness and respect, helped her to her feet.

They walked with her, the short distance to where the stump of a broad-leaf tree pushed defiantly up out of the ground. It had fallen many years ago during a great storm when a lightning bolt of such power and ferocity struck it a devastating and ruinous blow. Some days later, it had snapped close to its base and fallen back across the stream. Over time the stump had been eroded by weather and gnawed by countless minute jaws, which had created a structure that resembled a chair or throne. This had become known as the *Treóbryne: the fire tree,* and sometimes *Treóstol*: *the tree seat.* Whatever people chose to call it, it now provided a place for the great lady to rest.

As they approached, Renweard untied his wolf-fur stole and lay it across the stump before inviting Kendra to take her place and to rest. She did so gratefully and without objection, allowing herself to become one with the remains of the tree where she closed her eyes and drifted among the sounds of nature.

"Remain with my lady…" he said to his men "…should she wish for anything, you will oblige her!"

As one, they replied, "My lord. Of course!"

Renweard returned to Woden's side, who nodded his appreciation. He then addressed the gathering.

"*We* have reached a decision; *you* have been made aware of it. Debate is at an end…" he paused briefly, as though interrupted by a thought before continuing.

"…therefore, let no more be said! As soon as our lady is recovered, we shall proceed with the ceremony!" he turned to Colin and the Bernicians.

“I would now ask of you, my lords; will you please make your preparations so that the ceremony can begin as soon as Kendra is recovered?”

Colin stepped forward and, with a grace never before seen by his fellow Bernicians, said.

“My lord Woden; it will be our honour!”

Chapter 16: The Gift

A flurry of activity ensued, and as Colin gathered the Bernicians, Woden addressed Renweard and his men.

He felt tense, as though a great conflict was upon them, and Grimme sensed a nervousness in his lord that he had never before witnessed in one so resolute.

"It is time, brothers." He announced finally. "I am, however, unfamiliar with such proceedings. Such is the rareness of this event. I will therefore speak with Kendra to find out what is required of us… of you all…"

He paused momentarily, staring out across Haligsfeld toward the river. Through the trees, a ribbon of silver glinted and sparkled as the tide moved rapidly inland from the sea - the Anglo-Saxon highway.

Memories of longships, their sails still furled, held to the spar with heavy, pitch-covered rope, filled his mind. He could hear the creak of oar against thule: a 'thorn' of timber through which a loop of rope passed via a pre-drilled hole. This, in turn, held the oar in place and acted as a fulcrum against which the oar was strained, as forty oarsmen pulled hard and steady against the current; the helmsman, high in the stern, steer board tiller in hand and ever-vigilant as he steered the ninety-foot sea-going vessel along narrow channels between mud bank and shore; he could almost smell the air; a thick, heady mix, laden with salt, pitch and the sulphurous bite of river mud.

How long has it been? He asked himself; *How long since I stood among men; mortal?* Perhaps Kendra was right; Perhaps there was a time to move on - or move back!

"My lord...?" a warm, distant voice broke the spell. It was Grimme.

"My *lord…*?" It came again.

Woden started as he was torn, cruelly from his memories, far distant as they were.

"My apologies…" he said, "…I was reminiscing." His eye still glazed as though some part of him remained with the ship.

"Do you ever revisit the old world, Grimme? I mean *our* old world." He said, referring to the early fifth-century migrations.

"My lord; it is forbidden…!"

"In your mind, Grimme; your *mind*!"

It was indeed forbidden for Asgardians to travel between worlds. In truth, only the high elite could do so, and then only with the assistance of a prophet and Woden's express permission. None had ever done so; None had ever needed to…until now.

"I have occasionally looked into my mind, my lord, to see what is left there of the old world, but there has been little to tempt me. My duty is to Asgard; As it was, so it shall ever be!"

Woden looked at Grimme with both pride and disappointment. Pride: that he would remain, loyally by Woden's side; ever faithful. Disappointed: that he had no desire for that which had gone before; no wish to savour the burning fear of mortality; for it is that which causes us to *live* our lives.

"You are truly a god, Grimme. And I, for one, am glad that you live among us!"

Grimme bowed an acknowledgement before saying

"In which case, may I respectfully remind my lord that he is to speak with Kendra? And that she awaits you by the Treóbryne?"

Grimme's words finally plucked Woden from his reverie, and turning promptly on his heels, he marched purposefully away to where Kendra sat resting, calling as he went, "Of course; we must away!"

With a palm, Grimme gestured to the Renweard and his men that they should remain.

“I will follow our lord to find out what is required of you. For now, rest in this place.” Then he, too, hurried away after Woden.

“Well, I don’t know about anyone else, but I’m exhausted!” It was Garberend

“These incantations and portals have drained me; I am happy to rest!”

As he spoke, he settled himself on the ground by the stream and lay back, shielding his eyes from the Sun by covering them with his forearm. Almost immediately, he began to snore. The rest of the eight were stunned momentarily but then erupted with laughter at this most unflappable of companions.

“I believe…” Renweard stated, “…That Garberend may have a point!” as he, too, joined him by the stream.

“Rest, my brothers; there is little to be achieved by standing by and vexing.”

The men did as Renweard instructed; some laying, others sitting, but all relaxing, as conversation slowly faded into quiet contemplation.

***

Across on the other side of the portal, things could not be more different. For one thing, it was dark, and instead of a blazing Sun, they were working under a Third Quarter moon.

“It’ll be a Waning Gibbous next!” Jon had announced proudly.

“Did he just say ‘wailing gibbons?’” Colin mocked as Jon rolled his eyes skyward, adding playfully, “Peasant!”

As promised, Colin and the Bernicians went about preparing for the upcoming ceremony.

The weapons and other offerings that had been gifted still lay untouched on the tarpaulin where they had been placed earlier that evening. Fortunately though, Jon, with the help of Angela and a couple of the others, had had the foresight to cover them with blankets which they had weighted down against the autumn breeze with a few large stones that had lain strewn about the site. The temperature had dropped quite suddenly since the Sun had dipped below the horizon, and the evening air now hung heavy with moisture.

“Can I have your attention, please, everyone?” Colin called as the group gathered around him.

“Thank you…” he said as the last few individuals joined the ranks. “…right then, looks like this is it. Don’t ask me what’s about to happen, though, cos I haven’t got a clue; I’m not sure *they’re* any the wiser, to be honest, so if we just go about getting everything safely across to the pit, at least we'll have, played our part."

Rab stood alongside Colin and regarded him as he led the group on through this momentous occasion. He couldn't help thinking that it was only a very few nights ago that Colin had accused him of having hallucinations; in fact, hadn't he said that he thought Rab was having some sort of mental break-down? Even so, he bore him no ill will; it had taken *him* more than a little while to accept that this really was happening. Who wouldn't think you'd lost the plot? This was the stuff of fairy tales; of myth, and legend.

"Blimey!"

Colin acknowledged his good friend.

"You alright there, Rab?"

Realising that he had just spoken aloud, Rab quickly responded.

"Yes, mate. I'm fine, thanks. I was just thinking how a couple of nights ago, this was nothing more than a field with some pretty cool archaeology; now look at it! Gods, Anglo-Saxons - actual and modern day; portals; a prophetess. They should make a bloody film out of this!"

Colin laughed. "I think it'd be too far-fetched even for that lot!"

They laughed together.

Jon cleared his throat. “Yes, well, when you two have finished your reminiscing, perhaps we could make a start?”

Colin flashed Rab an ‘oops!’ before saying.

“Absolutely, Jon; you’re quite right. So… listen up, everyone!”

He stepped up onto an upturned sample bucket so that everyone had a clear view and continued.

“Right. Well, what I thought was: if we form a line between here…” he gestured to the tarpaulin “…and the pit…” He pointed across the site to where the circle of bonfires was being tended by a lone Bernician “…we could pass everything along the line and pop it down into the ground?”

The crowd seemed to favour this idea; it seemed fairly straightforward, and the small sea of heads nodded their approval.

“Good; so, Jon and Ange’, if you wouldn’t mind manning things this end, Rab and me will be over at the pit. Is that OK?”

Jon and Angela, too were in agreement.

“That sounds absolutely fine dear boy; It will save a lot of leg-work, plus it will make for less congestion on each side of the site; good thinking!”

Pleased that his plan had been so well received, Colin said,

“Right then; unless anyone’s got any questions, let’s get to it!”

What followed was not unlike a military operation. They began by sorting the team into two groups of fourteen. These were then asked to spread out to create two lines between the tarpaulin at one end and the pit at the other but offset to one another so that between them, both lines formed a kind of saw-tooth pattern. Finally, they turned to face inward and were ready to begin.

The system, although unfamiliar to most, was, in itself, quite straightforward: Jon would select an item and pass it to Angela, who would pass it to the first person in line. They would then pass it across to the person obliquely opposite them, who would do likewise, and so on. As each person passed the item along to the next, it would zig-zag its way down the line to reach the far end.

This method meant that not only did each individual avoid having to twist their back in order to pass the object along but also that they were less likely to drop it in the process.

And so, it began.

"Take your time, everyone; this is not a race, and we do not want any of our precious items damaged!" Jon called as he selected a leather-sheathed Seax and handed it to Angela, who in turn passed it to Graeme at the head of the line.

He needn't have worried; No one was in a hurry, and all wanted to see those precious items arrive intact.

At the far end of the line, objects started to arrive out of the semi-darkness. Colin had positioned himself down inside the pit, which had been completely lined with branches of Yew: the tree of transformation and rebirth.

The positioning of the weapons had been the only instruction they had received from Kendra so far, which, although in itself hugely frustrating, was completely understandable under the circumstances.

"no one item must touch another…" she had said, "…and each weapon must lay so that the grip of one lays opposite the tip of the next, and so on…"

"We understand, Kendra; we'll see it's done as you ask."

"…and each layer must be separate from the one below…" she continued until she was quite sure that Colin and Rab completely understood the importance of her instruction.

"It will be done exactly as you have asked, my lady," Rab said earnestly. Finally, with his reassurance Kendra seemed to relax; a little, anyway. She almost literally had the weight of the world on her shoulders today, and for the first time ever, she felt it.

"Very well. I shall say no more."

And so, that moment had arrived, and as Rab received each item, he passed it carefully down to his friend, who laid it gently and respectfully among the branches.

As one layer of weapons was completed, another of yew brush was placed on top, sealing it. The next layer of weapons was laid over this and more yew above that until the successive layers eventually filled the pit with only around three feet to spare from the top.

As Colin worked, every breath he took carried with it the smell of both life and death; beginning and end: a heady mixture of damp soil and freshly cut timber accentuated by the cold air that trickled down into the pit like unseen water.

"How we doing, Rab?" he called after about ten minutes of work.

"Not sure, Col; they're still coming, so…" Rab strained his eyes back down along the line into the darkness.

"I think these might be the last few items," he said as the bag containing the lyre reached the end of its journey in this life.

As he handed it to Colin, who was now out of the pit for fear of crushing the items within with his feet, Rab heard a voice behind him.

"Please, do be careful with my lyre!"

It was Jon.

"We absolutely will, Jon…" Colin said, "…we've created a small space for it just off to the side. Look…" he pointed to a small hollow among the yew branches that resembled a reasonably sized, albeit rectangular, nest. "…It's lined with yew *and* moss, so it'll be nice and snug in there!"

Jon smiled. "Thank you, dear boy; I will miss her!"

"She's going to an amazing new home, though…" Colin pointed out. "…who'd have thought she'd be played by someone from the sixth century? Can you imagine it, eh?"

It did seem completely fantastic: the idea that all those months of selecting the right timber; measuring, cutting and planing; polishing, and finally stringing and tuning the instrument, only for it to be passed through a time portal to be used by a late-departed Anglo-Saxon in Asgard.

"You are, of course, correct, Colin. This is, in fact, a wonderous day."

"Don't you know it! Are we all done now, then, Jon?" Colin asked with compassion, knowing that Jon's lyre had been a labour of love over many, many months.

Jon replied softly, acknowledging Colin's thoughtfulness. "Indeed, we are, dear boy; my lyre… *Eadig's* lyre… was the very last item."

"Come on then…" Colin said encouragingly, "… let's go and see if anything's been decided, eh?"

As he wiped dirt from his hands, Colin, Rab, and Jon started to make their way back down the line toward the portal, indicating as they went that the others should join them.

Once there, they gathered as they had previously, in front of the portal, forming a loose semi-circle with Colin, Rab, Angela, and Jon at its front and centre.

And there they stood, looking in on Asgard, awaiting their next instruction as the night grew ever colder, the sky ever darker.

***

Kendra reclined serenely into the Treóbryne and listened.

It was as though she had been absorbed by the seat to become one with it, and her comfort there was total.

Over the softest of breezes, she could hear the distant bubble of laughter and conversation as the eight patiently awaited her counsel one last time; she could hear birds chatter and pip as they went about the business of collecting food for their recently hatched young - even in Asgard such things took precedence over all else; and she could hear the footfall of a powerful, albeit anxious, warrior.

Without opening her eyes to look, she said

"My Lord Woden approaches!"

Woden smiled admiringly.

"My lady displays the vigilance of a hind!"

It was Kendra's turn to smile.

"That may be so, but I could detect the presence of you, my lord, on the darkest of nights… such is the manner with which you breathe!"

They laughed together as Woden acknowledged his tendency to breath noisily through his nose whenever he was tense or pensive.

Long ago, when still a young man, he led a small hunting party comprising some of his best warriors into the forest.

Their quarry, an enormous boar, had gone to ground, so they elected to dismount their horses and followed it into the scrub, where it lurked dangerously.

Having become separated from his men, Woden advanced carefully, his spear in the low position, ready to strike.

Meanwhile, the rest of his party, on hearing the heavy breathing of a wild and savage beast, closed in on their prize, and on the command of Bordan, the *valley dweller*, they struck, attacking from both sides simultaneously and wrestled the snarling, thrashing beast to the ground.

The struggle was brief, though, for no sooner had they pounced than the beast began cursing and railing; it was Woden!

Realising at once their grave error, the men released their captive and, with sweating brows and heaving chests, stepped back expecting his wrath. None came!

Woden, helpless with laughter, lay on the leaf-strewn forest floor, his spear now in two parts and his hair and beard a tangle of leaf and twig.

The men, relieved that Woden had seen the absurdity of the moment, were helpless and could do nothing but join him in his merriment as taunts of "Green Man" and "Herne" rang out among the trees.

In the melee that followed, the animal they hunted had slipped away unnoticed, surviving to fight another day.

"My lady is…?"

"My lady is NOT!" Kendra interrupted. "I am, for the time being, happy to rest a while longer."

Woden smiled, admiring, not for the first time, the pluck of this most noble of creatures. *I will miss you, my lady!* He thought to himself.

"My lady must take all the time she needs, and as soon as she is ready…"

"She will inform you of it!" she interrupted again, smiling playfully.

In truth, although she felt comfortable and at ease, she did not yet feel rested. But she also knew that she could not delay the inevitable for very much longer as the portal must be closed before night crossed over into morning in the old world. If she did not conclude the ceremony by then, it was unlikely that she would have strength enough to attempt it a second time; she was not certain she had strength enough for the first!

Her mind whirled as she considered alternatives to her original plan, concluding that were none and that the pursuit of any such was folly and a waste of time that they simply did not have.

And so, she sat in quiet contemplation, a picture of calm and serenity. Yet despite her outward appearance, her mind was in turmoil; so much so that her thoughts came to her as a drove of leaping hares who darted, frolicked, and boxed their way through the tangled undergrowth of her wearied mind and were, in all likelihood using as much of her reserves as performing the ceremony itself. *Enough!* She thought to herself.

Kendra's eyes flicked suddenly open, catching Woden off-guard.

"My lady…?"

Kendra sighed wearily "…is well and has concluded that we must begin the ceremony," she said, "For once, time is *not* on our side!"

Woden turned to Grimme, who, having arrived at the Treóbryne moments after his master, had waited patiently and silently in the background since.

"Grimme, would you be so kind as to inform my lord Renweard and his men that the ceremony will begin shortly?"

As Grimme turned to do his lord's bidding, Kendra added.

"Ask them, if you will, Grimme, to return once more to their death bed in Haligsfeld and to wait within. They are to remain there; I will attend shortly, and the ceremony will begin the *moment* I arrive."

With a nod, Grimme made his way back to the men, striding purposefully away to his task.

Woden turned his gaze back to Kendra.

"I am grateful to you, Kendra…" he said, using her name rather than her title.

It was more usual to address those of high status by title, as to do so was not only a mark of respect but also demonstrated loyalty and acceptance of those who served them.

By referring to Kendra by name, Woden was paying her a great honour; coming from one of such hight standing - the highest - it was an indication of their closeness, and rarely did he bestow such an honour. The gesture also reaffirmed the bond they had made over many centuries; perhaps too many to consider.

"… you have been both friend and counsel, and I have had need of both. I will be… *incomplete* without your presence."

Kendra drew herself up to deliver a riposte as was usually her way, but she sensed the sincerity with which Woden addressed her and was, for the first time in days, saddened at the need for her inevitable departure to the old world.

She had cared for her people and cherished them above all else, having seen countless numbers of them arrive in Valhalla; most confused; some even afraid for the first time in their lives, and she had welcomed them; comforted them, and helped them come to terms with their new lives.

The thought that she would soon be leaving all of this behind filled her with dread. She sighed, allowing the discarded quip to dissolve undelivered in the air.

"You believe I am to depart Asgard then, my lord?"

Woden slowly nodded his confirmation.

"I do, as I believe you, too, have accepted this as your fate."

Kendra smiled knowingly; Even now, she held on to the hope that the Bernician weapons could be transferred without her having to follow them, but in truth, she knew, deep in her heart-of-hearts, that this could not be the case; without knowing it themselves, the gods called for a sacrifice.

"My lord may have but one eye, yet still his sagacity would shame a *hall* full of scholars!"

Woden laughed heartily, then Kendra said suddenly.

"Come, help me up from my seat; the people have waited long enough; I shall linger here no more!"

Woden extended a strong arm which Kendra took gratefully, using it to pull herself up into a standing position.

Despite her apparent frailty, Woden was surprised to note that as her thin fingers wrapped around his forearm and took the strain, her grip was as strong as any who wielded a blade, and for one of such a slight frame, he felt he could sense the weight of her very soul.

She stood for a moment, still using Woden's arm to steady herself, before indicating with the wave of a dismissive hand that she would now proceed without further assistance.

"My lady is sure?"

Taking a deep, readying breath, Kendra replied.

"She is. Come; we must away!"

***

The Sun had reached its zenith by the time Grimme arrived back at Haligsfeld, where the eight Wandle's Ham warriors now lay snoring and murmuring in the heat of the day.

The stream by which they had lazed for the past hour gently babbled and tinkled as it made its way ever downhill to join the main body of the river, where after a journey of some four leagues, it was carried out to sea, through and beyond the broad estuary that sat low and wide in the landscape; its silver-grey fingers stretching out toward the far blue horizon. For as long as anyone could remember, sailors had used this as their landmark and their way home, and after a long and arduous journey, it was a sight that was welcomed by all.

He stood over them for a moment, watching as they slept, wondering whether they dreamt of this world or the old.

Woden's words came to him momentarily: '*Do you ever revisit the old world...?*' He stirred uncomfortably at the thought of ever having to leave Asgard, wondering whether, if he were called to do so, he could make the ultimate sacrifice as Kendra was now preparing to do.

Whichever sleep-realm they had chosen to roam, they seemed content within, and he felt a momentary pang of guilt as he made to disturb them from their slumber, though not enough to delay the event.

"My lord Renweard; warriors of Wandle's Ham; it is time!"

Renweard, who had heard Grimme's approach, did not move, choosing instead to address Grimme from where he rested in the long grass.

“We are glad of it, my lord Grimme; we were starting to decay into the landscape such is the comfort with which we rest.”

Grimme smiled.

“You will most likely wish you *had* decayed; the lady Kendra instructs you to, once again, sit within your death bed…” he gestured to the spot in which the men had been buried together what seemed, ironically, like a life-time ago “…it is her wish that you remain there until her arrival, at which point the ceremony will begin.”

Hearing voices, the rest of the men began to rouse from their slumber, stretching and yawning as they did so.

“Wha’shapp’nin’? Di’some’un shay death bed?” Abrecan slurred as he propped himself up on one elbow to face the direction from which the voices came, squinting painfully in the brightness of the sun.

Garberend, the first to have fallen asleep, did not stir until a gentle prod from the tip of Grimme’s staff brought him cursing back to consciousness.

Watching as his men slowly returned from the realm of sleep, Renweard could not help but admire them for their patience and their fortitude; a warrior without weapons was unthinkable and diminished the man, yet here they were, able and willing to fight on regardless; empty handed if need be.

Suddenly heeding the subtle warning in Grimme's words, Renweard returned from his reverie and called the men to arms.

"My brothers! It is time!"

They all, to a man, sprang to their feet, brushing themselves down and adjusting their clothing as they did so; belts were tightened; tunics straightened and leg wraps retied so that once more they sat comfortably about their person.

"It is time? Did my lord say it is time?" Eadig asked enthusiastically, Renweard replying,

"He did, old friend..." and then to them all, "Come! Let us hasten onto Haligsfeld so that this most evil of times be banished, once and for all!"

At Renweard's command, they strode excitedly away from the stream, some wringing cool water from linen cloths onto their head and neck as they walked, such was the intensity of the afternoon sun, and onto the plateau that had, in the old world, been their final resting place.

The graves lay within sight of the stream whose restful music had aided their peace and tranquillity. It was, therefore, only a short walk to reach them, and they covered the distance in a matter of a few minutes.

Nevertheless, each man was glad to arrive, for although barely a handful of days had passed since their precious weapons had begun to fade in the great hall, there had been no way of telling how long the curse might last or whether they would *ever* see their valued possessions again.

Now though, they were here; now they were being rearmed for battle; now they could become whole again!

Anfeald spoke first.

"Are we to occupy the original bed, my lord? As I, for one, do not recall which of these is mine."

For once, Renweard did not have the answer; the idea that they may need to identify a specific grave: the actual bed into which they had been placed, had not occurred to him, although, he thought, perhaps it should have.

He looked to Grimme, but the expression on his face told Renweard that he was as much at a loss for an answer as he was.

"We do not know, Anfeald..." Renweard replied honestly, "...in which case, I suggest we simply choose one and wait within. If Kendra wishes us to move, she will, no doubt, know to where."

This seemed as good a plan as any under the circumstances, so the men chose the grave closest to them and began moving toward it.

The graves themselves were not, as might have been expected, a deep pit in the ground, nor were they a raised mound of earth. Instead, eight shallow scrapes, indicated by the presence of slightly darker soil and a concentration of sharp, black tool stones, were the only evidence that anything had ever occurred on this spot; Still, this was evidence enough.

First to arrive was Eadig. It felt to him somewhat disrespectful to be placing his heavy, leather-shod feet into the last resting place of one of the fallen, and he stepped carefully, lest he steps on and offends whoever lay there.

For a moment, he stood and looked about him, wondering what to do next. The others were still in the process of occupying their chosen spot, so he decided to sit in the grave as he had been instructed and began lowering himself to the ground.

As he pitched forward, something at the opposite end caught his eye: a flash of light, a glimpse of something other-worldly. He paused halfway between earth and sky and peered at the strange sight in front of him.

Momentarily taken aback, he nevertheless recognised something familiar in this new magic, and gathering his senses, he leaped from the grave, calling excitedly.

"MY LORDS; LOOK!"

There was no tension in his voice. There was, however, excitement and fascination.

Renweard and Grimme, cutting short the conversation in which they had been deeply immersed, looked to the man, concern emblazoned on each of their faces, before hurrying to his side, where they found him staring, wide-eyed and open-mouthed at the ground in front of him.

"Is there no end to this wonder?" Renweard mused, overwhelmed once more by this demonstration of other-worldly power. "How can this be?"

Only one person could know the answer; only one, and she was yet to arrive.

Grimme looked down on the grave by which Eadig stood and was in awe. He had experienced many strange and wonderous events during his time in Asgard, yet the breadth of foresight and control displayed before him was breath-taking.

"I believe, my lord Renweard, that Kendra foresaw this… complication and has provided us with the answer we seek!"

As the rest of the men gathered around Eadig and the grave, it became clear that this was *not* the place in which he had been laid to rest; clearly, though, one of the eight *had* been placed there.

At the eastern head end of the grave, a collection of glistening white quartz stones formed a near-perfect circle; about the size of a human head. Within this, a pool of pale-blue light rippled and moved like water which now and then emitted a spark of such intensity that even the glare of the midday sun could not subdue it as it flew up and away on the breeze.

Nine astonished faces gazed in on the light-pool. But what was more astonishing was that one gazed back! It was Renweard; this was his grave.

"This is Kendra's hand; she is lighting the way!"

Grimme shook his head in admiration.

"I believe you are correct, Abrecan; I have known the lady Kendra for millennia, and still she has the capacity with which to astound and render me speechless..." then, remembering his instruction from the prophetess, continued, "...If this *is* the way, might I respectfully suggest that you follow it and return to your respective graves before she arrives."

Renweard, too, shook his head, marvelling at the apparent simplicity of the phenomenon.

"There *is* hope..." he whispered to himself "...this *will* work!"

Without warning, Grimme slapped Renweard hard, but affably, on the shoulder, as was his way when he wanted to convey pleasure or satisfaction.

As ever, it stung, and as ever, Renweard refused to show it.

“This too is correct, my lord Renweard, but might I suggest that you also follow the sign and take your place among your men? The Lady Kendra and Woden are on their way!”

Renweard looked back across Haligsfeld, following the line indicated by Grimme as he pointed back toward the stream.

There, two figures, distorted by the heat of the day, shimmered in the heat haze that billowed up out of the sandy soil, as though viewed through a waterfall; their movement strange and alien, their form unrecognisable, as they made their way slowly across Haligsfeld.

Chapter 17: The Departure.

And so, at last, the wait was over; debate was at an end; decisions made and finalised, and in the past hour, the Bernicians, having followed Kendra's precise instructions, had placed the many and varied offerings carefully and deferentially within the new ceremonial pit as the eight awaited her return.

The great ill that had befallen Valhalla was soon to be purged and their status as warriors restored; they were finally to be rearmed and re-provisioned, having looked on helplessly as the possessions with which they had gone to their graves had faded, becoming ghosts, before finally vanishing altogether.

The phenomenon was relatively new to the Asgardians who, although having witnessed many strange and mysterious occurrences over millennia, had seen nothing like this; at least not on this scale.

There had been a few, very few, such occasions - both Woden and Kendra having witnessed a handful of individuals sullied in this way - but nothing to match the events of the past few days. Over the past two hundred years, this had become an increasingly common event culminating in the mass desecration they were now witnessing. Now, at least, they knew the cause.

The tension was palpable as Kendra and Woden emerged from their mirage, approaching Haligsfeld, where the eight sat quietly, deep in thought.

Grimme greeted them both with a bow and was met with a smile from Kendra.

"I see you discovered my markers…" she said as she re-joined the group "…a stroke of genius if I do say so myself!"

Grimme smiled

"As do we all, my lady; in all my years, I have never witnessed the like…"

"Nor will you again…" Kendra interrupted casually, intending humour.

No sooner had she uttered the words than she saw darkness spread across the faces of the men, and realising, as they had, that these were likely to be her last few moments in Asgard, she chose not to complete her sentence.

"Yes, well… let us…" she struggled to regain her composure "…let us continue!" she said, finally.

Meanwhile, Colin and the Bernicians, having completed the task of filling the ceremonial pit, had gathered excitedly around the portal, where they watched as the Asgardians had eventually taken their place in the eight original graves.

There had been a sudden flurry of activity in Asgard with much calling and some deliberation on the part of Renweard and the tall golden warrior, after which the men had moved among the graves, which now emitted a soft blue light, apparently searching for something within.

It was impossible, from where the Bernicians stood, to see what this might be, but as each man found 'his' grave, he stepped into it and sat down.

Jon had a theory. "It would seem…" he said earnestly "…that each man has somehow been directed to the grave in which they were originally buried; otherwise, they could have simply chosen a grave at random and stepped into it."

"Reckon, you're right, boy…" Colin agreed "…looks like this is it then, eh?"

And so they waited, some making themselves comfortable in fold-up camping chairs - notably, Jon and Colin - while others simply sat on the ground. Most, though, chose to remain standing, but all faced the portal, and to those of this world, had they stumbled across the scene, they appeared as an audience watching an open-air movie.

It felt strange, almost voyeuristic, watching as the eight men of Asgard awoke and talked among themselves, having been joined by the tall, dark warrior in gold; listening as Eadig called to his lords who, along with the six remaining warriors, had hurried to his side; and marvelling as strange, blue light began radiating up from out of the ground.

The phenomenon was familiar to some, but to others, it was new, astonishing magic, and although no one could see into the grave from their position in the old world, all sensed that this was a truly profound moment.

The entire episode unfolded in front of them like a highly sophisticated science fiction movie, capturing and holding them there, bewitched, eager to know the outcome, until finally, as the ending drew near, the spell was broken by Grimme's hail.

"Bernicians! Prepare yourselves; my Lord Woden and the Lady Kendra approach; The ceremony begins!"

Tension continued to build as Asgard, and the Old World watched and waited together, the crushing silence becoming more and more unbearable as the blood, now pulsing and ringing in their ears, became a deafening, pounding roar.

Kendra positioned herself alongside the portal that had, for the past three hours, both connected and separated Asgard and the Bernicians. She paused for a moment, her gaze alternating between them, her eyes drifting over a sea of anxious, expectant faces; allies all.

Such suffering... she thought *...and such sacrifice.*

She wondered for a moment whose had been the greater: The seekers? They had certainly shown much courage and generosity; How *could* they have known of the great conflict their actions would unleash in Asgard? Like children, eager to learn, they had gone about their business without realising that by doing so, they were tearing apart the fabric of the very world they sought to understand.

In the end, though, they were wise, wiser than any in Asgard could have imagined, especially for a people so far removed from the old ways.

Or perhaps Renweard of the eight? Courage was their business; honour, the code by which they lived and died, yet to be deprived of that which makes you whole; to be stripped of that which makes you the person you are and still face adversity head-on, that was the mark of a true warrior and the men of Wandle's Ham had earned the respect and veneration of the Gods, the Einherjar and Valkyries alike.

Finally, her thoughts alighted, like one of the many butterflies that fluttered and skipped among the meadow flowers around them, on herself.

She immediately dismissed the notion that her part in all of this was anything more than that which was to be expected of someone of her high standing and that to refer to her passing through the portal and away from Asgard for all eternity as anything more than duty, was arrogant and self-fulfilling.

Despite this, there was no overlooking the fact that hers was the only outcome that might *not* end favourably.

The seekers were set to lose that which was most precious to them, and their sacrifice was great; but in time, these could be rcplaced, and they would, in the meantime, carry on with their lives much as they always had and the eight were about to see the end to their suffering with the return to warriorhood.

No, Kendra's sacrifice could not be overstated. *If* she survived the transfer, she would become mortal; she would be forever stranded in a world with which she had long since lost touch and may even lose the powers she had, for so long, taken for granted.

Kendra's sacrifice was total, and everyone present, including finally, Kendra herself, acknowledged it.

"It begins!" she said suddenly, catching everybody unawares.

Woden, who had fixed his gaze on his beloved lady, made to speak.

"My Lady Kendra, a few words..."

“NO, THERE MUST BE NO DISTRACTION!” she called, her mouth dry, her words hoarse yet losing none of their meaning.

“Time is slipping away, and I must summon all of my strength to perform this: the final act!”

Woden froze, mouth agape, his face awash with frustration and sorrow before finally letting it go with a sigh, the great man visibly deflating as though his very soul was in the process of leaving him; such was his despair.

Kendra now spoke to Asgardian and Bernician alike.

“My people...!” she smiled warmly, the meaning of her words becoming apparent “…*my* people; It is time. I must first ask you to move away from the portal and to be seated on the ground. Move now; one chain…you must walk the distance of one chain… I shall send a signal when you have reached the place.”

There was a gentle murmur, and the bustle of people on the move as forty-one pairs of leather-clad feet complied with Kendra’s instruction.

“Here we go, then!” Rab said as he walked alongside Angela and Colin. For once, Colin remained silent, deep in thought as to the potential outcome of the upcoming event.

“Col…?”

“Mmm… oh, yeah, yeah…Sorry, Rab!”

“How much further?” Angela was asking.

“I think I heard ‘a chain?’, whatever that is!”

“Sixty-six feet; a chain is sixty-six feet…” It was Jon “…and by my calculations, we’re about there.”

No sooner had the words left his mouth than there came the sound of a war horn, its tone deep and mournful, befitting the occasion. This was the signal that they had reached the required distance.

“As I was saying…” Jon concluded, taking a seat on the ground.

The flurry of activity continued for the next few minutes as people on both sides of the portal turned to face the way they had come before taking a seat on the ground as instructed, then, all fell silent as they looked on, waiting nervously.

Kendra now turned to Woden.

“My Lord, I have asked your son, Thunor, to assist me with the ceremony. May I have your blessing?”

Woden started at the mention of his son, surprised as much as anything else that Kendra had been able to trace his whereabouts. Thunor was his own man and, as such, often spent weeks away from Asgard. Any opportunity to see his son was welcomed, and he was, therefore, more than happy to oblige.

"Of course, my Lady; it is given, but…"

Pre-empting Woden's question, Kendra cut in.

"I have the means with which to trace your sons; Thunor, Loki, and I have, over the years, maintained a closeness that transcends the physical; I have merely to reach out to them with my mind, and we become connected."

Woden smiled, shaking his head in wonder at the audacity of their guile. "Indeed; it would explain many of their exploits while they were yet boys!"

Kendra returned the smile but, sensing that they were on the pathway to reminiscence, quickly moved on with the ceremony, closing her eyes and becoming still, focusing.

For a while, nothing happened, and several minutes passed before there was an unmistakable change in the atmosphere that both sides felt simultaneously.

At first, it was nothing more than a faint breeze that blew in toward the portal, as though the pressure within had dropped, yet despite the chill of the Bernician night, none there felt the need to swaddle themselves against it.

Conversely, those under the glare of the Asgardian Sun felt no cooling benefit, despite the fact that it now seemed to be growing in intensity, lifting dust and leaf and scattering the busy insects away from their labours.

Thus, they waited.

Before long, ripples of excited conversation and nervous laughter began drifting across Haligsfeld as the air suddenly became charged and alive with static electricity. The gathering looked around at one another incredulously as the hair on their heads - those who had it - and arms began standing comically on end while at the same time causing them to tingle, sending shivers down the spine.

And then, nothing, but at the same time, everything!

Light; sound; motion; all came at once, yet none existed.

It was as though everything endured together, yet not at all.

Time hung motionless in a vacuum before finally, a shock wave, driven down from on high, spread out across Haligsfeld and on both sides of the portal.

Those who had been seated now lay flat on the ground; whether they chose it or not, many instinctively drew their knees up into a foetal position as the tumult passed violently over them, carrying away anything that wasn't either tied down or held firmly, and all screwed their eyes tightly shut against the flying debris.

The finale could only be perceived through closed eyelids as flashes of intense blue and white, created as multiple bolts of lightning ripped the air and assaulted the ground, forming a vault of light with, at its apex, Thunor, Woden's son; rightful keeper of Mjöllnir: the great weather hammer, who rode his creation to the ground, announcing his arrival with one final ear-splitting clap of thunder that rendered all but Woden, Kendra and Grimme defenceless and devoid of hearing.

What seemed like an age passed before, their ears still ringing, Colin, Rab, Angela, and Jon attempted to communicate.

"What the f…?"

"…flaming hell was that?" Rab intercepted Colin's pert line of questioning.

"Summat like that, yeah. Blimey, was that it? Did the weapons arrive?" he asked.

Ever astute, Jon offered his version of what had just happened. "I believe that was merely another party arriving; perhaps to assist with proceedings? And given the nature of their arrival…" he continued excitedly, "…I believe we are now also in the presence of Thor, or to give him his Anglo-Saxon name: Thunor."

Rab had just managed to bring himself up onto his knees and was in the process of sitting back on his haunches.

"My God! As if everything else wasn't enough; We'll be meeting The Guardians soon!"

A series of puzzled looks flashed in Rab's direction.

"…Of the *Galaxy*? …doesn't matter…"

"Indeed not…" Jon replied, "…I believe the poor boy may be concussed!"

"My son!" Woden greeted Thunor with open, outstretched arms.

"Father! It has been too long!"

"And yet you come to us now, in our hour of need," Woden remarked proudly.

"As was ever the way, father; my service to Asgard is absolute."

They embraced as a family before, finally, he turned to Kendra.

Dropping to one knee, Thunor bowed his head and greeted her as though she were his own mother, such was the reverence in which she was held.

"My Lady Kendra; I am, as always, at your service."

Irritated at Thunor's formal tone, Kendra became flustered and hurried the boy before her to his feet.

"Enough, enough! I am grateful for your presence; there need be no more said than that!"

Thunor lifted his head from its bowed position and looked straight into Kendra's dark eyes, his lips barely containing a mischievous smile as he failed in his attempt to appear cowed.

Meeting the ice-blue pools of Thunor's eyes, she could contain herself no longer, and leaping to his feet, the two embraced as she both wept and laughed all at once, such was her joy.

"Oh, my boy! My boy!" she repeated over again.

Like Woden before him, Kendra had mentored Thunor and Loki as children, teaching them the mystical ways of Asgard; of bird and beast; of essence and spirit; of earth, water, fire, and sky but above all, of respect: respect for all things, because to lack respect breeds resentment and if the spirits and the beasts and nature herself were to turn upon us, not even the mighty Woden could prevent the destruction that would inevitably follow.

"Come, come, there is little time. We must prepare for…"

Thunor's face dropped at Kendra's bidding. He was fully aware of what was required of him, having 'discussed' it with Kendra through the meeting of minds, and he was no happier at the idea now than he was then.

"There is no other way?"

"We have discussed this, Thunor. Please do not harry me with further questions; we must prepare for the transfer *as we discussed*. I shall say no more on the subject!"

"Very well, my Lady; you are, indeed, as great as you are wise."

Kendra swelled at the compliment, though not through mention of her qualities. Rather, pride for the man Thunor had become.

"I have taught you well; you are a credit to the house of Woden."

"What's happening?" it was Colin.

Jon, as ever, had a suggestion.

"I believe we are witnessing a family reunion; certainly, Kendra and Thunor appear to be well acquainted."

"Well, that's nice an'all, but they need to get a move on; have you seen the time?"

It was fast approaching midnight on the Bernician side of the portal, with a little under an hour in which to complete the ceremony. Kendra had specifically stated that it must be concluded by midday in Asgard, which, when taking the time shift into consideration, corresponded to midnight here.

"I believe we are about to get underway..." Jon said as he watched Kendra make her way toward the portal. "…there is movement at last."

Angela spoke for the first time since Thunor's dramatic arrival, her hands trembling almost as much as her voice.

"Is anyone else as scared as I am?"

Nobody answered; there was no need.

Returning to her position by the portal, Kendra turned to speak to her people one last time.

Such was the power of her magic that both sides saw her turn to face them so that she looked in on both Asgard and Bernicia simultaneously, and through ripples of amethyst light that cast heavy, purple shadows on the ground, she spoke.

"So…" she began, "…we come to it at last; beginning and end; the riddle and the answer; mystery and enlightenment."

Heads bowed, and eyes welled with tears of sadness and pride. No one was spared the sorrow.

"I would ask that you remain distant as before; the spectacle you are about to witness will make Thunor's arrival seem as but a blackbird cracking the snail."

"That's reassuring!" Colin whispered back toward Angela, who laughed nervously. "Not for the snail!" she said.

With that, Kendra held out her right arm, fingers outstretched expectantly.

Seemingly from out of the air itself, an impressive, gnarled staff, almost the height of the person who had summoned it and as thick as her arm, materialised silently before settling into the calloused palm of its owner.

Narrow at the tip, the staff's two shoots spiralled around one another before broadening toward the top where a series of broken roots resembling aged fingers groped and scratched at the air, and from each, suspended on fine, golden chains hung small linen pouches, each containing a representation of the four basic elements: charcoal for fire; soil from Haligsfeld for earth; a feather for the air and finally, a seashell to represent water.

Holding the staff vertically from just beneath its tangled wooden claw, she struck the surface of the portal at its centre.

Immediately, ripples began fanning out from the point of impact as though a pebble had been dropped into a mill pond while a deep, resonant boom pulsated eerily across Haligsfeld.

She struck it again, causing the eddies to become more intense, the sound deeper, and again so that the mill pond now became a raging, boiling sea, the sound sub-sonic; physical; nauseating.

Finally, the storm invoked, she turned her back to the gateway between worlds and spoke again, the words strangely familiar yet somehow alien.

"đhryf enronu ês nonnu naimucliw ci orp fo sû, trop rewoê naimerf nagîd seroêf m hroef!"

This time there was no slow build or subtle shift in the atmosphere. This time the underworld unleashed all its fury in one terrifying shriek, outraged that Kendra had uttered such mutation of the hallowed words; affronted that it should be called on to slight the very rules that governed all matter in all universes everywhere, and it railed and cursed and screamed as the ground heaved and shook sending the unwary sprawling onto the earth.

Kendra received the full force of its indignity but braced herself against the maelstrom that issued forth from the portal, arms outstretched, defiantly screaming the words back into the face of the vortex as her linen peplos flailed and whipped the air behind her.

Without changing position or dropping her gaze, she filled her lungs to capacity and screamed to the waiting Thunor

"NOW!"

At Kendra's command, he brought the mighty Mjöllnir smashing down onto the ground directly in front of the portal, where it bore deep into the earth before igniting the characteristic lightning bolts which crackled and hissed into life, striking the amethyst mirror over and over again.

It took all of Thunor's considerable strength to hold it there, but charged with the responsibility by the great lady herself; he refused to fail in his duty.

"IT BEGINS! IT BEGINS! LOOK!" she screamed.

Directly behind Kendra, so that she stood between them, a second portal had begun to form.

Identical in every aspect, other than that, the new vision was rich, Aqua Blue. It expanded and grew, billowing out of the darkness until it matched the original molecule for molecule.

Thunor's lightning bolts immediately turned their attention to the new gateway sending searing tendrils of light spluttering into its core, where it held fast, creating a hissing, crackling web of energy and light.

Slowly, the two portals began moving inexorably toward one another.

In the old world, thirty-one terrified Bernicians clung to each other as the spectacle unfolded with growing ferocity. All now lay on the ground; Rab and Angela held on to each other tightly as, around them, chaos prevailed. The cries and screams of some of the party occasionally pierced the night air as light and sound pulsed painfully, and dust and debris flailed around them.

Through it all, Colin managed a brief glimpse of the pit that contained the offerings, and, shielding his eyes against the squall, he forced himself to look across to where they had earlier worked in the still, cold night air.

Light was starting to build from somewhere deep down in the ground, from deep inside the pit itself. It pulsed slowly, illuminating the ground and those laying nearby, each time exposing a scared and frightened face, each pulse brighter than the last and each pulse accompanied by a sound that burrowed deep into the mind, confusing and disorienting the observer.

As the portals moved closer, the howling storm that raged between them intensified as bolt after bolt of blue-white lightning struck the wrathful vortices, their once tranquil surface now seething as they screamed dissonantly in protest.

And still, Kendra screamed defiantly while Thunor held Mjöllnir firm in the earth.

The effort was beginning to show now, even on one as powerful as he, as sweat beaded heavily on his brow before trickling away, hesitating for the briefest moment, before finally dripping slowly from the tip of his nose, and then, as if to rally himself, he began a long, defiant roar, refusing to be broken by this fiendish spirit, and as he lifted his head, he saw the end come, and it was as beautiful as it was painful to behold.

The two portals now concluded their advance as they closed in on Kendra, surrounding her completely, bathing her in amethyst-aqua blue light that grabbed and snatched and held her firm until she became entirely enveloped in its terrifying beauty.

She no longer screamed at the apparition. Its menace held no fear for her, and she bore it no ill; it was, after all, of her making and had answered her call. Instead, she closed her eyes and waited. Waited for the end and the outcome that all were so eager to have happen, yet none wished for.

One last defiant scream shredded the air across Haligsfeld as the portals finally collided and energy ripped and tore and rent the air asunder. Hands quickly covered ears in an attempt to protect them as the screeching reached its peak and was now becoming physically painful.

"MY LORD!" Eadig called out.

"HAVE COURAGE, MY BROTHERS!" Renweard called through the confusion of noise.

"MY LORD; IT IS GARBEREND!"

Renweard shielded his eyes against the blast as he turned to look at his noble spearman.

"IS HE UNCONSCIOUS?"

No one could have anticipated Eadig's response.

"NO, MY LORD; HE SLUMBERS!"

The seven warriors roared with laughter at the improbability of the sight.

In Bernicia, Colin turned to Rab, who still held on to Angela.

"WHAT THE BLOODY HELL HAVE THEY GOT TO LAUGH ABOUT!"

Rab was unable to see through the maelstrom but shrugged his uncertainty anyway.

The pit was fully aglow now, with aqua-blue light radiating steadily, blindingly out from the ground.

Then everything stopped.

Thunor, the resistance now lifted, recoiled from the earth; Mjöllnir, free and weightless once more. Momentarily caught off balance, he quickly regained his posture before drawing himself up to full height, stretching away the efforts of the past few minutes. He felt groggy, drained, as though inebriated. He frowned, disoriented. But as his senses returned, he remembered what had just taken place and why!

His mind suddenly clear, he looked uneasily across to where Kendra had confronted the portals; all was quiet.

Here and there, and from both sides, the sounds of movement began drifting out into the still, eerie silence as others began to recover from the spectacle they, too, had just witnessed. Some wept, traumatised; others appeared stunned, their trauma, for now, contained. Voices, the words incomprehensible, began rising as friend comforted friend, and here and there, a body lay still on the ground.

A dense mist hung still in the air as an occasional spark crackled defiantly out of the ground, hot and blue; the earth itself scorched and burnt, smouldered still, and the air was heavy with the smell of ozone that invaded and burned the nostrils.

Then at once, it came to him, and his blood ran cold, his greatest fear realised:

Kendra was gone.

Chapter 18: The Return

Angela sobbed quietly as Rab continued to hold her close to him.

"It's OK, Ange, it's over now; it's over!"

"Are you sure?" a softly muffled voice replied.

"Come and see for yourself; look!"

He released her, encouraging her to sit up and look around, and so, uncoiling slowly, she pushed herself up from the ground after what had seemed like forever.

"I thought it was never going to end!" she said, looking around as the rest of the group emerged from their places of safety.

In truth, there had been little in the way of cover, and most simply lay on the ground, having wrapped themselves tightly in cloaks or blankets. Others just held on to one another.

"I know..." Rab said, "...but it has."

He smiled kindly into the dirt-streaked face of his close friend. He had never seen Angela look so vulnerable; She was always the self-assured, confident one who knew what, how, and when she wanted something done.

"You OK?" he asked.

"I feel such an idiot; crying like that..." she said, eyes downcast, trying to avoid eye contact out of embarrassment.

"*Why*? I felt like it myself, to be honest; Christ, none of us have seen anything remotely like that outside of..." he searched for an example "... outside of a movie. Please don't apologise..." he took her hand gently "...it's nice to know you're human!"

Sensing that Rab was reaching out as a friend, she smiled for what seemed like the first time that evening; a genuine, heartfelt smile.

"Come on; better go and check on the oldies, eh?"

"OI! I heard that!" it was Colin.

"Eh? Oh... you OK, Col?" Rab asked, genuinely concerned.

"I am, ta. You two?"

"We're fine, thanks; just a bit shaken up, s'all."

Colin was genuinely relieved.

"Thank God for that! Have either of you seen Jon?"

The three scanned the immediate area, suddenly aware that he was no longer with them.

Peering across the site, they saw, through a heavy mist, Bernicians helping each other; some being assisted up from the ground, others just sat motionless, holding on to one another; and here and there, lone souls checking that everyone was safe and uninjured before heading off to the site huts to make hot drinks. Just then, Rab spotted him.

"There he is, look; over there, leading the recovery."

Jon was indeed heading up the recovery team, as ever, Bernician welfare was very much at the very top of his list.

"Is anyone injured? Graeme, are you OK? Yes?... Jolly good! Perhaps you'd be kind enough to assist Jules. She seems to have grit or some other foreign body in her eye… she's having the devil of a job of it… AHH! Craig would you…?" and so it went on.

"Looks like everything is in hand there then…" Colin smiled through a bemused frown "…how does he always stay so spotlessly clean, though? All three shook their heads.

"Teflon coated?"

"Must be!" Angela agreed.

"Come on; let's give 'em a hand.

They were about to head over to help Jon and the others when Angela spotted something: a body!

"Who's that?" she said, pointing toward the pit, which still smouldered ominously.

“Eh? where?” Colin asked as he glanced casually back over his shoulder.

“Over there by the pit; Look, there’s someone laying on the ground!”

Peering with some difficulty through dense smoke into the gloom, they could just make out a shape. It could just as easily have been a discarded cloak or blanket, but as their eyes adjusted to the light and the smoke began to clear a little, parted by a gentle breeze, they recognised the unmistakable silhouette of a body.

Laying on their side, motionless, their clothes smouldering like the ground around them, was a frail, elderly woman.

As one, the cold realisation hit them; It was Kendra!

Setting off at a run, the three archaeologists quickly made their way over to her, avoiding post-holes and pits; burning branches of Yew, and countless unrecognisable objects that lay scattered across the site as they leaped and sprinted over the sandy soil, desperately trying to avoid a twisted ankle, or worse.

“Oh God, let her be alive…!” Colin said through deep, rasping breaths.

“She’s moving, LOOK!” Angela called as she rushed ahead of the others.

They arrived at Kendra's side, instantly dropping to their knees, but despite their concern for her wellbeing, for the briefest of moments, nobody seemed to know what to do and so remained there, motionless. Staring in blind panic, they hovered, feeling completely helpless before common sense and first aid training finally kicked in. Rab, being in the best position to do so, placed one hand on Kendra's hip, the other on her shoulder, before turning her gently onto her back and peering anxiously into the prophetess's face.

The old lady sighed gently, involuntarily, as she was moved, and it sounded to Rab as though she had just taken her last breath. He felt the ice-cold hand of fear sweep over him.

"Should we move her like this?" Colin asked.

"I don't know…" Angela replied nervously, "… but we need to check she's breathing so…" she shrugged, perplexed.

Kendra's eyes remained tightly closed, her expression one of having borne great strife, and her breathing came in short, shallow gasps.

Remembering some of his first aid training, Colin shook her shoulders, albeit a little too enthusiastically.

"KENDRA! Is she breathing, Ange'?" He shook her again.

“She is…!” came a tired, irritated voice from the frail, dishevelled body that lay in front of them “…but she would do so more freely were she not hemmed in by concerned onlookers!”

Chaos was unleashed as three startled archaeologists scrambled to give the Lady Kendra more room, apologising profusely as they crashed headlong into one another, tripping and cursing and jostling for space and throwing up dust in their wake.

Such was their confusion that it took a while for them to recognise the unmistakable sound of laughter as Kendra rolled helplessly on the ground, tears streaming down both cheeks that washed pink streaks into the dirt and grime.

Momentarily speechless, all three froze, bewildered.

“Are you OK?” Rab ventured. “Is everything alright?”

“Alright? Am I alright?” she replied through fits of recurring laughter. “I haven’t laughed like this in an age; to think that I should be greeted in the Old World by such a performance… and after such an ordeal; Wonderful! Wonderful!”

A large crowd started to gather around them now, as having witnessed the drama of a knot of people running headlong toward the pit and hearing their calls for help, they had responded instantly.

One by one, the concerned Bernicians arrived, only to find the "casualty" laughing and teasing her gallant heroes, and gradually, realising that all was well, the tension eased, and they too relaxed, joining in the hilarity and seeing the funny side; though some more cautiously than others.

"Oh… come…" Kendra said as she swallowed her laughter, "…come, help me to my feet; I need to check."

Colin was confused. "Check?"

"The pit, dear boy; the pit! I believe Kendra is referring to the weapons." Jon had joined them.

Having made sure that everyone who needed help received it and those who were unharmed provided it, he'd left the rest of the group making tea and relaxing as they came slowly back down to earth, talking excitedly about the events of the past few hours.

"Indeed, I am…Jon?" Jon swelled with pride at Kendra, having remembered his name "…I must look into the pit to see whether the weapons have arrived in Asgard."

"How will we know? I mean, the portals… they're gone." It was Angela.

"Your point is valid, child, but let us face one unknown at a time; come!" Kendra insisted as she made to walk toward the pit.

With that, the entire group shifted, parting as she moved among them, her short, delicate form dwarfed by even the smallest Bernician until they stood alongside the smouldering hollow.

It was completely dark now, the unearthly blue light long since extinguished, and apart from an occasional spark, only mist and smoke remained as evidence that anything had ever occurred there at all.

"I cannot see; I must have light! Is there a flame?"

"I can do better than that… my Lady."

It was Colin. For a moment, Kendra froze. It was as though she had suddenly remembered something, something important, something she needed to do. Rushing forward, she wrapped her slender arms around him and pulled him to her in an unexpectedly firm embrace.

"Colin…Colin…oh, my dear boy… and Rab… where is Rab?"

Rab stepped forward nervously as Kendra threw herself at him, repeating the process.

"Rab… my first contact with the Old World!" she said matter-of-factly as she kissed him on both cheeks.

Releasing him, she addressed the crowd.

"Seeing you all in the flesh; so strange… so strange… yet so… *normal*."

Then in an instant, her expression changed; she was no longer the over-excited, frail, elderly lady who babbled enthusiastically to everyone around her. Instead, the Kendra they all recognised returned; proud and strong; reborn and renewed; and with new vigour to take on the life that she had been destined to lead, and with great dignity, she addressed the gathering.

"We must see to the weapons; we must know that they have passed into Asgard. The flame! You have the flame?"

Colin reached into the hip pocket of his famed gilet and produced a small black, military-style torch, and pressing the rubber-covered button at its base, he adjusted the beam and shone it down into the pit, filling the interior with light.

"Like I said: I can do better than a flame."

"I see already that there is much to learn about the Old World…" Kendra mused.

"Not so *old* perhaps, though, eh?" Colin noted.

Kendra nodded wistfully.

The crowd gathered fervently around the pit, vying for the best vantage point yet without pushing or competing for space, and stared anxiously down into the void.

Where there had once been iron and gold; glass, wood, and wool, now, there was nothing: No swords; no lyre; not even the Yew that had so gently cradled their precious charge.

"Has it worked!" called a small voice from the back of the crowd.

"Well, there's nothing in the pit," replied Colin enthusiastically.

"...nothing in the pit..." Kendra repeated distantly, imagining what might now be occurring back in Asgard.

Jon had a question.

"My Lady, may I ask: as you are here with us and the pit is quite clearly devoid of content, might we assume that the weapons have indeed arrived safely in Asgard?

Kendra looked deep into Jon's eyes. She saw a man of learning and wisdom, not unlike Woden himself.

"I believe there can be no other explanation; as you have correctly stated: *I* am here; therefore, it stands to reason that the weapons must be on the other side, in Asgard; it was the reason for my forfeit after all." She smiled wistfully before continuing.

"Although, as Angela has already observed, with the portals destroyed, there is no way of knowing for certain; we must therefore assume that our endeavours have been a success; Asgard owes all of you… of *us*… a great debt.”

For a few seconds, nobody moved, remaining instead calm and pensive, looking at one another tentatively.

Rab glanced at Colin only to find him staring back, a wry smile spreading swiftly across his face.

“We’ve only gone an’ done it!” he said softly.

Few heard the words, but their tone was enough; Haligsfeld erupted in celebration.

~

“My Lord!” Grimme shook the shoulders of the man who lay still and unresponsive on the ground “My Lord Woden!”

Woden’s eyelids fluttered and blinked several times before opening fully; his one, seeing eye staring straight up into the anxious face of one of his most trustworthy subjects.

More than that, Grimme had been a loyal and faithful friend for as long as he could remember, and his counsel was much valued and respected.

“Come closer…” Woden whispered hoarsely.

Grimme leaned in so that he could hear his master's voice clearly, straining against the restriction of his armour, concern drifting darkly across his face.

"...I believe the Lady Kendra may have outdone even herself this day!" he said solemnly before breaking into self-appreciative laughter.

Grimme frowned in mock disapproval.

"My Lord would do well to remember that..."

Woden could do nothing and laughed all the harder as Grimme bristled peevishly.

"My Lord Woden would..." but it was no good; Woden's laugh was loud and infectious, and so, shaking his head in disbelief, he joined the great warrior lord in his merriment.

Thunor, having joined them, exchanged looks with Grimme and smiled.

"This is the father I have always known!"

"I can see where your brother, Loki, learned his craft!" Grimme retorted wryly.

"And learned it well!" Woden added, laughing all the more.

A few feet away, Renweard and his men lay on the ground breathing hard from the exertion of the past few minutes.

Not only had they endured the turmoil and ferocious down-blasts created as Kendra's portals collided, but they ached from having laughed so heartily at having seen Garberend lying sound asleep as all around him chaos reigned.

"This will fuel my fireside stories in the mead hall for many years to come!" Eadig had promised.

"Well, we could do with a change!" Abrecan teased Eadig's feigned indignity.

"Come then…" Renweard called above the laughter as he climbed to his feet, "…we have much to discover!"

As the men took to their feet and began brushing themselves down, a cloud of dust billowed around them, turning the air apricot-pink, each man becoming nothing more than a ghostly shadow backlit by sunshine, each surrounded by the earthy haze.

Such had been the force of the blast that not only were they now coated with the heavy, red earth of the Asgardian countryside, but small twigs had been forced through the linen cloth of their tunics; some, deeply piercing flesh which they removed carefully.

Garberend groaned as Anfeald shoved him with his foot, waking the slumbering hulk. He rolled grudgingly onto his side, cursing the fool who had disturbed his sleep, revealing as he did so, a clear demarcation line where dust-laden chaos met pristine calm. The laughter resumed and had anyone wandered across Haligsfeld at just that moment. They might have assumed that either it was the happiest, most joyous place to exist or that the air was heavy with one of Kendra's mind potions.

Whatever the cause, it was the release the men needed to recover from their ordeal, as being warrior clan, they would not - *could* not - outwardly display the fear that had gripped and ensnared them throughout the ordeal.

Woden, on hearing the sudden outpouring of laughter, turned to see what gave his warriors cause for such merriment.

Shaking his head, he looked on in wonder at the men who, having endured such calamity, were now making so merry as though what they had just witnessed was an everyday occurrence.

"If my army possesses such souls, who could stand against them and hope to prevail!"

Grimme nodded adding

"Indeed, my lord, and were they still to do so, their folly would soon be known; their dead, beyond the count, strewn lifeless beneath their feet as they retreated back into their filthy mire!"

"Come Grimme…Thunor… let us join our brothers."

Despite the layer of dirt, their armour flashed and glinted, shining almost as brightly as the light of the fierce afternoon sun, as they moved toward Renweard's company, who, in turn, gathered to receive them.

As they approached, the laughter petered out almost immediately as the eight presented themselves to their Lords; But it was Renweard who spoke for his men.

"My lords, we have endured; it brings us great joy to see that you have made likewise."

Woden regarded the eight warriors that stood before him, proud and eager to serve. Nodding his approval, he remained silent, preferring instead to look at the scene; as though burning it into his memory. Finally, he drew a long, deep breath and spoke.

"Brothers; in my long life, I have witnessed many things: war and wyrm; demon and dragon; angry skies and vast, foaming, mountainous seas. But that which I have seen this day will surely remain, long after the event which brought it railing and screaming into being has been buried and forgotten in our minds..."

The men nodded in silent agreement.

"...however, before that day is upon us, we have yet to discover whether Kendra's endeavours have, indeed, been fruitful; to discover whether the Bernician hoard has, in fact, arrived."

This had never been far from Renweard's mind; In fact, he had been about to muster the men in order to seek out the offerings when Woden, Grimme, and Thunor had arrived.

"My lord..." Renweard began, "...we are ready to learn of our fate. Would you have us search for the hoard?"

"There is no need, Renweard...!" a voice rang out across Haligsfeld "...I believe I have it!"

The men turned as one to peer in the direction from which the voice had come.

About the distance of a single chain, and quite some way from the graves where the ground began to break slope, Thunor stood alongside a small mound. At around six feet in height, it appeared to be constructed from alternating layers of yew branches and objects fashioned from wood and various metals which protruded from within. The whole assemblage smoked and smouldered dangerously in the heat of the day as though it might ignite at any moment.

“I believe you do, my son; come then!”

Woden set off toward his son and the mound as the others followed eagerly, walking purposefully to join Thunor, who had already begun the process of dismantling it when they arrived.

“My lord is that…” Eadig gazed in wonder as from the very top of the mound and wrapped in a sheepskin bag, a lyre appeared.

Renweard accepted it from Thunor, dusting it off carefully before handing it to Eadig, who received his new charge delicately with both hands. Then, as though it were a newborn infant, he held it gently, gazing tenderly down at its form.

The eight looked on, spellbound before Anfeald spoke softly.

“Make it sing, Eadig!”

“Yes, do!” “You must!” a murmur of voices echoed in agreement.

With shaking hands, Eadig released the leather thong that held the bag closed and slid the lyre gently from its sheepskin covering.

To all, it was as though they had, indeed, witnessed a birth, as though a new voice were about to sound in Asgard.

Woden sensed this, and all present understood the significance of what was about to take place.

Eadig's audience gathered where they could; some stood, others sat on the ground while Eadig himself sat leaning against a tree stump, and after a few fine adjustments to the tuning, he began.

Brothers, will you hear my tale

Of those whose need beyond the veil

Was answered by a maiden, bold

Whose story hence must now be told.

An evil that beset us all

Was met with magic, fire and squall

Was met by friends who held us dear

Whose offerings now gather here

And in the mist, a maiden, brave

Replenishes the warrior's grave

Kendra: prophetess; earth mother

Diminisher of woe for others

As firmament and tempest rung

She conjured with an ancient tongue

The gateway to allow our kin

To reunite, to join within

When finally, the chaos ebbed

And all was well, and evil left

So too our prophetess was gone

Left only in the words of Eadig's lonely song.

As Eadig resolved his lament, the last chord faded, drifting sweetly away on the hot breeze as though it carried with it the soul of the one for whom it had been written.

Haligsfeld fell silent and remained so for what seemed an age, a hot breeze the only thing to resemble a sound as the men sat in contemplation. Even Garberend, who had once been accused of having a river-worn cobble for a heart, stared longingly into the middle distance, grieving.

"You have a rare gift, my friend!" Woden said, finally breaking the silence.

"My lord honours me!"

"As he should, Eadig… Come, brothers…" Woden continued, "…let us assemble the offerings that have been so generously afforded us by our Bernician kin and made obtainable by our dear sister's sacrifice."

Slowly they unpicked the mound until a selection of weapons lay on the ground. One-by-one, seax, sword, shield, spear, helmet, and knife were pulled reverently from the smouldering pile to be laid alongside the others as slowly and surely the armoury grew until finally, along with the two sets of chainmail, the drinking horns, battle horns, and leather shoes, everything was recovered.

Remarkably, despite its fiery appearance, both the mound and its contents were cool to the touch, and none of the weapons had suffered any sort of damage, at least so far as anyone could tell.

Beadurof took a step toward the cache.

"With my lord's permission…?"

He said, and without waiting for a response, he chose a sword of such high quality it could only have been made for a king.

Oiled sheep's wool lined a red leather scabbard, within which slumbered a double-edged, razor-sharp slayer of men; a beast that, with one well-aimed swing, could separate a head from its body. Yet, for all its macabre intent, it was the most beautiful thing any of them had seen. Adorned with gilt metal and Millefiori glass inlay, it was, by far and away, the finest weapon of the entire collection.

For a moment, the men assumed that Beadurof, a man celebrated for his selfless, generous nature, had been overcome by the sight of this magnificent bounty or, at the very least, by the desire to be armed once more, to be whole again.

They could not have been more wrong. Beadurof turned slowly toward Renweard and, having taken the few paces between them, dropped reverently down onto one knee. Holding the sword with both hands, he raised it high above his head and finally spoke his intent.

"With or without a weapon, you have ever been our leader. Will my lord accept this noble blade as a token of our love, our kinship, and our loyalty? With it to make our enemy tremble and quail? With it to make the warriors of Wandle's Ham whole and honourable once more?"

The remaining six warriors called out in unison, inviting Renweard's response, "GIESE!"

Renweard stepped forward and placed a hand atop the crown of Beadurof's head. Then, lifting the sword from Beadurof's cradling hands, he drew the blade in one swift motion and admired its perilous beauty. It felt good; it felt completely natural, its weight, as ever, forcing hand and wrist forward, ever seeking its prey. Renweard felt the life force of the beast, and he was at one with it. He kissed the flat, patterned edge of the blade as the men waited.

"My brothers. You have shown me the meaning of honour; Have we not endured without protest…?"

Once more, the shout went up, "GIESE!"

"…have we not carried ourselves as warriors, despite those who would seek to diminish our title…?"

Once more, "GIESE!"

"…and do we now reclaim that title for our own so that once more, we might bring down the FURY OF ASGARD *AND* WANDLE'S HAM ON OUR FOE?"

Again "GIESE! GIESE!"

Renweard, his arm outstretched, pointed to the weapons cache with the tip of his pattern-welded sword.

"Arm yourselves then; make yourself whole again and join me in Woden's Einherjar; for tonight…" he smiled mischievously "…we feast in Valhalla, warriors all; whole once more!"

With a cheer, the men busied themselves about the weapons cache as Grimme, Thunor, and Woden looked on.

"The twilight begins," Woden said pensively.

"My Lord?" it was Grimme.

"It is said, Grimme, that Ragnorök is the 'twilight of the gods"; that the world will be cleansed by a great flood and that the surviving gods will reunite and the world be repopulated by Lif and Lifthrasir, the only two survivors of mankind…"

He paused momentarily as a shadow of regret passed over his face.

"…it is also told that Thunor and I will *not* be among them!"

Grimme frowned dismissively.

"I have heard these tales, my Lord, but I have never held them to be true…?"

Woden placed a reassuring hand on both Grimme and Thunor's shoulders and smiled.

"If this is to be our fate, then let us meet it full on, blow-for-blow; shield-for-shield. Let us take flesh and steel into the foray, knowing that the world will be reborn and refreshed; surely there can be no finer legacy than this?"

Grimme snorted, ejecting a private thought.

"Grimme?" Woden looked at his counsel questioningly.

"A stray thought, my lord… of a *maiden, bold.*"

The men nodded sagely as their thoughts dwelt briefly on their lady, pride now the overriding emotion.

After a while, Woden drew a long, thoughtful breath before exhaling noisily.

"I feel that the wyrd has more in store for us…" he nodded, confirming the thought to himself "…I feel too that our paths, those of the Lady Kendra and Asgard, will cross one last time. Yes, I believe it so!" Woden responded mysteriously and without further explanation.

Thunor and Grimme glanced at one another, each attempting to read the others' thoughts. They smiled warmly as brothers, and without further question, they set off.

"Come, let us join our Wandle's Ham kin in celebration; tomorrow… we make for the field at Vigrith!"

And with that, they departed Haligsfeld.

CPSIA information can be obtained
at www.ICGtesting.com
Printed in the USA
LVHW080007061222
734629LV00016B/1335

9 781915 852052